Los Angeles Stories

Los Angeles Stories

Ry Cooder

City Lights • San Francisco

Many thanks are due to Lynell George, Mister Jalopy, Colin Nairne, Dave
Frevele, Michael Dawson, Carolyn Kozo Cole, Glen Creason, Gene Agu-
ilera, Alec Wilkinson, Danny McKinney, and Craig Alexander.

Cover photo of Bunker Hill cottage by Arnold Hylen, courtesy of the California History Room, Arnold Hylen Collection, California State Library,
Sacramento, California.

"Sin Ti" by Pepe Guizar
Copyright 1948 by Promotora Hispano Americana de Música, S.A.
Copyright Renewed
Administered by Peer International Corporation
All Rights reserved. Used by Permission

"La Vida Es Un Sueño" by Arsenio Rodríguez Scull
Copyright 1947, 1948 by Peer International Corporation
Copyright Renewed
All Rights Reserved. Used by Permission

"Fine And Mellow" by Billie Holiday
Used by Permission of Edward B. Marks Company

Library of Congress Cataloging-in-Publication Data
on file

City Lights Books are published at the City Lights Bookstore,
261 Columbus Avenue, San Francisco, CA 94133.
Visit our website: www.citylights.com

For Susie, Joachim & Juliette

Contents

All in a day's work

1940

—〰—

I WORK FOR the *Los Angeles City Directory*, a book of names, ad-
dresses, and job descriptions. I am one of many. Our job is to
go out and collect the facts and bring them back. Other people
take our work and put it in the Book, but we do the important
part. Los Angeles is a big city, and the *City Directory* is a big book.

"How would you like to be listed in the *Directory*?" I show
people what it is. They're afraid you'll ask embarrassing questions like "Do you have a toilet?" and "Can I see it?" I tell them
they can list whatever they want — the job, the husband's name,
the wife's name — simple things that most people don't mind.
Most people like to be noticed, they like being asked.

The supervisor said I have the right manner and appearance: medium size, medium age, dark hair, and glasses. I received
a week's training, and then I was given a territory. The Book is
published yearly. I'm paid at the rate of twenty-five cents an entry.

I live in a one-room apartment on Alta Vista, in the old
Bunker Hill district, so Bunker Hill is part of my territory. You

have to do a lot of climbing, but I like the feeling of being elsewhere. Apartment houses are convenient for this work, and Bunker Hill has a lot of them. The population is older, and older people don't mind taking a little time since they're not going anywhere. I don't expect to be asked in, and that puts people at ease. It's easy to be listed in the *Directory*, that's my message.

I made the acquaintance of a Mr. John Casaroli. Mr. John, as he was known, was a retired opera singer and teacher. I listed him as *Casaroli, John, vcl tchr, New Grand Hotel 257 Grand Ave*. It turned out we got along, and I was often a guest in his apartment. One evening I arrived there to find police and onlookers crowded around what looked like a body on the sidewalk. The police said Mr. John had jumped from the roof just minutes before and was dead. They asked me if I was an "associate" of his, and I explained that he was my friend and I'd been invited for a spaghetti dinner. They took me to police headquarters and I was questioned for an hour. When I asked why, the officer told me it was routine. That's when I learned that Mr. John had made a will and left his record player and all his records and Italian poetry books to me. I spent the next few evenings moving them to my apartment, one block away. I discovered he owned a copy of the *City Directory*. It had been hollowed out, and inside was five thousand dollars — in hundred-dollar bills! I had never even seen a hundred-dollar bill. I decided to leave the money where it was and go on about my business. I didn't tell anyone, since there was no one to tell. Mr. John was the one friend I had. But I wondered — why would a man, an Italian, make all that spaghetti and then jump off the roof?

Mr. John's treasures made life much more interesting. I started listening to the records in the evenings and drinking the Cribari red wine in the way he used to do, a new experience for me. Then I thought I might try to learn Italian so I could read the poetry books. Why not? There was an Italian woman in my building I knew only as Cousin Lizzie. She agreed to teach me for fifty cents an hour. I listed her as *Giordano, Lizzie (wid Benito), smstrs, Alta Vista Apts. 255 Bunker Hill Ave.*

We use abbreviations for the jobs: *smstrs* for seamstress; *lab* for laborer; *pntsprsr* for pants presser; *shtmtlwkr* for sheet-metal worker, and so on. Even with the abbreviations, the *Directory* is huge and the lettering is so tiny, some readers have to use a magnifying glass. We're trained to be very particular about the spelling of names. I meet people who are poorly educated and aren't sure how to spell their own names. In that case, I have to ask other family members, or neighbors, or check their mail, if they don't object. I don't mind taking the time; it's all part of the job.

One day, I knocked at the apartment of a Mr. and Mrs. H. D. Clark, and a woman answered. There was some kind of a service going on inside. I heard someone reading from the Bible. The woman picked up a small case off the floor and shoved it at me, shouting, "You can't leave him alone, can you? He's dead, but you bastards can't leave him alone!" She slammed the door. I took the case home and opened it, and it was a clarinet. There was a card pasted inside the lid that read, "If found, please return to Howdy Clark." I looked him up in the *Directory*. He was listed as *Clarke, Howard D. (Margaret), music, New Grand Hotel 257 Grand Ave.* I made a note to relist Margaret Clark as *wid*, the abbreviation for widow, but when I returned the following week to confirm the spelling of Clark, she was gone, *no frwrdng.* The old Italian moving man saw me looking at mailboxes. "They move in, they move out," he said.

I heard music. I went up the steps to the front porch, and there a man was playing the ukulele. "No vacancy," he said when he saw me.

"The widow Clark is gone," I said.

"I don't like the cops hanging around."

"I'm not a cop, or a bill collector," I said. I showed him the book.

"A lousy book that costs twenty-five dollars? Nobody has that kind of money to throw around, but nobody."

I thought of Mr. John. "You can't judge a book by the cover," I said, but he was right in a way. The Book is not really meant for the ordinary home; it's a service to the business world, that's the official point of view. I once had the idea of offering it to homeowners on the time payment plan of fifty cents a week, but my supervisor said, "Can't be done, just do your job."

I was reassigned to the district near the L.A. River called Aliso Flats, or just The Flats. Many of the local residents are Mexican, and Russians of the Molokan faith. Mexican women are usually at home, and I'm offered a little lunch sometimes — you never know what. Women often make lunches for sale in the home to make extra money. I list those as "lunch rooms." Some homes have rented rooms so I need to talk to the roomers as well. My first week in the Flats, a housewife showed me to the back where the roomer lived. I knocked, but there was no reply. I said, "Hello, I'm from the *City Directory*, and I would like to ask you a few questions. It only takes five minutes." I heard a radio playing. I knocked again. I pushed open the screen door and saw a man's feet. His body was in the kitchen. There was blood on the floor and blood on the walls. The woman screamed and ran back inside the front house. I used the neighbor's phone to call the police. That's part of our training. The police asked if I knew the man, if I was an associate of his. I showed my business card like we're trained to do. They took my name and address and told me not to leave town. I asked the officers if they would like to be listed in the *City Directory*. "Not on duty," they said, but one officer gave me his home address and suggested I call on him later.

I had difficulty in the Flats after the story got around. I

overheard one Molokan woman, Sadie Tolstoy, telling her friend, "He takes the names to the dark side." Finally, I stopped going down there, but I missed the little chili stand on Utah Street. It was only fifteen cents a bowl and very good.

Thanks to Mr. John, I can eat wherever I want, but I usually make my own lunch. Pershing Square is a perfect place to sit and watch people. There are big shade trees and flowers and religious speakers. One day, I sat across from a woman dressed in black with tangled hair and strange fingernails that had grown out long and curved back. She shook her Bible at me. "False prophet!" she croaked. Another man walked by, and she shook the Bible at him. "Judas!" The man ducked his head down and hurried along the path. "Whore of Babylon!" she shouted to a woman in high heels pushing a baby stroller.

I ate my ham sandwich and made entries in my daybook. A man on the bench next to me said, "What are you writing? Tales of the sordid, the lurid?" I showed him the Book. He was very old and poorly dressed, but you can't judge on appearances. He put out his hand, saying, "Finchley by name, hobo by trade, no permanent address."

"The *Directory* doesn't recognize that occupation," I replied.

"Oh, I've been many things. If you want the whole story, it's going to cost you."

"The *Directory* doesn't pay for information."

"They'll pay. It's a first-rate yarn. Comedy, tragedy, sin — the worst kind! I'll cancel all previous engagements. Just open an account at Gordon's liquor store for the duration." He shuffled off.

I spent the rest of the day in the Japanese district called Little Tokyo. I interviewed three dentists, two lawyers, a doctor, and ten restaurant cooks in one building — all single men. The professional types spoke good English but the cooks thought I was checking white cards, so they clammed up. It took a long time, and the building was hot and stuffy. There was a bar on the street level called Tokyo Big Shot, a tiny little place with a counter and eight bar stools. It was empty except for the Japanese bartender and a white woman. I ordered Brew 102 — it's cheap and it hits. The bartender poured one and sneered at me. "You a checker?" he asked suspiciously.

"He don't look like a checker," the woman said. She was missing some of her lower front teeth, so it came out like "shecker."

"What a goddamn checker look like?" the bartender said.

"He's got a satchel like they got, but his eyes are bad. He ain't a checker."

"What's a checker?" I asked.

"State liquor board," said the woman. Aside from her teeth and a slight tremor in one hand, she was not so bad looking. I put the Book down on the bar. "This is what I do," I told her. "How'd you like to be listed? It's free."

"A shnooper," she said.

"Told you," said the bartender.

"Aren't there any Japanese women around here?" I asked.

"What's he want 'em for?" the woman said.

The bartender shook his finger at me. "Goddamn checker. You drink up, go home."

The *Directory* doesn't list bars. I paid up and left.

"Won't turn any tricksh for him," the woman called out after me.

The next day, Billy the office boy came looking for me in Pershing Square. "Super wants you," he said in his unfriendly way. I don't like Billy.

"What for?" I asked, just to irritate him. Billy hates questions, hates to give answers.

"Hell do I know," he said.

I put my ham sandwich back in my bag. "And Daniel was

cast in the lion's den," the woman in black said from her bench across the path.

They call it the City Directory Library. I've never seen any of the public there, so it must be a library in name only for business reasons. In point of fact, the supervisor is the only person there, in my experience. You address him as Sir or Mr. Supervisor. I don't even know his name.

"Got a call about you from a Sergeant Spangler at police headquarters." The supervisor has a way of talking to you without looking up from his desk. "Two dead men, so they wonder why."

"Three, if we count Howdy Clark the clarinet player."

"Unreported?"

"He was in his apartment, in his coffin. I spoke to Mrs. Clark, but she declined to be listed." That was the wrong thing to say. The supervisor blew up.

"I don't *give* a damn about any woman named Clark, you just forget all about *that*. I'll tell you *this*, and I want you to understand *this*. No dead bodies. Any more of that and you are *out*," he shouted, stabbing the desk with his finger.

"But it's bound to happen, look at the numbers," I said.

"You listen to *me*. Don't contradict *me*. I'm reassigning you to beauty parlors, as of *right now*. Get moving."

"You heard him," Billy said as I was leaving.

Sounds easy, doesn't it? But you have to go out and find them, and that can take up all your time. I have what you might call "hound-dog reckoning" — a nose for where to look — and it comes in handy. I started with Beauty by Rene, next door to a fancy dress shop. I walked in and the smell hit me. I was unprepared for that! And the noise — hair dryers going, women talking in loud voices a mile a minute like crows in a tree. I spoke to the first operator. "Your business could be listed in the *City Directory*." She kept right on yammering to the woman in the chair. I moved on. I held the Book open for the next one. "Beauty by Rene, bold type, no extra charge," I said cheerfully.

"Boss!" she yelled.

"Where is he?" I yelled back.

"She! In the back!" A very thin woman was sitting at a tiny desk talking into a telephone. She slammed the receiver down and stared at me and said, "Well, what?"

I held the Book open. "This is a wonderful opportunity to list with the *City Directory* at no cost to you, the businessman."

"Don't hand me that," she said. "I run this place. Everyone out there is a mad dog from hell until proven otherwise, including you and that son of a bitch landlord on the telephone." She lit a cigarette and blew smoke at me. "Trying to break my balls, can you believe the son of a bitch?"

"Why not give the Book a try for a year?"

"All right, hotshot, what's your name?"

"Frank."

"As in what?"

"Frank St. Claire."

"Nice. So lead off with it. Don't start with the 'no charge' bit, make it sound good, give it a little class, dress it up for cris-sakes." She filled out the form. "What made you come in here?"

"That's my assignment, beauty shops."

"There's too damn many. It's a cutthroat business, it's very competitive. Do me a favor and don't list all of 'em right around this neck of the woods. Make me look good. The Biltmore, that's a ritzy crowd, they got sheckles in their pants." I told her thanks, I'd do my best. I left, but then I went back.

"Let me ask you something," I said.

"Fire away, Frankie."

"How long can fingernails grow if you don't cut them?"

"Who knows? They keep growing, like hair. It's molecular."

"Thanks."

"Why?"

"I see this woman in Pershing Square every day where I eat lunch. Her nails are about a foot long, but curved back around."

"Tell her to drop in for a manicure, I'll give her the professional discount."

"Thanks."

"You're a very thankful guy, Frankie. Go get yourself a new pair of glasses."

I walked back to Pershing Square. The woman in black was gone. It was getting on toward evening, and I closed my eyes and fell asleep. When I woke up, she was back. "Precept upon precept, line upon line, here a little, there a little." She seemed to be in a relaxed frame of mind. "Of money, some have coveted. They have erred from the faith and pierced themselves through with many sorrows." I waited, hoping to hear more. I tried to give her a quarter, but she hid her face behind the Bible and wouldn't look at me. I left.

There's a bar at the top of Grand Avenue called the Los Amigos. They have a coin-operated player piano, a shuffleboard table game, and booths along the side. The bartender's name is Russell. It was late, and the place was quiet. Russell saw me come in.

"Hiya, Frank. Haven't seen you around lately. The usual?"

"No. I want a whiskey sour. That's a good drink, right?"

"Sure, Frank, sure. One whiskey sour." There was a woman alone in a booth, and she looked up when she heard my voice. It was the manager from Beauty by Rene.

"Thankful Frankie," she said. I sat down across from her.

"How are you this evening, Rene? I guess I'm surprised to see you in my neighborhood."

"Don't be."

"How's it going with the landlord?" I asked, just trying to be delicate.

"That ball-busting son of a bitch? I can't move now, things are just starting to pick up. Downtown's gonna take off when the war hits."

"War?" I wasn't sure what she was talking about or how many drinks she'd had.

"War, kiddo. As in Adolf H.? You heard about him?"

"I'm not sure. I haven't seen the papers lately. Where is the war?"

"Get lost. Nobody's that out to lunch, but nobody. You better get your nose out of that book. Get yourself a girl, there's one on every corner."

I was starting to pick up a slight drawl in her talk. "Where are you from, originally?" In Los Angeles, it's a harmless question.

"Amarillo, Texas. I caught the first thing smokin'. End of story."

"How'd you get started in the beauty line?" I asked.

"I was a bartender in Amarillo. The L.A. cops won't let a woman tend bar in their precious town. I went to cosmetology school, I'm legal."

Russell brought fresh drinks. "This whiskey sour is not bad," I said.

"Look, I can't figure you out. I mean, you're all right, aren't you? Upstairs?" She pointed to her head and made a circle with her finger. "It's no act — the book and your job and all that?"

"It's no act. I work very hard. My boss is a bastard, like your landlord. I'll tell you a little story if you want to hear it."

"Fire away, Frankie. Fire away and fall back."

"I had one friend here on the Hill. Mr. John, an Italian opera singer. But he doesn't sing anymore, and you want to know why? Because he's dead, that's why. He jumped off the roof of the New Grand Hotel."

"A jumper."

"You come back to my place and I'll show you something you never seen in a month of Sundays. I can't believe it myself."

"I got to get down the Hill before the train stops. Tomorrow is another day to be beautiful, right, Frankie boy?"

"You don't believe me. You think I'm one of those mad dogs, like you said."

"Maybe, maybe not. Whiskey sour is a damn good drink." She got up and left, just like that.

Russell walked by, checking tables for tips. "Can't win 'em all!" he said, clapping me on the back so hard I almost choked. I thought about leaving, but then Louie Castro walked up. Louie is a very fat, oily man with a fat, oily voice. Not the kind of man you'd care to know too well. He owns the Los Amigos and lives upstairs.

"Nice to see you, Frank. Always nice to see an old friend." He slid into the booth. "Of course I heard about Mr. John. Tragic." I nodded, like I was too sad to say anything. "I understand you came into a nice little bequest. That's the kind of man he was, generous to his friends." Louie makes it his business to know about things; he likes to know the value of people and things. He sat there, looking at me, sizing me up.

I had to say something. "That's right. Records and books, Italian stuff. I don't understand Italian." Basically true.

"Sentimental, that's the kind of man Mr. John was. And I'm very emotional, Frank. That's why I'm so upset about Mr. John." Louie waited for a reply, but I couldn't think of anything emotional, so I kept quiet. "I'm glad we had this little talk," he said. He maneuvered his big body out of the booth and went upstairs. Russell fussed around for a while. "Gotta close, pal. See you real soon!" I left.

Down below, the city sparkled and hummed like a giant beehive. I walked home. My apartment building is the oldest wooden structure on Bunker Hill. Each floor has a covered porch across the front, and the rooms open out onto it. At night, you can see the lights of the city stretching away to the east. The river, the train tracks, the gasworks, Lincoln Heights, El Sereno, and beyond. I like living there, even though the showers are downstairs. When I got back I checked the directory to make sure the money was all there. I listened to some opera records and looked at the poetry books. I hadn't been doing so well with my lessons. I knew some of the words but I didn't understand the poems. "Try harder," Cousin Lizzie kept saying.

Next morning I went out to buy a paper from Lou Lubin, the gray-haired newsboy who hangs out by the Angel's Flight platform. "'Lo, Lou." I said. I always use that line with him. "What's this I hear about war?"

"Where you been, in the jug?" He's short, and he cocks his head to the side, looking up.

"I'm a working man, Lou, I don't have time to know all these things. Fill me in."

"Hitler and Mussolini got it all sewn up tight. I haven't heard from the family in two years, don't know where they're at. It's all sewn up tighter'n Aunt Fannie's girdle." Lou used to be a nightclub dancer and an extra in the movies.

"Sorry to hear it, Lou. I hope they're okay."

"Thanks."

"You know anything about Mr. John?"

Lou turned so that his back was to the street. "Some guys were talking to him. Very tough guys in a Cadillac. A Cadillac sticks out."

"What'd they want?"

"I'm just the newsy on the street here. Gotta keep the nose clean. You were a friend of his. It was something they thought he had. Something small, something he had hidden in his place. They didn't find it, and they went away. Then they came back."

"The police said it was suicide."

"The Catholics would be out of business."

"Where would a man go for clarinet lessons?"

"Look it up."

Lou was getting nervous, he wanted me to leave. I looked up "Music Teachers." It was mostly women teaching in the home. Mostly piano and violin. I came across *The Saxophone Shop, Leo Schenck, 319 Spring St. R1121.* I called the number from a pay phone. He sounded like an older man.

"This is Leo."

"Do you teach clarinet?"

"Age?"

"Thirty-eight."

"Too old."

"I'd like to try."

"Why?"

"I was given a clarinet."

"Bring it in." Leo sounded tired, and it was only eleven in the morning. I walked there. It was Saturday and the downtown streets were crowded with shoppers. Every restaurant had a line of people waiting to eat, but I had a salami sandwich in my pocket. The shop on Spring Street was tiny and dark, with saxophones hanging up and saxophone parts lying all around. Leo was a skinny bald man with horn-rim glasses and a green visor like pawnbrokers wear. He opened the clarinet case and stood there looking at it. Inside the case, the clarinet was broken down into four sections. You could see it was old, but it had been well cared for. Leo looked at me through his thick glasses.

"I don't want to know how you got this," he said. "I don't want to know about you or who sent you." He closed the lid and snapped the latches. "I got a sawed-off. I made it myself. You try anything, I'm taking you with me."

"I represent the *City Directory.* No other medium can —"

"I got double-ought buck here. They'll just turn the hose on you and wash you into the street." He brought it up from under the counter and showed it to me, the meanest looking little thing I ever saw. I took the case and left. I started walking fast down Spring Street. I walked right through every red light and didn't stop until I got to my bench in Pershing Square.

I tried to calm down. People were coming and going all

around me: kids, old folks, men and women, laughing and talking, friends meeting and calling out to each other. I was too scared to move. After a while, I opened up the case and looked at the four sections of the clarinet as Leo had done. I took the pieces out and turned them around in my hands, but it meant nothing. It was just one more thing I didn't understand.

"You don't look like a reed man," said a voice next me. I jumped, but it was only Finchley, the retired hobo. He took the case and began assembling the pieces like he knew all about it. "Le Blanc, very nice. Something's stuck in here." He fingered around inside one of the sections and brought out a rolled-up piece of paper. "There's your problem," he said, handing it to me. There was a little box in the case and thin pieces of wood inside the box. He took one out and moistened it with his tongue; then he fitted the wood into the end of the clarinet and put the end in his mouth and began to play a little tune. I recognized it. "Over the Waves," which everyone has heard at some point. The woman in black appeared. She came out from behind a palm tree holding her arms straight out to the side and twirling around with the music. She had her Bible in one hand, but she seemed to have forgotten about it. People passing by stopped to watch her. She was a sight, with her torn black dress and her matted hair and those fingernails! After a while, Finchley stopped playing and tipped his hat. "Thank you, friends and neighbors, you're very kind, I'm sure." He passed it around. Some people put money in the hat, others walked off. The woman sat down on her bench across the path and seemed to go right to sleep. "We did good business," Finchley said. "Let us repair to a nice, cool bar. Should we ask your friend?" I shook my head. "She'll be fine," I said "I need a drink bad."

The nice, cool bar turned out to be the Tokyo Big Shot.

"Finchley!" said the Japanese bartender. His gold teeth lit up.

"And the shecker," said the snaggletooth woman at the end of the bar.

"My friend is in a quandary, at a crossroads, and we have come here today to find resolution. For this purpose, we require your back table and a bottle of your cheapest whiskey, *tout suite*," Finchley said. The woman grabbed her glass and made a beeline for the curtain behind the bar, but Finchley said, "You'd best remain on watch, my dear. Be on the lookout for a midget carrying an umbrella."

Behind the curtain was a tiny room with a round table and four chairs. There was nothing else in the room except a telephone and a Mexican pinup calendar from 1936. A lightbulb hung from a nail in the ceiling. The bartender brought a bottle and two glasses. "That will be all, Sammy. We'll call if we need you." Sammy laughed and went back out front.

"A man conceals something inside a clarinet. He assumes it will be found by someone in particular, someone who will understand." Finchley unrolled the paper and smoothed it out on the table. It was a photograph of three men, taken at a restaurant table. The men were looking straight at the camera. Their faces were flat and bright, like a flashbulb had been used. The picture was old, and the men were wearing clothes from another time.

I recognized one man. "It's Mr. John," I said. "He was my friend, up on the Hill. He's dead now. But this is him, a long time ago. I know it's him."

"You have the clarinet, and you know this man."

"But I don't know why I have it," I said. I explained how the widow Clark mistook me for someone else.

"But you might have been the right man. She was expecting somebody. She blamed them." I told Finchley about Leo and the shotgun. "We'll get to that presently," he said.

"But what if they're looking for me now?" I said. "Leo was scared. I'm scared."

"That's good. Danger sharpens up the mind." The woman came in through the curtain. "The midget was ashking for you. I shaid you'd been here and gone," she said.

"That's fine, Lydia. Have a drink."

"Well, I don' mind if I do." She held out her glass. Finchley poured her a tall one, and she tossed it down in one gulp.

"Shammysh rotgut is the worsht shince canned heat," she said.

"Have one more," said Finchley. She took her drink in both hands and went out through the curtain.

"What's that about a midget?" I asked.

"Just a fellow I know. Trouble follows him, he's like a human lightning rod. A sure sign that something's up." Finchley rubbed his hands with enthusiasm.

I was beginning to form an opinion of Finchley. Had I fallen in with a madman? I kept hearing Leo, "They'll wash you into the street." It wasn't hard to imagine: The gutter on Spring Street. Sewer pipes. Garbage in the riverbed down by Aliso Flats. "What about the dead man on Utah Street?" I said.

"Omit nothing," said Finchley. I tried to remember details. The blood caught his attention. "Blood on the walls, delightful! Sprayed, smeared, how was it done? Think, man, think!"

"Smeared, I would say. I didn't stick around there, I had to find a telephone."

"Smeared how? Up high? Down low?"

"Low, definitely. It looked a little like letters. Maybe it meant something."

"Close your eyes. What do you see? You knock. You open the screen door. You look about for someone in the house. Something makes you look down. Is something moving?"

"No, it's just feet."

"Do you smell anything?"

"Frying lard."

"Music?"

"A radio. A soap opera. *Ma Perkins*?"

"Excellent. Eleven o'clock to eleven fifteen, followed by *Our Gal Sunday*. You get the idea?"

"No, I don't."

"My friend, consider. A man is listening to the radio while making lunch, sometime between eleven and eleven fifteen. But by the time you arrive, he's been murdered, his blood smeared on the wall down by the floor. I suggest he named the killer with his own blood, then crawled into the kitchen and died. What did the blood spell?"

Then I saw it. "It spelled 'Book.'" Finchley picked up the telephone and dialed.

"Homicide," he said into the receiver. He waited. Then he said, "They're putting me through."

After what seemed like days and days, a big man in a suit came into the room and sat down at the desk. I was handcuffed to a chair. He shuffled some papers around and looked over at me.

"So, Mr. St. Claire. Frank St. Claire. I wouldn't be here, wouldn't waste my time, but there's too many connections."

My mouth was dry and my tongue felt like an ironing board, but I had to say something. "What do you mean, connections?"

"A suicide on Bunker Hill, a dead musician in hock to the bookies, and a spic dismemberment down in the Flats. And Frank St. Claire knew them all."

"I meet people in my job, I don't know them. Except for Mr. John."

"John Casaroli jumps off the roof and you inherit. Why? Tell me that. Make it sound good."

"I really don't know."

"A couple of bright boys were seen hanging around there. Friends of yours?"

"I don't have any friends since Mr. John died."

"You create a disturbance at the Clark home while a service is going on. No respect for the dead, it seems. Why's that?"

"I was doing my job, how could I know?"

"The widow says you told her to hand over the clarinet. Says you threatened her."

"She's lying. She gave it to me."

"Why would she lie?"

"I don't know."

"All right, Utah Street. Some character slices this guy's arm off and beats him with it. There's blood on the walls. Maybe it spells 'book,' maybe he was overdue at the library, I wouldn't know. But, here's Frank St. Claire at the scene, within minutes, and that's just one too many times in my book."

"The supervisor makes all the decisions. I think he was punishing me for the trouble with Howdy Clark. Nobody wants to work the Flats."

The detective got up. "Nobody's as dumb as you act," he said. He left the room. After a while, an officer in uniform came and took me down the hall to another room. A man in a white coat was seated behind a desk. He told me to sit down and relax. Relax! How could I?

"I'm Dr. Sonderborg," the man said. "I'm going to ask you some questions."

"I've done nothing," I said.

"Begin, if you will, by telling me about yourself. Anything that comes to mind."

"Nothing comes to mind."

"I see you're a single man, living alone. Do you have a girlfriend?"

"I know a girl. I know three girls altogether, but I recently met one in particular."

"Tell me about her. What's her name?"

"Rene. She runs a beauty parlor on Olive and Fifth."

"Is she kind to you, is she affectionate? Responsive?"

"She says I might be a mad dog from hell. 'The jury's out,' is how she puts it."

"And that makes you angry."

"No."

"Would you say her behavior towards you is cruel? Belittling?"

"Oh, no. She's really a nice person."

"Do you ever ask her to hurt you, to punish you?"

"What? What is this, who are you?" Maybe the police are crazy, I thought.

"Do you hate the police?"

"No."

"Are you plotting against the government of the United States?"

"No."

"Are you a Communist?"

"What's that?" I said. The doctor pushed a button on the desk and the detective came in the room.

"What do we got?" he asked.

"Why do you waste my time? Get him out of my office. Drop him off in Griffith Park. I went to medical school for eight years, Spangler. Eight goddamn years."

"And you got a *very tough* job here, Sonderborg," Spangler said with obvious distaste.

Detective Spangler gave me back my briefcase and told me not to leave town. I left the police building and walked up the Hill. The police believe everything is a pattern. Once they see a pattern, they think they know it all, and they think they got you. That's not the way life is. Take it from me, life is random and inscrutable, like the *City Directory*. Or my name isn't *St. Claire, Frank, chkr, Alta Vista Apts 255 Alta Vista Ave., Ls Angls.*

Who do you know that I don't?

1949

—⚊—

THE STREETCAR STOPPED on the corner to pick up a load of early risers on their way to the little piece of job. A solitary rider got out and walked south on Berendo, a dusty street in a dingy neighborhood just west of downtown. He unlocked the front door at number 39, a two-story brick building in need of paint since elephants roamed the La Brea Tar Pits.

"Jazz Man Records" read the sign in the front window, unwashed since Joaquin Murietta shot up Laurel Canyon. The man stooped to pick up the circulars from the scarred linoleum floor and then closed and locked the door behind him. Shelves lined the walls. On the shelf were ancient 78-speed records, thousands of them. There was a small desk covered with dust, a desk lamp designed by Abraham Lincoln, and a black telephone. The man pulled a curtain aside and walked back to another room lined with shelves. 78s, thousands more. A portable record player sat on a small table next to an overstuffed chair salvaged from the Edwin Hotel fire of 1910. The man took a disc over to the table. "Clarinet Marmalade" with Johnny Dodds, on the Okeh label, recorded in 1927. He sat back in the chair, lit his pipe, and closed his eyes. The scratchy old record played, and the little tune got moving — an unsolved riddle from the past: 4/4 time on the bass drum by brother Baby Dodds, top melody from the clarinet, suggestive interplay on trumpet and trombone. Chankchankchank went the banjo. The man's face settled into an unconscious mask. In four minutes the record was done, and the steel needle in the heavy stylus arm began to drag across the center grooves, making a sshh, sshh, sshh sound that went on and on.

Nobody wants to get measured for a suit on Friday. Our people believe that the mortician dresses you on Friday for the last time. But still, in he came — Johnny "The Ace of Spades" Mumford. And he says, "Ray, I want the one-piece back! I want the French shoulders! Three-pleat pants all the way up, and I need my trick waistband, you hear me, Ray? Purple gabardine and cocoa brown, and I want 'em in two weeks!"

"Who do you know that I don't, Johnny?" I laughed.

"Look, man, I got the number one rhythm-and-blues record right now. I'm so hot, I'm burnin' up, and money don't mean a thing," said Johnny, a good looking, chocolate-colored man, five-feet-seven and rangy. I made an appointment to see him again in two Fridays. Johnny pulled away in his new Cadillac, all done up special for him in two-tone lilac and cream, a beautiful car.

I got the job done right to the day. I got his fit, and no doubt about it. Then Lenny, from the Stylin' Smilin' and Profilin' barbershop, stuck his head in the door. "You get the news about Johnny Mumford?"

"Man, what news?" I said.

"Johnny shot dead, backstage, at the 54 Ballroom!"

"The 54? Somebody killed old Johnny?"

"He killed himself playin' with a gun! Lawd, have mercy where's the po' boy gone!" I ran out for a paper. "Self-inflicted," it read. I closed the shop and went straight down there. I told them to let me talk to the reporter, that I had information about Johnny Mumford. They brought me to a fellow upstairs. I said, "Look here, you got it wrong. No chance Johnny did this, and I'll tell you why. He had me make up two fancy suits, two weeks ago today. No way the Ace of Spades would order clothes like that and then go out and shoot himself in the head."

"Let's have your name and address." The newspaper man didn't even look at me.

The funeral was big. African Methodist on Twenty-fifth was packed. Ebenezer Brothers Mortuary did the best they could, what with Johnny's head blown out in back. I brought the suits over, and his mother chose the purple. Oopie McCurn, the bass singer with the Pilgrim Travelers, took me aside after the service. "The suit was a nice gesture, Ray. We all agreed. Ray does shoulders, no need to go further." He gave me a look. "If you take my meaning, brother." The Travelers did their rendition of "See How They Done My Lord" for Johnny. Little Cousin Tommy took the lead on "Somewhere to Lay My Head," and Johnny's mother and sister fainted and had to be carried out. Tommy is a short man, five feet in shoes, but he has a big voice and he can use it. "Overreaches," as Bill Johnson of the Golden Gates observed later on at the repast, and you don't dispute a man like Bill.

A police Ford was situated outside the church. Two plain-clothes stepped up, looking plain. "Have a seat in the office," one said. Breezy. No sense kickin', as Jimmy Scott says, and he should know. I sat.

"I'm Detective McClure. You been stirring things up a little, haven't you? Some people we know are getting a little concerned. You should concentrate more on your little tailoring job, that's our line of thinking."

"I've been trying to get at the truth. Nobody seems interested."

"You were seen talking to that boy from the *Sentinel*. What'd he offer you, 'cause we can top it."

"You can top the truth?"

"Very definitely. We can let you breathe. Have a pleasant afternoon, Mr. Montalvo."

"Ray Montalvo, Custom Vootie Tailoring! If It's All Vootie, It's All Rootie!" That was Slim Gaillard's idea, he likes everything strictly all rootie and reetie pootie. Slim is a very good-looking, well-set-up man, and talented, but he's what you might call a floater — he's never in one place for very long. I'm from down around the District. It's been mixed for a long time — black, Mexican, and Italian. I'm what you might call mixed, myself. Momma is from the West Indies, and Daddy was a Sicilian — Pietro, or Pete, as he was called. Daddy came out here to play professional baseball, but he was underbuilt and passed over. He worked as a stonemason until he died, a frustrated little man with a wicked fast pitch, wasted. I learned tailoring from Uncle Gustavo. Gus, as he was called. Gus was an expert in charro out-fits for the mariachis that hang out over in Boyle Heights. That's a very good clientele, very reliable. If they dig you, they stay with you. And the style never changes! You just keep doing the same short black coat and tight pants with no pockets, silver buttons, brocade, and big hat.

Gus would shake his head at me and say, "Looka, Ray, whadda you wanna do, eh? Why you don' wanna work for me, I don' know! I gotta good business, the Mexicans. Good boys, they pay alla time on time. Whadda you got, jazza musicians! They don' pay, I know! I'm an old man. I got no sons a passa the job! Big waste! Whatsa matta you, Ray?" Two weeks to the day after

Johnny Mumford's funeral, he had his third heart attack, the big one. No pockets in a shroud, Uncle Gus.

Maybe I was wrong, but I never could see it — a black-skinned man with an Italian name cutting charro suits for the rest of my life? Thing is, I liked music! Jazz, jump, jive, rhythm and blues! I tried, but I couldn't play anything very well. I studied harmony and all that, but you can't get tone out of a book. Down around the District, you got to get hot or go home, so I made clothes for the players instead. Gus was right about the money though. Jazz musicians are a little unreliable, they're always leaving town, they float.

My mother told me I had a responsibility to Gus's family, so I went over to talk to his wife, Graziesa. She was in bad shape, hysterical, and the girls were terrified. I said I would look into it and see what might be done. The truth is you could almost see the cloud over my shop since Johnny died. Lenny the barber had stopped coming by for coffee when the two cops started parking out in front at lunchtime giving everybody the eye and tossing their cigarette butts all over the sidewalk.

A custom tailor is sort of a confidence man. It's a confidential job, and it makes a man watchful and a little lonely. Other people wear the clothes you make, they go out and drink and do the Hucklebuck. That's all right, it's in the nature of the work. But a tailor under surveillance is all through. The vout just ran out. T-Bone Walker stopped by in his new Lincoln Continental. He said, "I think you better *mooove* way out on the outskirts of town!" T-Bone was on his way up. I had heard something about a new tailor on Sunset Boulevard.

"Ramildo of Hollywood! El Último en Charro!" read the new business card. I moved my sewing machine and the gabardine over to Gus's place on First, two blocks down from the Mariachi Hotel in Garibaldi Plaza. I told everyone that I was taking over and discounting all work ten dollars just to get acquainted. They were all very polite and very sorry about Gus. He was family to them, but

I am a different color, see, and they didn't quite believe the whole nephew bit. You've noticed how furniture salesmen stand in the door and watch the street? I started doing the same thing, looking up and down the street for hours at a time. I announced a 30 percent discount and free hat, one to a customer. Folks waved and smiled, but nobody wanted a suit or a hat or even a belt buckle. I tried hanging out in Garibaldi Plaza, but every time they started up blasting those trumpets, it made my teeth hurt.

One day, two pachuco kids came into the shop. They looked to be about twenty, five-six and very skinny, not your charro body type. Kiko and Smiley, by name. They employed a trick handshake I wasn't familiar with. "What can Ramildo of Hollywood do for you cats?" I asked cheerfully. "The first sombrero is free!"

"Queremos un zoot," they both said at once.

"Reet! I cut suits for the Ace of Spades, rest his soul. Maybe you heard of him?"

"Ay te huatcho, vato." Seemed like they had.

"So, two full-drape zoots. Color?"

Smiley said, "Uno. We trade off."

"Oh, I dig you now, you want to share it. Well, it happens this is zoot special week, and I can do you a suit and two pair of pants for the price. That way, you're dressed, you both look good."

"Órale! En púrpuro!" They laid twenty dollars in ones on me as a deposit without being asked and bopped off down the street. Two days later they were back with more ones and some silver, but I said make it twenty bucks total, a steal. They were ecstatic about it, and they both looked sharp and ready. "Fall by any time," I told them. "Don't be strangers."

The big deal in retail ready-to-wear was the Victor Clothing Company, at 214 South Broadway. Leo "Sunshine" Fonerow had dreamed up the idea of credit layaway. You could buy anything in the store for $2.50 down and $2.50 a week. It worked like a charm and Leo became a rich man dressing the poor. He kept six tailors working around the clock doing alterations. One old man, Daddy Bassey, dropped dead pinning trouser cuffs, and I hurried in to see if I could nail the position. I told Leo I would do the work at home at a discount, and he hired me. Alterations were due back Friday night for customer pickup on the weekend. Leo reckoned that working people would appreciate it if he kept the store open on Sundays. Families came in after church, excited and happy to be downtown, like it was a special event. A Mexican girl did good business selling tamales out in front of the store. I thought she was beautiful — compact and solid, about five-four, with a big hairdo and a sly look. I tried to talk to her, but she didn't speak English and I didn't have the lingo down, so I just pointed and held up two fingers. "De qué?" she asked. "Make mine soft and easy, but I mean good and greasy!" I replied. She laughed; she got the message.

I was motorvating home late one Friday after dropping off a load of pants, when I came upon a police roadblock at Broadway and Second. It had been raining, and the street was glowing red from squad car lights. I made a quick right turn and saw two guys, one in a suit and the other in trousers and a sleeveless undershirt, running down the sidewalk. That's what caught my eye in the dark, the undershirt. I pulled alongside and shouted out the one phrase I knew from movies, "Vamos muchachos!" They jumped in. I ran the light at Spring, made a bad left and pulled up in the alley behind the Times building. I cut the lights.

"Zoot patrol," said Smiley. "They will catch all Mexicans wearing clothes!"

"Pendejos! Pinches gabachos!" said Kiko. Two police Fords went flying by on Spring, their sirens blasting.

"I happen to have a friend here," I said. "Let's go say hello to Herman." Herman "JuJu" Doxey, the night watchman at the *Los Angeles Times,* spent most evenings in the backseat of his '37 Buick, listening to the radio, off the street and out of sight.

I knocked twice on the window. Herman rolled it down and peered out through a thick cloud of cigarette smoke.

"Here we have Brother Ray and two young fellas," Herman said. "I'm always glad to make the acquaintance of young people. Gettin' hectic over on Broadway, it's protrudin' on my mood."

"We have to get off the street for just a little while." I said. I sat up front; Kiko and Smiley got settled in back.

"You boys just relax," said Herman. "Listen, there's Johnny Mumford on the radio, and now he's crossed over Jordan. Ain't that a shame?" He passed the Chesterfield pack around and we all lit up.

"Chonny was over there at the Big Union, we saw him!" Kiko said. "He sang 'My Heart Is in My Hands.'"

"With his eyes to Florencia," Smiley said.

"Florencia?" I asked.

"Qué chula chulita!" Smiley whistled.

"I know you got some fine, healthy mamacitas, and that's a fact," Herman said.

"Healthy?"

"You know, solid."

"Solid?"

"Man, dig it and pick up on it!" Herman motioned for quiet while poor Johnny's last platter got moving on the radio — a slow-thudding blues, the horns sustaining in big harmony blasts, like the Southern Pacific Daylight pulling into Union Station:

> Got me a fine healthy mama, she's long and she's tall
> Built up solid, like the L.A. City Hall
> From the top of her head right down to her feet
> She's a high-grade load of sugar freightin' up Main Street
> Fine and healthy, yes she fine and healthy
> So doggone fine and healthy, boys, and she ain't no
>   hand-me-down!

"High-grade load of sugar?" Kiko pronounced it *sookar*.

"As in, juicy!" Herman said.

"Sólido!"

Herman began. "All right, then. John Mumford. Born, Los Angeles, 1923; died, 1949, cut down in his prime. The prodigal son was a forward child; his mind was not to obey. But he gave his all. The band would lead off so as to get the beat planted in the mind. At the turnaround, Johnny would move up to the front. Very smooth. But on the chorus, he might start slappin' his left knee in time whilst holdin' the microphone in his right hand. Ol' Johnny's gettin' ready! On the second verse, John hold back just a little, walkin' around and shakin' his shoulders out, like a fighter. Next chorus, he tighten up! He grab a handful of Ray's gabardine, 'bout midthigh! Clutchin' at it! Them little gals run forward as close as they can get. He let the guitar work. He back up. Last chorus, he commence to stompin'! He grab his waistband and jerk his pants up, on the beat! All the gals throw pocketbooks, handkerchiefs, anything they ain't gone need later on. They don't throw they hatpins or they guns, nossir, they don't throw that! Heh, heh, nossir, they don't."

I said, "Was it a woman got him killed? You know he didn't do it." Herman had the inside dope on all subjects known heretofore and as yet undesignated.

"Right now, I got to make my rounds. What good it is, I don't really know. Look like a newspaper building to you? It's a Temple of Secrets, the High and Mighty Church of the Next Dollar, and ain't nary a one of 'em mine. What they need a watchman for? Our Lord and Savior had a marvelous trick bag, I'm told, but even he couldn't break in here." Kiko and Smiley crossed themselves. Herman laughed. "Don't you boys be concerned, I'm strictly spiritual! My mind is stayin' on Jesus! I'm a deacon in the Church of the Rapid Bible and the First Born, on Thirty-third. Worship services are spontaneous and unscheduled, but all are welcome! Right now, you folks better sit tight and let me have a look around on the boulevard. I'll be back."

Kiko said, "Man, he's been at a lot of shows."

"Actually, no. You dig Herman right here, every night. No need to go further. He'll be on the radio in a little while. We don't check him with no lightweight stuff."

Saturday and Sunday nights it was Leon the Lounge Lizard's radio show, *The Rump Steak Serenade*. Leon featured the cool sounds of jazz from midnight to 3:00 a.m., broadcasting live from Doctor Brownie's Famous Big Needle, the jazz record shop on San Pedro open twenty-four hours a day. At two o'clock, Herman came on for a fifteen-minute interlude: "It's time once again for *Dig It and Pick Up On It*, with Herman the Human Jukebox!" Folks would call in with questions and try to stump JuJu, but it had never been done. If a caller asked about a record, he could name all the players, the label color, matrix number, and chart position. He'd know how many suits Billy Eckstine had and what brand of gin Fats Waller preferred. Tonight JuJu was sharp and on the money, as always. A white man in Glendale, who wouldn't give his name, asked, "Is it legal for colored men to call themselves 'King,' 'Duke,' and 'Count'?" JuJu answered politely, "Yes, if jazz is legal. If not, all bets are off, and you had better stay right there in Glendale!" Next came a brother from Watts, one Horace Sprott. "How many times has guitarist Irving Ashby been stopped by the LAPD on his way home from the nightclub job with Nat Cole?" Answer: "Eighty-seven times to date, and always by the same motorcycle officer, William 'Bitter Bill' Spangler, badge 666. Officer Bill asserts that John has been entertained in their home by his wife, Mabel, repeatedly and often, whilst he is out on patrol. 'She plays those records by that spade, Cole. I hate music! Every time I come in from work, the place stinks like fish. I hate fish!'" The third caller was a white woman with an East Tennessee drawl that made a question out of everything: "Hello, Herman? This is Ida from Thirty-third Street, and I have a garage full of old 78 records? They belonged to my husband; he liked that music you like? I'm moving to Spokane, so what should I do?"

"'Scuse the hat, Miss Ida, ma'am, but that's me you hear a-knockin'!" JuJu laughed. "I declare now, don't you go answering that door for nobody else!"

We were sitting in front of their house in Chavez Ravine, up in the hills behind Chinatown. Kiko got a jug from the house and we passed it around, listening to Billie Holiday on the communal jukebox that was wired up to the lone streetlight.

My man, he don't love me, he treats me awful mean
He's the lowest man I've ever seen

"Help me out, lay something on me," I said. "Like, 'May I ask your name?', 'When do you get off work?', 'Would you like a drink?', that kind of thing."

Kiko laughed, "Man, pick up on *theese* and dig it!"

"What you wanna do, man?" asked Smiley.

"I want to take this girl out, man, what do you think?" I said.

"You wanna take out one of our girls, pendejo?"

"Yeah. You know, for a drink."

"A drink?"

"Yeah, just for a drink."

"Oh."

He wears high-drape pants, stripes of lovely yellow
When he starts in lovin' me, he is so fine and mellow

"Where did the jukebox come from? What's it doing in the street?" I asked.

"Cousin Beto SixFingers found it. Nobody over here has dinero por radios."

"He found a brand-new Wurlitzer jukebox?"

"Cousin Beto finds things for people."

"Do you help him?" I asked, wondering what Kiko and Smiley did all day and night. I kept seeing them in the strangest places. "What happens when it rains?"

"It moves," said Smiley.

Love is like a faucet, it turns off and on
Just when you think it's on, baby, it's turned off and gone.

The record finished. The fancy colored lights switched off, and the machine went to sleep.

～

The last rays of the sun fell upon the dirty front window and died trying to get through. The man sat in the front room of the record shop studying an auction circular of rare 78s. He made little checks next to certain entries with a red pencil, drinking occasionally from a greasy water glass. A pint bottle of Four Roses bourbon sat near to hand.

The red lightbulb in the ceiling went on. The man put the paper down and walked through the curtain to the back door. He checked the peephole, then opened the door partway. "Boss," said a confidential voice in the dark. An ancient panel truck was parked in the alley behind the shop, "Cousin Beto's Scrap Metal" painted on its side. A short, slightly built man with a large cardboard box stood waiting.

The box contained 78 records which the man with the pipe began to take out and examine. He handled the records expertly, like a bank teller counting money. The short man was Mexican, or Mexican and something else like Greek, with oily black hair ducktailed in the pachuco style and a wide leering mouth full of gold teeth. He watched the man closely.

"*Nice*, boss. Look at the *condition*," he whispered. The man with the pipe regarded the Mexican and spoke for the first time with the pipestem clenched in his teeth. "Whiteman, Whiteman, Whiteman, Nick Lucas, Vernon Dalhart. Bunch of crap. Where are the sleeves?"

"I had to get out of there *fast*, boss, I had to leave the sleeves. But I got something special, something you really gonna *like*. Columbia Black Label, *brand new*." He held it properly, as the man had taught him always to do, by the edges. His gold rings flashed in the light, especially the ones on his right hand, since there were six fingers instead of the routine five.

The man took the record and turned it this way and that, examining the grooves and the silver inscription that read "Ma Rainey, colored singer with piano acc. by Clarence Williams, recorded in New York, 1923."

"Where'd you get this?" he said in a flat, accusing tone.

"Boss, *listen*. It's a lady, down on Thirty-third. Her old man was a collector, like you. They're in the garage! Bluebird, Paramount, Columbia, Okeh! This is el mero mero, boss.

"What's the setup?"

"She's a gabacha. In the house twenty years. Two poodle dogs inside. Garage is in the back. Original boxes. You gonna *love* it, boss!"

"Who else knows?"

"A kid brings her groceries from the tienda on the corner. He's always looking for old cars down there. He got the key and went into the garage. He found this. He says it's got muchos hermanos más!"

"The key?"

"She likes him, she lets him see."

"Get it."

"She keeps the keys on a string around la cintura."

"Get the key."

The deliveryman pointed to the box of records on the table. "Y éstos?"

"Junk," said the man, turning back into the doorway. The deliveryman took the box and put it back in the truck. It had seen better days and was full of rust, but the motor made almost no sound as he drove away.

～◌

Sunday morning, the shop doorbell rang and it was Herman. "Brother Ray, what you got planned for today?"

"Just trying to decide between a bench in Union Station and a bench in Pershing Square."

"We going to pay a social call on a high-tone Christian white lady named Ida."

"The one with all the records?"

"That's just what I'm talkin' about! See, we tryin' to be a little more visible over at the church. We got some old people need help and some young people that's gonna need help. Those that haven't had all the advantages like you and me."

"All the advantages?"

"Yes. You learned a useful trade, didn't you? You just getting relocated now, but you'll do all right. Some of these young ones, here, they might wake up one day and find they ain't got nothin' now, and ain't never gonna get a doggone thing. What then? So we tryin' to raise a little money to start a night school. I told Ida, she can take it off her income tax!"

It took most of Sunday to move the record boxes over to the church social hall. "Gonna have a big sale with all these babies! We gonna call it 'Jumpin' at the Record Shop!'" Herman was thrilled, Ida was pleased. She gave us iced tea.

That's a drink I never cared for, but it helped wash away

the dust. It was an old-style bungalow with giant pink and blue hydrangeas all around the outside and white lace doilies everywhere on the inside. Plenty of photographs of Ida with a weak-eyed, weak-chinned man I took to be the late Mr. Ida. I was afraid to get dust all over the doilies, so I had my tea standing up. "Well, if it's of some use to your people, then I feel satisfied. My late husband wanted to be interred with his records, but I was disinclined. Korla Pandit played the organ for us at the funeral service, in person. Such a kind man. Very comforting. He had a vision in which he saw me moving towards a new life in Spokane, Washington. Korla says Spokane is an important spiritual center. You know, another man expressed interest in the records, but I didn't particularly care for his aura. And, there were six fingers on his right hand? Six and five is eleven, a sinister signpost, as Korla would say. Sit down, young man, don't be bashful. More tea?" I sat. One of her French poodles tried to bite my leg. "My late husband read his evening paper there. He always listened to his records out in the garage when we had our circle. Frank was very thoughtful and considerate."

My back hurt from lifting all day. I changed clothes and drove downtown. The girl was there with her tamale setup. "Dos de pollo," I said. She was surprised.

"Bueno, habla español?" she asked.

"How 'bout vamos por some nice quiet place?"

"Tiene un carro?" The same in any language.

"I got a car, un Chevy."

"Una ranfla!"

"Cuándo you get finito?"

"A las siete." She had me there, I didn't know the numbers. She took hold of my wrist and pointed to seven on my watch.

"Solid!" I said.

"Qué?"

"I mean, that's good. Hasta seven o'clock?"

"Hasta las siete en punto." It seemed easy, maybe a little too easy.

I came back at 6:30 and parked down the street where I could watch the girl. I couldn't figure out what the hell I was going to do. Invite her out for Mexican food? Invite her out to learn English? Maybe some people don't care about English, like they're fine how they are. It started to rain. At 6:45, an old Ford delivery truck pulled up. Two guys got out and put the tamale cart in the back. I could see the thing was heavy, and they were little guys. Kiko had the coat this time, and Smiley had the undershirt. So, how do they decide? That's the thing that puzzled me the most. The girl got in and the truck pulled out.

Kiko and Smiley knew my car, but all Chevys look alike in the dark, so I followed them. Whoever was driving did a very nimble job dodging trolleys and beating the stoplights. The truck was a lot faster than it looked. They headed west on Pico Boulevard, past Hoover, past Vermont, and turned right at the alley behind Berendo. I parked around the corner and ran back. A little ways up the alley, I could see a headlight beam coming from a white stucco garage with a curved roof and open double doors. I got down low to have a look, like they do in Westerns. The truck was inside with the motor running, "Cousin Beto's Scrap Metal" painted on the side. Other cars were parked diagonally against one wall. Fancy cars, like Cadillacs and Lincolns. Jukeboxes, fifty or more, were lined up along the opposite wall. There was a stairway leading up to a second-floor landing.

A man came out on the landing. He saw the delivery truck and walked down the stairs. "Where's Beto?" he asked in a gruff, unfriendly way. I couldn't hear the answer, but the man didn't like it. "You tell him I don't want any gaddamn greaseballs in here!" Kiko and Smiley got the tamale cart out and pushed it up against the wall. The man walked over to the truck and looked in. "What have we got here?" He sounded a little drunk. The girl stared straight ahead.

"Meester O'Leedy, es mi hermana, Florencia. She sells tamales es muy buena, she makes *goood* money por you!"

"Maybe we ought to have a little drink, maybe I was a little hasty back there. No offence meant and none taken, right, *sister*?" A jovial tone, hollow and mean.

"No entiendo," the girl said to Smiley.

"Sorry, Meester, pero, she no speak much English, que lástima! Es Sunday, so she wanna go por the church! La madre es gonna make *big* trouble when I don' go straight over there! Es okay?"

The man waved them away in disgust. "Gaddamn bunch of churchgoing monkeys!" He turned and walked back up the stairs. I sprinted down the alley and made it around the corner to the Chevy just as the truck shot out of the alley and hustled back down Pico Boulevard.

The rain was picking up. I sat there in my wet clothes, trying to think. What had I learned? Almost nothing, except for one little thing. The light in the garage was bad, but I recognized one of the cars parked in the back. A brand-new Cadillac, sporting a custom lilac-and-cream paint job. Lilac and cream. No mistake, there was only one car in Los Angeles like that, and it belonged to the late, great Johnny Mumford, the Ace of Spades. When a man is buried in a suit you made for him, then you got a responsibility.

I drove back to the shop. I lay down on the bed in the back and turned on the radio. It was ten o'clock, and the Lounge Lizard didn't come on until midnight. I had time, I dozed off. The next thing I heard was a woman's voice. "This is Judy from Echo Park. Who killed the Ace of Spades?" There was a pause, then Herman answered in a strange, sad tone: "The Ace was killed by the 39 Backbiters and Syndicaters, an organization of paid assassins under the direction of —" But he never finished. A shot rang out over the airwaves. There was a minute of dead air, then "Jumpin' at the Woodside" with Count Basie came on. I panicked. I jumped out of bed and tore out of there in the Chevy and headed straight for Doctor Brownie's record shop. Leon was getting ready to go on the air. "What's the action, Jackson?" he asked.

"Man, where's Herman!"

"He's not due 'til two!"

"Look, man, I got to find him! If he gets here, don't let him go on the air!"

"What's the gag? Why the fright bag?"

"I had a vision. If Herman goes on the show tonight, something terrible will happen, I've seen it! You just got to believe me and keep him off the air 'til I get back!"

"Reet! Bring me back a double order of areechiepoochies!" Leon was gone, swinging out in radio-land jive.

I figured I had one chance to warn Herman. I drove down San Pedro to Thirty-third and turned left. I took the block at two miles an hour, looking for anything out of place. The Buick was parked in front of the Invisible Church, right behind Cousin Beto's panel truck. I parked and cut the motor. If I live ten thousand years nothing will ever surprise me again, I thought. I knocked, and the door swung open. "Right on time, Ray," Herman said. He was seated on a straight-back chair in a small circle of chairs in the front room of the church. Ida was on his left, dressed in a gown of something thin and pale. On his right was Kiko, then Smiley and Florencia. Between Florencia and Ida was a man in pajamas and a fancy piled up do-rag. "Sit right down, Ray," Herman said. I took the empty chair. In the center was a glass ball on a pedestal, lit up from inside. The light kept changing in some trick way. I said, "I had a powerful dream, there's gonna be trouble on the radio!" Herman said, "That's all right, we hip to it, we gonna take care of it right now. Just settle back and relax." He closed his eyes.

The room got dark. The light in the glass ball dimmed, and

the do-rag man spoke. "Let us join hands." Hands found mine. "Let us pray." His voice was rich and deep, like a radio announcer's. There was silence for a minute. "Let us begin. Fascination lies in the magic of the extraordinary," he intoned.

"The world is a beautiful place to be born into," the group responded.

"Now and then it's good to pause in the pursuit of happiness," he continued.

"The world is a beautiful place to be born into," the group repeated.

". . . and just be happy. Who asks for guidance?" The question hung in the air. Ida was first, she was ready. "Will I be happy in Spokane?"

The do-rag man shifted around in his chair. I watched his face undergo a change. He grinned, he tilted his head to one side, then the other, and began to speak in a woman's voice and make piano-playing motions with his hands. "*Happiness is just a smile away . . .*"

"Who's that speaking?" Ida wanted to know.

"I'm Billy Tipton. *Spokane is a little cold sometimes / A little rainy maybe / But it's all right / If you're white.*"

"But will I belong there? I need to belong to a place," Ida said.

"Where are you calling from?" asked Billy.

"Los Angeles."

Do-rag made piano chording motions and sang in a woman's contralto range, drawing out the vowels in the manner of Marlene Dietrich: "*You don't belong to Los Angeles / There's nothing left to tie you down / Drop by and see me / Spokane's where I can be / Found.* The Billy Tipton Trio, Fridays and Saturdays at the Rumpus Room, 517 North E Street. *It's not a cool room / It's a don't be fooled room / It's not a polite room / But it's the right room / For someone like yoooou.*"

He settled back, his eyes remained closed. "Who asks for

clarification?" Suddenly I wasn't sure what I wanted to know. What difference did it make who killed Johnny Mumford? Who cared where his Cadillac had got to?

Then Florencia began to cry. She raised her head and looked up toward the ceiling and spoke through the tears. "Chonny, mi amor, mi corazón," she pleaded. "Tu hijo is coming soon. Your child. What can I do? It's a sad world for me now. I have nothing. No tengo nada. Please help me, Chonny." It was pitiful and heartbreaking. The do-rag man leaned forward and rested one elbow on his knee and rolled an imaginary cigarette, just like Johnny Mumford used to do. He smiled a sad smile. "Hey baby, I'm sorry for the way it worked out. I didn't mean no harm. They got to me when I was high. I was onstage, doin' my hit. The crowd was goin' wild, streamin' and tryin.'" Do-rag blew imaginary smoke and waved it away. "They said, 'Some guy wants yo' autograph.' I said, 'I'll be rat down!' This man put a paper in my hand, and whilst I was signin', he pulled his pistol and shot me dead. I never even saw his face. If you have a boy, please name him after me. If it's a girl, name her Florence. I know she gone be fine and healthy, jus' like you, baby. Jus' like you." His voice began to fade away.

Smiley's hand shot up like he was in school.

"Chonny! Wait! En heaven, what kine of car does Jesus drive?"

Johnny replied with a chuckle. "Well, pardner, soon as we get up here, we take an oath not to tell. It'd be unfair to the competition. But I'll say this, it's low and slow, and it's all dolled up! Lots of lights and mirrors and trick stuff on the inside. The Lord looks *goood* when he come cruisin' by! That's all I got for you, my telephone is ringin'. But, one thing we all agree on, there ain't *nobody* up here that does shoulders like Ray Montalvo! No need to go further! I'll see you when the swallows come home to Central Avenue!"

Do-rag collapsed. He sat there with his head on his chest

and didn't move a peg. I thought that was going to be the end of the performance, but then Herman spoke up.

"I have a question for Korla Pandit. Can you hear me, Korla? Someone wants to kill me. They will, if I go on the radio. Why?" Korla do-rag seemed to struggle inside himself, as if he was fighting against something or someone. His head jerked around and he started talking fast, too fast. "This is Billy Tipton again. Who's the tailor out there?"

"That's me," I managed to say.

"Great, listen, I can't wear off-the-rack, see, and my tailor died last month, he froze to death in two inches of water, can you beat that, so suppose I send you my specs, because I got to get some new suits made and I—"

"Hold it!" Herman said in a tough tone I'd never heard before. "Get back! That's not Billy Tipton, it's someone else, someone close by. Who are you! What do you want!" Nothing happened, nothing came through. "We're none of us going to break the circle until you come out in the open and give it up!" Herman was bearing down, and it scared me bad. Korla just sat there with his head down and said nothing, he didn't even breathe. Then all hell broke loose. Ida started hissing and snarling like a bobcat. Her face got all pinched up, and she said through clenched teeth in a voice like a buzz saw, "I want my records you took my records those records are MINE!!!" She fell on the floor and lay there writhing and hissing and clawing at herself. Herman got up and went out of the room. He came back with a hammer and one of Mr. Ida's 78s. He read the label out loud: "The Growlin' Baby Blues, Blind Lemon Jefferson, colored blues singer with guitar, the Paramount label, 1926." Herman took the record over to the wall and put a nail through the middle and hammered it all the way in. Every time he hit the nail, Ida's body jumped a foot. When he was done, she lay still and seemed to relax and breathe regular.

Herman switched on the lights. "That's all, folks. Just got

to find out who it is that wants a bunch of old records that had." I helped Ida up off the floor. She seemed a little dazed. "Very kind of you, I'm sure," she said. Herman and I walked her home, and Herman thanked her for organizing the circle on short notice. "Well, if it was of some use, then I'm satisfied. I feel very confident about Spokane now." She didn't seem to remember about the records, which was a damn good thing. I walked over to the truck. Florencia was sitting in the front seat, between Kiko and Smiley. She didn't look up. I said, "I'm sorry. I hope it's going to be all right for you." The truck pulled out. Herman checked his watch. "Got to make the gig, can't disappoint the folks in radio land."

"What happens now?" I asked.

"Don't you worry, I'll take it from here." He took off in the Buick. Thirty-third Street went back to sleep. I looked all around for Korla Pandit, but he was gone, and I never saw him or Florencia again.

~

Fifteen people were injured in a freak explosion in a quiet neighborhood on Berendo Street, near downtown Los Angeles. The blast originated at 39 Berendo, a record shop operated by one Don Brown. The building was completely destroyed. Police and firemen at the scene found the charred and fused remains of what must have been an extensive stockpile of shellac recordings. Sergeant Blaine McClure, of the Los Angeles Police Department, speculated that chemicals may have triggered the blast. "In a case like this, we overlook nothing. Our science boys are very alert, I can assure you." When asked if the FBI had been notified, Sergeant McClure replied, "The LAPD is on the job, buster." When asked if Don Brown had been located, McClure said, "We are very interested in Mr. Brown. We'll find him."

Off-duty motorcycle officer William "Bill" Spangler was taken into custody yesterday after neighbors reported that he chased his wife, Mabel, down the sidewalk brandishing his service revolver. Spangler, who had been drinking, told police that his wife had served him a tuna sandwich for lunch that had paper in it, which he showed detectives. The paper was identified as the label from a 78 recording by Louis Armstrong, a colored singer with trumpet. Sergeant Mc-Clure of the LAPD speculated that it was flotsam from the recent explosion on Berendo, one block away. The Spanglers reside at 33 Catalina Street. Neighbors told police the couple quarreled frequently and often. Spangler was quoted as saying, "I'm expected to take it and like it and go out and do this stinking job?" Mabel Spangler was unharmed, and has been released.

'My Dear Mr. Montalvo. I trust this note finds you well. I have found a new home here in Spokane. I find I am enjoying new things, for instance, music! Thanks to Mr. Billy Tipton, who has proven to be a real gentleman, and you know how rare that is! Please remember me to your friend Herman. Kindest regards, Ida Kirby, General Delivery, Spokane, Washington.'

The manager of the Bundy Theatre at Pico Boulevard and Thirty-fourth Street in Santa Monica stood outside eating a candy bar and watching the traffic. It was Wednesday, a slow night for neighborhood moviegoing. The manager was a big man, three hundred pounds easy, from eating candy bars on the job. A Santa Monica city bus pulled up across the street, headed westbound toward the beach, thirty-four blocks away. A solitary rider got out and unlocked the front door at number 3406 West Pico. A sign in the window read "Jazz Man Records." The manager watched the man enter the store and close the door. "New guy," he said to himself. "Who the hell cares about records?" Above his head, the marquee lights stuttered on and off, making a buzzing sound like Morse code. Goddamn salt air, like I don't have expenses, he thought, and the thought made him hungry. He turned and walked back inside the theater.

The new owners at 968 East Thirty-third Street loved the house. It was in perfect shape and priced just right for a young couple. It was after they'd been in the place a little while that the problem arose. Their dog hated the garage. He wouldn't even go out in the backyard. He stayed in the house and shook and wouldn't hardly eat. It drove the man crazy. "There's nothing out there, Jerry," he told the dog. Jerry whined and shook. Just to prove it to himself, the man got his flashlight and went out to have a look around. When he came back, he was spooked. "Honey, there's a man in the garage sitting in the big chair. I went up to him, but he was gone. The chair was warm. I don't know, maybe Jerry's right after all. What the hell . . ." The woman watched the man and said nothing. Christ, she thought, I was doing all right in Spokane.

La vida es un sueño

1950

—⚡—

A TRIO MAN is a man who stands on a stage, in the spotlight. He plays the requinto, he sings the bolero, and he watches. He watches you, señor, and you, señorita — especially you. He observes the audience, a nocturnal conveyor belt of lovers, haters, and drunks — stretching from the earth to the moon.

He must have the knowledge, the repertoire of songs that tell the simple stories of life, la historia of every man and woman: romance, religion, and death. He must have the touch, the sense of the crowd, their mood. Happy and gay? The songs must correspond. Borracho and melancholy? Then, there is a desire for the songs of la lucha, the struggle of living.

Some of us are better than others. Some are even men of wealth and fame from the sale of discos and autographed pictures. That is a rare category, the famous ones of the Mexican silver screen: Trio Los Panchos, Trio Los Tres Reyes. They wear the tailored draped gabardine and smile as the beautiful star glides by: Ninon Sevilla, Maria Felix. But I am not one of these.

No, I am somewhere in the middle. I am not conocido, but I am not desconocido. My instrument is old, but the maker was respected. Hernando Aviles of Los Panchos once commented that my tone is acceptable. Los Angeles is not Mexico City, but we have many fine nightclubs and restaurants here. It is enough. One must not aim too high. "Ya Estoy Con Mi Destino."

I choose not to interfere. Sometimes there are disagreements. Over what? An insult on the dance floor, a look of disrespect to the esposa, a dispute over a song lyric? Rough language is used, knives are drawn, that sort of thing. The Trio man never takes sides: "And now, señoras y señores, muchísimas gracias a todos, a marvelous new song from the poet laureate of love, the genius of sentiment, El Unico, Agustin Lara! And it is my privilege to announce that the great man is with us in the Club La Bamba, en ésta noche! Viva!" In this way, calm is restored. If one lacks sensitivity, women will lose interest. If one seems effeminate, men will feel compromised. I am known in the world of Trio as a man of skill and finesse. I am not associated with any one particular trio, but prefer to work freelance. This marks me as something of an oddity.

Los Angeles is a maze of class distinctions. I live in the great barrio of East Los Angeles, overlooking Hollenbeck Park. My street is one of large, older homes and one small residence hotel, the Edmund, where I have a room with a balcony. Flower boxes, trees, gardens — a bit bohemian, you may say, but not leftist; that milieu lies further north, in Boyle Heights. There you may find the authors of revolutionary political tracts and those of the poorer class of scholars and professors. My district is favored by entertainers. Not celebrities, but those who have regular positions like myself. We are not mariachis! Mariachis are hardly more than street beggars! You will find them congregated in Garibaldi square, on First Street, near the Aliso Flats district, a squalid area. Mariachis are of the mestizo class, specializing in the primitive music of the migrant and the homesick. I am educated. I read the staff, I know the ostinato, crescendo, obbligato. Trio is refined and elegant.

The Trio man is a night man. I return home between one and two in the morning, and I arise at noon. It is my custom to have coffee at Graziesa's Squeeze Inn. Graziesa makes my coffee with hot milk, the way I like it. She is just my height, barely five feet tall, but always cheerful. She greets me with a song when I arrive. I tell her, "Graziesa, I will present you at La Bamba. You will be a sensation." She says the public wouldn't pay money to see such a short, fat woman, and she had better stick to making tamales and café con leche.

I read both the Spanish and the English newspapers. I am not limited in my thinking in the usual ways of the musician who cares only for boxing and women. I am interested in everything around me — literature, art, science, politics — but most of all, I love the cinema!

On this particular Saturday afternoon, I was in a state of intense excitement. The latest film from Mexico City featuring the Diva of Sorrow, La Reina of Shame, Marga Lopez, was opening at the Million Dollar on Broadway. I was first in line. Rain was forecast, so I carried a light overcoat and an umbrella. My clothes are specially tailored by Ramildo of Hollywood — they do not make ready-to-wear for a man of my build. "Look as good as you can" is my motto. I took my usual seat in the back row, on the aisle, where visibility is better for me.

In they came, rushing to their seats. The lights dimmed, a thrilling moment! Suddenly, a ripple of anxiety swept through the crowd. Heads turned, faces peered out, regarding the figure of a portly man standing by the door. I recognized him at once. Alberto Salazar! Salazar dared to show his face in this moment, before this audience, in this theater? Unspeakable! Unacceptable! Alberto Salazar was, in fact, the film critic for *La Opinion*, the leading Spanish-language newspaper of East Los Angeles, and a scheming, grasping egotist who spent his time pontificating to a retinue of craven sycophants in the cafes and slandering everybody in his newspaper columns. For years, he had nurtured a vendetta against Marga Lopez, trumpeting some flaw in her performance or gloating over some base rumor of scandal in her personal life. To my complete horror, Salazar took his seat in the row in front of me! Directly in front! I was appalled! The last row is essential for me. There, the slope of the floor is such that I may see the entire screen, and now, this hijo de la puta sat there, blocking my view.

The film began. Well, there was no choice, every seat but one was taken. It was quite impossible, but I tried to follow the story, which seemed to concern itself with the double life of a poor woman of Mexico City who sacrifices her own happiness in order to support her younger sister in an upper-class religious boarding school. By night, the woman earns a little money as a taxi dancer in the famous dance hall, Salon Mexico, a place we musicians know well. The principal male character was that of a sympathetic policeman, played by the great Miguel Inclan, who watches over her in a fervor of unrequited love. Que emoción!

A half hour had gone by when a latecomer arrived and took the empty seat next to Salazar. A man, slender, with wavy black hair worn long and heavy with pomade in the manner of the Filipino. His coat was wet, so it had begun to rain. A little time went by. I listened, I concentrated. The Marga Lopez character was trapped in a brutal relationship with a dance-hall pimp, played by the repulsive Rodolfo Acosta — a bully who forces her into danzón contests and then takes the prize money for himself. Desperate, she steals the money back, the pimp beats her, but the heroic policeman bursts in on the scene and declares, "Hit a man, you are so macho!" The two men struggle. The woman escapes. The policeman is victorious but wounded. He looks for her at Salon Mexico. She weeps with gratitude. The policeman weeps with gratitude for having had the opportunity of defending her honor! Wonderful! Sensational!

At that point the Filipino rose from his seat and left. Odd, I thought. Unless, of course, he can no longer tolerate the noxious presence of Salazar, who actually seemed to be asleep. Ay caramba, por eso! The monster sleeps through the film, then goes out and butchers it in the newspaper! But I was now able to see the top half of the screen. The policeman reveals his love and devotion. He offers his hand; he is not offended by her degraded lifestyle, her humiliation. But she refuses him! She is unworthy, his reputation and position are at stake, and so on. The social order must be maintained, the woman must pay the price; it was ever thus. "No llores más," the policeman entreats her, but we know the trail of tears must go on and on. "Pa' Qué Me Sirve La Vida," as the mariachis say.

Suddenly, shouts rang out in the theater. "Sangre! Mucha sangre!" The house lights came on. I smelled blood, it was true. I know the smell, my uncle was a poultry butcher and it was my task as a child to pluck the chickens. I saw at once that the blood flowed from beneath Salazar's chair. I touched his back, and he toppled over onto the floor. A butcher's flaying knife protruded from the back of his neck. "Le gusta el pleito, el Filipino," as my grandmother used to say. She was very old, but I remember her well, with her pince-nez glasses and her habit of cigar smoking, in the manner of the comic actress Doña Sara Garcia.

The police arrived. Sergeant Morales was put in command of the situation. Morales is a man necessary to the conduct of police business among the Spanish-speaking population. Owing to my proximity to the deceased, I was the first to be questioned.

"Did you accompany Salazar to the theatre?"

"Certainly not!"

"But he sat very near to you."

"Yes, unfortunately."

"Why do you say that?"

"Because I couldn't see the screen."

"What did you have against him?"

"He was a man despised by everyone in this theater. Ask them all, you will get the same answer." The innocent man has nothing to fear, nothing to hide, my grandfather was fond of saying, pero, no diga a la policía tu nombre proprio.

"Why?"

"He was a one-man judge, jury, and executioner. He abused his position. He insulted Marga Lopez, myself, everyone."

"How did he insult you? Who are you? What is your trade?"

"I am no tradesman, but an artiste, a musician and singer. 'Acts like a man, looks like a chicken!' He's better off dead, I assure you!"

"This was an execution. Did you do it?"

"I salute the man who did."

"We will speak with you again. Please do not leave town."

"Here I was born, here I remain, here I shall die. 'Hasta la Tumba Final.'"

"My wife enjoys Trio. Where do you appear?"

"The Bamba Club, Thursday, Friday, and Saturday. Please allow me to invite you and your esposa as my guests."

"Thank you, it would be a pleasure. Hasta la próxima, señor."

"A sus órdenes, Capitán Morales."

"Sergeant Morales."

An honest man, not unlike the policeman of the film, I thought. But the film had been interrupted. What happened to Marga Lopez? The truth is, these film stories are all alike; the end is always the same. Real life is so much more uncertain, take Salazar, for instance! And now, something new had been added. I had become involved in a mysterious thing, a crime. I had told Morales nothing of the sinister Filipino. Without thinking, I had become an accomplice.

I TAKE THE "A" streetcar at Sixth and Boyle and get off at Spring Street, a ten-minute ride. I often meet fellow musicians on the streetcars — the code-talking black men of jazz, the card-playing Filipinos of the Temple Street dance halls, the nihilistic pachuco boogie boys — we all ride the Big Red Cars, except for the mariachis, who prefer to walk. The La Bamba Club is located in the heart of downtown. Mexicans are under curfew in the downtown area since the riots, but La Bamba enjoys a good reputation and is exempt. Modest on the outside you may say, but once inside the effect is marvelous. Brightly colored paper lanterns with tiny lights give a festive atmosphere, and there are live plants and dwarf palm trees everywhere. At one end, a good-sized stage and an ample dance floor. Full bar and dinner menu featuring Mexican dishes, such as chile rellenos a la casa and chicken enchiladas supreme. Very nice. Julio "Kid" Quiñones is the bartender, with his happy-to-be-alive grin and boxer's ears. Showtime is nine o'clock. The master of ceremonies, Manuel "El Flaco" Zepeda, welcomes the audience, and then we are introduced. We usually begin with a selection of popular boleros. Boleros have a soothing effect the diners appreciate. I take requests. Ladies enjoy passing a note up to the stage, it excites them.

This particular evening, it was the following Friday, I received a note that read: Sra Morales requests "Sin Ti." I caught the eye of Sergeant Morales, who was accompanied by his wife and their companions de la noche. I had already made arrangements. He inclined his head toward me — everything was perfectly understood. I turned to our trumpet soloist, Angel, and said, "the Harmon mute." The Harmon gives the trumpet a sensation of elegance and refined melancholy.

Sin ti
No podré vivir jamás
Y pensar que nunca más
Estarás junto a mi

Yes, it's true, I have sung this song, perhaps a thousand times. The effect is always the same. One is immediately drawn into contemplation and reverie. The composer gives us a gift of time, a brief moment following each lyric phrase, to fully savor its meaning before passing on to the next. It is a languid pace, but one that builds emotion and strength in a most subtle way, never to distract from the mood, the intimate world of the song.

Sin ti
Qué me puede ya importar
Si lo que me hace llorar
Está lejos de aquí

The poetry is simple, the sentiment is common. But there is the art! Effortless, comfortable, each thought set before the listener like pearls strung into a necklace by the hands of a beautiful woman, one by one.

Sin ti
No hay clemencia en mi dolor
La esperanza de mi amor
Te la llevas al fin

Now the trumpet joins in harmony as the wonderful conclusion is revealed. How did the composer build such a work of feeling from two words?

Sin ti
Es inútil vivir
Como inútil será
El quererte olvidar

"Gracias a todos! And now, for your dancing pleasure, the orchestra of Bebo Guerrero!" I left the stage. Couples rushed to the dance floor. I observed Sergeant Morales and his wife. A gentleman, he escorted her to the ladies' lounge and waited by the door.

"Buenas noches, Señor Morales. Are you enjoying yourself?"

"Ah, my friend, buenas noches! My wife is enchanted, I am delighted!"

"May one ask if there is progress in the matter of Alberto Salazar? The musicians were wondering. . . ."

"We have determined that there was a man seated next to Salazar. He left early. We are very interested in this man, his description, his type. We will find him, whoever he is. And now, con permiso, let me introduce my wife."

Was I undignified? Undoubtedly. Mute, even? Possibly. "Aquellos Ojos Verdes" . . . the song began to play in my mind. Odd, I thought — I know this face, I've seen her somewhere — the green eyes, the somber expression, the lustrous black hair. They returned to their table, and I left the building by the side door. The night was cool. Gradually, I recovered myself. In the alley, Angel was smoking a cigarette and drinking from his flask. I took it.

"Ay, hombre, qué pasó? You, drinking? Órale!" He laughed. It is not my custom to drink during performances. "Ah, sí, ya comprendo, la muchacha with the green eyes, I saw her! Que chula! But her man is a cop, I know him! Cuidado, mi carnalito!"

"It's nothing. The music affected me." I felt something else. In the darkness, someone was watching. Angel went back inside to look for women. The frenzied beat of a rumba was making the wall of the building beat like a drum. To me, the rumba is primitive and unmusical. I remained outside. Further down the alley, someone began to cough — a harsh, rattling sound.

"Tuberculosis loves Mexicans," my grandfather said as he lay dying of the dread disease that was to take him, both my parents, and my sister by the time I reached the age of fifteen. I can recall my mother crying and arguing with an Anglo doctor. Was I four years old? "This child was born with tuberculosis. He will never grow properly. He will always be sickly. He is going to cost the city of Los Angeles a lot of money!" I was in a tuberculosis ward in the children's wing of General Hospital, on Mission Avenue, but a ward for Mexican and Negro children only. Unforgettable! The long room — a contaminated yellow-green. The ancient iron beds — so jammed together as to be touching. And the endless coughing, the frightened faces.

But my mother was brave. One day, she took me in her arms and fled. The Anglo nurses ran after us, screaming for help, for the police. It was after dinnertime and the place was quiet. My uncle was waiting outside in the Ford truck he used for hauling chickens. We escaped. Much later, I learned that the police had tried to find us, to bring me back to the hospital, which was really a prison for the poor and the sick. They were afraid los gabachos would learn of the tubercular Mexican boy running loose on the streets of Los Angeles, resulting in widespread panic! Civil unrest! Political upheaval! But we fooled them. My mother took me to the little Mexican Hospital, on Hammel Street, behind the cemetery. She reasoned that the police would never go near the place; they were too afraid of catching the dread incurable Mexican Sickness.

Dr. Ricardo Chavez treated me for one year. I was allowed to live with my grandparents. The doctor discovered that both my mother and father were infected, my father in the advanced stage. He died within weeks of the diagnosis; my mother, one year later. Somehow, I survived. Dr. Chavez was mystified, but he told my grandmother I would be all right as long as I got enough to eat. This was not a problem since my uncle was a butcher, as I told you. So, we ate chicken! Yes, we ate chicken, and I remained healthy. My growth had nothing to do with tuberculosis. The Anglo doctors believed all Mexicans were born physically and morally tubercular, it explained all their problems. I no longer care to eat chicken, but I still visit the Mexican Hospital out of sentiment for my old doctor. Now, there are three doctors with Hispanic names there. Progress!

It was my uncle Chuy who gave me music to go with the chicken plucking. Everyone listened to the radio program *Los Madrugadores — The Early Risers*. Music to get up at 5:00 a.m. and hurry off to slave the day away by! Local musicians performed the popular Mexican tunes of the day. Uncle Chuy sang along as he singed each plucked chicken over a blue gas flame so as to remove the pin feathers. He would say to me, "You have good hands, I will teach you." But his guitar was too large for me, I couldn't hold it properly. Uncle Chuy knew a requinto player on Olvera Street who had a second instrument. On my tenth birthday, Tío Chuy traded a dozen pollos for it. The requinto is about one third smaller than the guitar in size and one fifth higher in pitch. It was created specifically for trio arrangements. My future was sealed: "The boy is too small for work. Pero, es possible he could survive as a musician, con la mano de dios." Yes, I survived. Often, I am in pain. My old doctor says my bones are weak. Often, I walk with difficulty. But I had a neighbor, a nurse, who lived at the Edmund Apartments. She had access to the medicine I needed. Morphine, it is called.

My nurse was Italian. Rose was her name, she worked at General Hospital. Rose's husband was killed in the war. Arriving home late, I sometimes heard accordion music coming from her apartment. Passing each other in the hallway one evening, we made introductions.

"I'm a musician myself, I appreciate the accordion."

"My husband played. Those are his records," she said. We became acquainted, friendly. One day there was a knock at the door. I had been lying on the sofa for days, unable to move. She called out to me: Was I there? Was I all right? I called back that the door was unlocked. She knew what was wrong.

"Osteoarthritis. In your case, nothing can be done, but there is a painkiller. It's controlled, you shouldn't tell anyone. I would lose my job, maybe jail." Paradiso! Next to music and the cinema, the drug was the most wonderful thing. Life could be beautiful. Rose told me she liked Mexican music. She actually listened to *Los Madrugadores* before leaving for work in the morning. Later, it was a little while after the assassination of Salazar, she came to my room. I thought she was there to inject me, but it was something else.

"Arturo, I have a story for you," she began. "I told you my husband was killed in Germany. He never fought in the war. He was killed by the police, right here in Los Angeles. My husband was a convinced Socialist and a union man, a printer. He worked against Mussolini. He had a comrade, a Filipino, who was trying to educate Filipinos about Fascism in Los Angeles. One night, there was a meeting on Temple Street. Someone informed and the police raided the meeting. They were looking for the leaders, particularly my husband's friend. The police opened fire, and my husband was shot. No doctor would touch him. I did what I could, but he died in my arms. That was seven years ago. Now the Filipino is a patient in General Hospital. He still leads the group through me. I tell the others and they do the work. He wants to talk to you. I don't know why, but it must be very important. The police don't know he's there, his name was never known outside the group, as far as I know."

I was astonished: behind every door, a strange world. "What do you want me to do?" I asked.

"Please come to the hospital tomorrow, in the afternoon. Go to the TB ward and tell them you are a relative of Mr. Bulosan. Carlos Bulosan."

"MUY BUENOS DIAS, M'IJO," said the walls. "You've been away so long!"

"Buenos dias," I answered back. The same yellow-green, the same iron beds, the terrible smell.

"The man you want is right over there. You grew a little, congratulations!"

The chart had a graph, the graph tended downward. Bulosan, C., seemed to be asleep. Compact, Asiatic face. Hair worn long, slicked back. Small bones, pain lines. He opened his eyes. Catlike, dreamy. They fooled you a little, I found out later.

"How do I look?" he asked.

"I've seen worse. My grandfather and my sister died in here."

"This room didn't take you. You're lucky, so far." A soft, high-pitched voice, like the top tenor in a trio. He coughed — a harsh rattle.

"I'm happy to have a little luck once and a while," I replied. Too much, and fate pays a call. La Visita, my grandmother called it.

"Rose chose you."

"I will do what Rose asks."

"You have a friend with the police. Sergeant Morales. He is investigating the death of Salazar, the newspaper man. What does he know? Whom does he suspect?"

"He questioned me, he mentioned an unknown man seen leaving the theater. I don't know what he is doing."

"Find out." Talking was a great strain. Bulosan began to cough with a force that lifted his body off the bed. I felt myself collapsing inside. Many eyes watched me leave the long room. Is he coming to stay with us? — the eyes wondered. "Come back soon, m'ijo, we'll have a party!" the walls called out.

I was in terrible pain. My bones hurt, my head hurt. Somehow, I got back to the Edmund. The TB ward had frightened me, it made me sick. La Bamba was out of the question, the thought of the place nauseated me. Rose had provided enough morphine. I injected myself, the first time without her. The needle hit a vein right away, gracias a dios. Right away. But I remained on edge. Wary. I lay on the sofa, drifting down the devil's highway of pain. A brutal road with little shrines to the dead everywhere: Aida Manzano, my mother; Mateo Manzano, my father; Ignacio Abrego, my grandfather. Then something called me back. There was a man in my room. Not a man, but a figure made of leaves. He made no sound, he had no outline, no substance, but the light from my reading lamp gave him form. He moved abruptly, gesturing in an anxious, pleading way. What do you want? I'm sick; leave me alone, I begged. He opened the door and turned back to me as if to say, you must follow.

I walked west on Sixth Street. The Leafman darted ahead, crouching here and there behind trees, appearing and disappearing in the light of the street lamps, leading me on. The Red Car came lumbering along, the "A" line. I climbed aboard and took a window seat. Leafman ran down the sidewalk, in and out of the light, hiding behind trees, watching me. The streetcar lurched and bucked along at a frantic rate of speed. You may say I was terrified. The conductor turned to me. Not a man, but an eggplant! An eggplant, dressed in a motorman's suit and cap! Faceless, featureless. He barked like a dog. The trolley door swung open directly in front of the Central Police Station. A black sedan pulled up to the curb, tires screeching. Sergeant Morales called out, "Buenas noches, my friend, I have been looking for you!" The rear door opened, unseen hands shoved me inside. The car pulled out onto Grand Avenue. "Where to, Sarge?" the driver turned his head to ask. A potato in an LAPD uniform.

"I asked for you at La Bamba. They suggested I try your apartment. I went there, the door was open. I became alarmed. The Edmund is known to the police. Unsavory, I'm very sorry to say. You should be more careful. By the way, I found a syringe and a drug vial in your room. We will speak of that later. I think you have something important to tell me?"

I was observing the streetlamps, an old habit. Styles change as one passes from one district to another, one era to another. Very interesting for one who travels by streetcar at night. But Morales was becoming impatient. My bones hurt, my head hurt. Where do old streetlamps go when they are no longer wanted? My eyes filled with tears at the thought.

"You must pay attention, my romantic friend. Listen to me. You were seen leaving General Hospital. What did you do there?"

"A sick man, I don't know him well. A favor."

"Who is the sick man? A musician?"

"A laborer, not a musician."

"Where did you get morphine?"

"I am afflicted with a bone disease, I was born with it."

"It is quite illegal to possess morphine. I thought we had an understanding. Need I remind you of the consequences of concealing information? I'm afraid we may have to detain you as a material witness. En El Tambo, no hay boleros, no hay morphine, no hay nada. I want you to tell me if this is the man you saw leaving the Million Dollar Theatre the day Salazar was murdered." He thrust a photograph in front of me, a picture of Carlos Bulosan.

My mind was starting to clear a little. "That is impossible. I saw this man, I spoke to him. He can't walk, let alone walk out of the hospital and get himself to the theater and kill someone. Only a poor fruit picker, and he is dying. I know it, I know the signs."

"I suggest that you and this fruit picker conspired to murder Alberto Salazar!" Morales's face was now inches from mine. He was enraged. "I further suggest that you were paid for your service in morphine!"

"You may suggest what you will, but I am sick, I must return home. It is useless to make these accusations."

"Of course. You are unwell, I'm very sorry for the inconvenience. Police work — sometimes, it is distasteful. My wife sends her regards. Buenas noches."

We had come to a halt in front of the Edmund Apartments. Morales sat back in the seat, his face composed into a mask. The driver appeared human in form. The police car drove away, leaving me there on the curb. I entered the building and walked up the stairs to my floor. My door was closed and locked. I used my key. I laid down on the sofa, trying to think why Morales wore no left shoe. Was his left foot cloven? With the dawn, I fell asleep.

MY GRANDFATHER IGNACIO was fond of saying, "If all the Mexicans in Los Angeles fought alongside Pancho Villa as they claim, the revolution would have triumphed on Olvera Street." There's a photograph of Villa with his arm around my grandfather, who is dressed as a woman, dated Durango, 1919. Grandfather carried a derringer in his boot and a very large bone-handled knife in his coat right up until his last days in the hospital. "They got Flores Magon, but they'll never get me," he declared, referring to the anarchist, whom he claimed to have hidden in the cellar. "The anglos were on the floor above in countless thousands. We fired, Ricardo and I, until our last bullet was gone. They took him then. I escaped — a tunnel underneath Chinatown." In another version, Flores Magon was shot in the back by an informer while straightening a photograph of Trotsky. "Porfiriato revanchist swine! Viva Tierra y Libertad!" The tears came.

My grandparents had been itinerant comic actors in Mexico before immigrating to Los Angeles in 1930. They made a success in the little provincial theaters of those times as "Mantequilla y Huevos." My grandfather appeared as a woman, my grandmother as a man. The man makes improper advances to the woman, the woman resists, the man is indefatigable. Aroused, the woman overpowers the man, at which point, the true sex of the actors is revealed in a licentious manner. Very popular with General Villa and his men! Popular, also, among Federal troops, which enabled my grandparents to ferret out strategic information, or so I have understood. "When an officer is así tan borracho, he can't tell the difference," Grandmother Beatrice would say, her cigar clamped in her teeth.

They arrived in Los Angeles with enough money saved to purchase a tiny bungalow on Bernard Street, in the neighborhood behind Chinatown. Mexican family orchestras were the rage in the thirties, so Grandfather Ignacio simply removed the enlarged papier-mâché genitalia from the theatrical costumes, hired extra musicians, and launched "Los Alegres de Los Angeles" in honor of their new hometown. My mother took over as lead singer when Beatrice retired. After mother died, my sister Encarnacion and I moved in with the abuelos. When my sister died, I moved out.

I woke up the morning after la noche de terror and realized the Edmund was not a good place for me anymore. The Trio man stands on the stage, in the spotlight, rendering the same bolero songs night after night, but outside the four walls of Club La Bamba? Maybe he knows very little about the world after all. I had a bad feeling about things. I didn't like being watched by the police, and I didn't at all like the idea of Leafman dropping by unannounced. I packed my trunk, took down the family pictures, and fled back to Bernard Street. The house of the abuelos had passed to my widowed aunt, Louisa, the only family I have left. She met me at the door. Her eyes grew big. "Pablito, you've come at last!" Her only son, Pablito, had been killed in the anti-Mexican riots — an eighteen-year-old pachuco boy, shot down by the LAPD for wearing high-drape pants.

"Not Pablito, tía mia. It's Arturo."

"Arturo and Encarnación! Gracias a dios!" Louisa still attended mass in the plaza church twice a day.

"Encarnación is in the convent. She has her habit now."

"By the grace of God the Father! I will light candles. You have brought me such good news, we will tell the padre! A blessed day!" Another blessed day of ignorance for her, a day of fear and uncertainty for me, a Trio man on the run. We sat on the little front porch with its sagging roof and peeling paint. Finches peeped in the old rose vine, now grown to epic proportions. Alameda Boulevard hummed along a few blocks away.

"How are your neighbors?" I asked.

"Getting older, like me. Los Chinos are good people to live with. They are not of the faith, but they appreciate peace and quiet. We help each other. I give tamales, they bring their strange food. I like it more now since my teeth are gone. I'm so lonely, Arturo. God the Father sent you to me."

"Yo tambien, tía Louisa. I have no one, only my job at La Bamba."

"You have your guitar, something most people never know. Is La Bamba a place of sin? Should I worry?"

"Harmless. Our people can forget their problems for a little while."

"God gave you a talent for music. Pablito loves music, he will be so pleased to see you!" Evening was coming on. I changed clothes, took the requinto, and walked the four blocks to Alameda. I boarded the "U" car line and rode west on Spring Street. "El Cho Time," as Grandfather Ignacio had whispered to me in the hospital, the crazy light fading from his yellow eyes at last.

"Órale, hermanito, you missed a big night over here!" Angel laughed, shaking his head. He was standing in the alley under the stage door light, smoking and drinking from his flask. He offered it to me. "The cop, Morales? He was looking for you. He got into it with the boss! Por eso!"

"What did he want?"

"Los ojos verdes wasn't with him. The boss says, 'If this is business, take it up with Cobby. You got yours.' Morales didn't like that! 'I'm not vice, I'm homicide,' he says. Tú sabes que the boss has got muchas problemas with that blond chica of his? Échale! She comes over, very drunk. 'What's the beef, what's with the cops all over the place,' she goes. Morales says, 'Tell her to sit down and be quiet.' She goes to the boss, 'You gonna let a spic cop come in here and talk to me like that?' Everybody was watching. The boss turns to her and says, 'Don't use that word in here if you're smart.' She goes, 'A spic cop in a spic joint full of spics!' Big night, hermanito!"

I drank from the flask. It was raw and it burned, but it steadied me. Angel said, "Keep it, you don't look so good." We went inside. The noise and the smoke almost knocked me down, but I made it to the stage. "Only one cho, hermanito, we take it easy." Angel helped me up. The microphone felt heavy as lead. "Señoras y señores, bienvenidos!" I announced. Angel passed me a note: Sra Morales requests, "Aquellos Ojos Verdes." We began. From a corner table, she was watching. She was alone.

It was during the second verse when I realized where I had seen her before — in the barbershop, on North Main Street. Nick Acosta cuts my hair the way I like it, he gives a nice close shave. Behind the chair hangs the calendar of the Mexican National Lottery, La Loteria National, with its glamorous painting of two Mexican girls. One is laughing, her head thrown back. The other regards the viewer with somber green eyes, her hands folded in her lap. I felt my self-confidence return. Why? What difference could it make? Sergeant Morales's esposa, an artist's model, so what? Do not imagine that I have any illusions when it comes to women. I know what they see when they look at me, I assure you. It was that suddenly my curiosity was working again, my interest in things!

We finished the set. The Bebo Guerrero orchestra started their pounding, and the dancers began flinging themselves about like zombie windup toys gone mad. Baila, mi gente! I made my way to her table. "Buenas noches, Señora Morales, I am so very pleased to see you here. I trust the sergeant is quite well?"

"Sergeant Morales is involved in police matters just now," she said. I took a chair. She was drinking something green from a tiny glass. "Your drink, does it agree with you?" I inquired.

"No. I hate this place, it is so vulgar, so *recherché*. I have an appointment, I can't be late. I want you to escort me. I have a car."

We left by the side door. A very large Cadillac sedan appeared. The driver opened the rear door for us. He was wearing a long overcoat and a fedora with a large brim, in the Mexico City style. We sat back in the enormous cushioned seats, something I had never seen except in films. In front, there was a passenger, a woman. She turned to greet us. "Good evening, Arturo, and thank you for coming," said Rose, my nurse.

"Don't thank me, thank madam," I said.

"My name is Florence." She pronounced it Flor*awnce*. My bar*baire* will be happy to know, I thought.

"Is it too much to ask to what place I am escorting you? A man likes to know."

"A man will know in due course."

"Some very important people want to thank you for your service, Arturo," Rose put in.

"Will I learn what service it is I have done?"

"Presently."

I sat back, I observed streetlamps. We left downtown and proceeded west on Sunset Boulevard. Inside the big car, it was a private world, quite the opposite of the streetcars I ride every day. On and on we went. I realized I had never been this far west in all my life. We turned off Sunset and headed north along a narrow canyon road that climbed up and up, ending at a pair of tall iron gates. The driver sounded the horn and the gates opened. We drove into the courtyard of the strangest house I have ever seen. Two long cement platforms, top and bottom, separated by giant glowing panes of glass. Behind the glass, people could be seen walking around bathed in light, as in a film. The structure appeared to be unsupported and about to topple into the blackness of the canyon below, but once inside, one had a feeling of weightlessness, almost of flight. There was an aura, a tone of serenity I had never before experienced. "Somebody must have won the Mexican lottery," I said, trying to take it all in. "At least try to be discreet," La Morales hissed at me.

Everyone was elegant, singular, in character. It was all new to me. Mexico City types in ascot ties, emaciated white women in peasant costumes laden with heavy gold jewelry, movie actor and actress types situated here and there. I walked by a very famous Hollywood leading man who had propped himself up behind a huge rubber plant. He was blind drunk, but his smile and dimpled chin were resplendent. "Good to see you again, amigo. Let's go to Mexico and make a picture together," he said, winking and leering at me. A portly Mexican with wavy hair and pencil mustache hurried over. "I saw you make the entrance with Florencia! I am Fernando Lazlo-Porro!"

"Arturo Manzano," I answered.

He turned to his group of friends. "Arturo Manzano, a great friend of Covarrubias! Florencia was so very charming with Covarrubias, was she not? But she has, what do I want, *evolved*, I know you will say that she has, ha ha! This house is my *homage* to Los Angeles!" The group of friends applauded. I felt a strong hand on my arm, a strong voice behind me. "Señor Manzano is needed elsewhere."

"Of course! In these times, everything is understood." The architect bowed, the friends withdrew. I looked around at my new handler. Could it be? A man appearing to be Miguel Inclán steered me through a door, perhaps the only door in the place. It was a library room with a low ceiling and soft light from lamps shaped like pink garden snails. In a large chair, in a gown of indigo colored silk, sat Marga López. "We are enchanted . . ." she began. I threw up my hands. "Stop! What is the meaning of all this? I am only a poor requinto player from East Los Angeles! I know nothing of architects and Cadillacs and movie actors who step off the screen and walk around in the glass houses of the rich! Somehow, there is a mistake!"

"There is no mistake," said a soft voice behind me. Carlos Bulosan coughed, a harsh, rattling sound.

The dashboard clock said twelve midnight when they left me out in front of La Bamba, which was closed and dark. The Cadillac whispered off and joined the late-night traffic. I caught the last Red Car of the evening, the "U" line, for Chinatown and Lincoln Heights. The motorman greeted me. Only a man, not a vegetable, thank God. "Har yew! Where's your guit-tar? Never knowed you to be without it! This here's my last run for the night, then I'm goin' home to bed!" The trolley clanked and ground its way along. Bernard Street was quiet as the grave. The little houses on Tía Louisa's side are six or eight steps up from the sidewalk and set back so that you may sit outside at night with privacy. Someone was there. Louisa retires at 8:00 p.m. sharp, and she doesn't smoke Olvidados. No self-respecting burglar would bother with the place, not on that street. I walked up. Sergeant Morales was asleep in the ancient wicker chair. He raised his head. "I need a drink," he said in a thick sort of way. I passed him Angel's flask. "Social or business?" I asked, a line from *Cry Danger* with Dick Powell.

"Where's my wife?" Morales asked.

"I don't know." It had the advantage of being true.

"Don't hand me that, my romantic friend. I think you know a lot of things, and I'm the man to find out all about it. Ay la madre, this is terrible!" He made a face at the flask, then drank it down.

"How did you know where to find me?"

"Estúpido! I'm Morales, sergeant over all! I know every taco-bender and pachucopunk and bolero-jockey in East Los

Angeles! And I got a message for one chiseling little sawed-off yockey punk who thinks he's gonna maniobrar pa' conseguir una posición buena in particular, and I'm gonna tell you exackly what it is, you want to hear what it is? Stay away from my wife! She's too big for you."

"That's a dirty crack, brother," I replied, unable to resist quoting Elisha Cook from *The Big Sleep*, a personal favorite of mine.

Morales hung his head. "Millones de perdones, you are entirely right. I'm a lousy cop. That's what the watch commander told me. 'Morales, you couldn't catch flies in a Chinese butcher shop. You are back on the beat.'" He was close to tears.

"I think my aunt has some cooking wine in the kitchen," I offered.

"You're a good man, Manzano, and here I am giving you a hard time. You played it straight with me, and I pushed you around. My wife despises me. I am *outré*, I am *déclassé*. What does it mean?" The tears came. I brought out a bottle and glasses. I poured two, saying, "Here's to plain speaking and good understanding." Sydney Greenstreet, *The Maltese Falcon*.

"I have some answers for you," I began.

"Doesn't mean a goddamn thing. I'm off the case. There is no case."

"Salazar was a police informer. More than that, a spy for the FBI."

"Creo que sí. Everything he gave us was hygenic, I knew it," said Morales.

"He interfered. He dragged red herrings across police investigations."

"He was shielded."

"Claro. But he was assassinated, just as you said. An itinerant fruit picker, who shall remain nameless, stabbed him in the Million Dollar Theatre that Saturday."

"But you told me the man was incapacitated!"

"I believed he was. Tonight, I learned he can operate for

brief periods with the help of esoteric Chinese drugs. He is dying, that's the truth. A martyr to la causa."

"Qué causa?"

"I understand Salazar informed on the labor movement here and its ties to the Mexican Communist Party. He identified labor leaders to the FBI, he invented suspects, he falsely accused even the most harmless and innocent. He was a vile man, a coward — but a pawn in the game, nada más. Mexican artists and writers are trying to build sympathy, but men like Salazar are a threat because they love power and will stop at nothing to hold onto it. You may say it's the cause of poor people who will never ride in a Cadillac or eat crab tacos in glass houses."

"This wine is not so bad," Morales said. Poor Morales, a tiny cog in the big wheel, like me. Somewhere up the street, music began to play softly and drift toward us. I knew it at once. "La Vida Es Un Sueño," the most extraordinarily moving of bolero songs. "Life Is a Dream," written by the great Cuban poet Arsenio Rodríguez, upon learning that his blindness could not be reversed. Morales and I sat there and listened. At three in the morning, the consolation of a Cuban song, floating by on a Chinese street in downtown Los Angeles. I felt relaxed and at ease knowing there was nothing more to fear from the police. Finally, everything had arranged itself.

Después que una vive veinte desengaños
Que importa uno más?
Después de conocer la acción de la vida
No debes llorar
Hay que darse cuenta que todo es mentira
Que nada es verdad
Hay que vivir el momento feliz
Hay que gozar lo que pueda gozar
Porque sacando la cuenta en total
La vida es un sueño y todo se va

Kill me, por favor

1952

—⚬—

WE HAD THREE weeks' work at a combination bowling alley and cocktail lounge in downtown Kingman, Arizona. Harry Spivak was the contractor and also the manager. That's technically in violation, since contractors are supposed to be players, not managers. It's a conflict of interest, but you got to put beans in the pot. Our previous engagement didn't pan out so well. I had to leave a good overcoat behind, and a good overcoat is sometimes hard to find, particularly if the salesman's got a suspicious attitude. So, there we were, in Kingman, not a very fast-stepping town. My partner's name was Ramon Sanchez, but he called himself Smokey Ray Saunders on these dance-band jobs. I go by the name of Al Maphis, but I use my given name, Alphonso Mephisto, if we work jobs on the Mexican side of town. Smokey is a bass player and I'm a drummer, so we find it convenient to contract out as a unit. I don't like to say two for the price of one, which is a violation, but you got to eat.

We found the last room in town, plunked down twenty

dollars apiece for the week, and climbed the well-worn stairs to wash up before going to work.

Hanging alongside the rusty bowl was a single towel — one towel and two guys to share it. I grabbed it, ran downstairs, waved it in the landlady's face, and demanded, "How come?"

"One towel to a room," she replied. "That's all my boarders get and you ain't no better. You ought to mind your manners and thank me."

"Thank you for what?" I asked.

"You behave or I'll have my husband throw you out. He won't like it that a Mex tried to pass, I run a clean place."

It's true. I have Spanish blood on my mother's side. So do half the people in Tulsa, Oklahoma. I smiled my best musician's smile and said, "Ma'am, you are entirely right. Being half Mexican myself, I know what it is you are afraid of. It's easy for a Mexican to take a life, I've heard them say they enjoy it, and that's why they like the knife; it gives pleasure. I have tried to better myself, but the urge to kill is strong, and one never knows. 'Que será, será,' as my mother used to say. Ramon, he's never even seen a toilet before. Pobrecito!"

If you get a job call at a bowling alley, take my advice and skip town. The noise is going to mess up your rhythm and concentration worse than plain drunks. But three weeks is three weeks. We set up and got going around six in the evening. Two trumpets, two trombones, tenor and alto, guitar, Smokey, and myself. All good union men and very copasetic.

I counted three couples on the dance floor and five people over at the bowling lanes. The dancers were on their way to being drunk, and the bowlers were already drunk, whooping and hollering every time they hit a pin. Harry Spivak passed out charts, and it was all standards, so I could get some sleep on the stand. The trick is to keep smiling. A girl wanted to hear "Sweet Lorraine," since her name was Lorraine, so we obliged. After three renditions, a man started a fracas on the dance floor, complaining that he was sick and tired of the same damn song, and play something else. Lorraine's boyfriend invited him to step outside and say that again, which he did. Spivak called intermission.

Smokey and I sat in the car and had a little drink and a smoke. "This dirty towel business has got me thinking," I said. "Suppose there was a trailer, a big trailer, but made specially for traveling men like ourselves. We could operate the thing and rent bunk space out to the guys we were working with and have a nice place to sleep and all the clean towels we want."

"I want pussy," Smokey said.

"All it takes is cash," I said.

The next day I found a trailer dealer in town. I asked him some questions, and at first he scoffed at the idea of a roving boardinghouse. Finally he said I should draw up my plans, submit them to a trailer manufacturer in Chicago, and sit back and wait. I'd either get a horselaugh for a reply or maybe one of the most unusual stables on wheels.

Next, I visited a local banker who luckily was sympathetic to trailers. He said he didn't see any reason why I couldn't get a loan, provided I could show good credit, a permanent address, reputable job, and good references — that being a white man to sign for the collateral.

Out on the main drag, I thought, now what? The trailer idea had a hold of my mind, and I couldn't let a little thing like money hold me back. "One monkey don't stop my show," I told Smokey.

Our landlady's husband had notified us that we weren't welcome around there. I made the point that these older wooden structures like his were highly combustible, which brought his way of thinking around to refunding us the whole forty dollars plus a little extra for good fellowship.

The Buick had been our home often enough. I bought it

from the wife of an evangelist, a professional man on his way to the Texas State Penitentiary. It was a 1938 seven-passenger with the backseats removed. The blessed reverend had it equipped with a bed, a collapsible ironing board and electric iron, a marine toilet and sink, and an exterior shower nozzle supplied from a forty-gallon water tank mounted on the roof. As you might know, a musician often finds himself compelled to go straight from the street to the stage with no access to facilities, and a man looking at a matinee and two evening shows needs a place to take a crap, wash up, and press his pants. Some of these dance joints don't have a backstage, let alone backstage plumbing, and oftentimes the management doesn't like the help to mix with the customers, as if it lowers the tone to have to piss alongside a drummer.

All the towns along Highway 66 are laid out identically. Whites on the north side, coloreds to the south, the highway up the middle. We found a little tamale joint on the dark side of town called Berta's Pollo Encantado. Smokey dug Berta; she was fat and soft like yesterday's bacon sandwich. Not my favorite dish, but I'll take it as I find it.

We ordered tamales and beers and sat down at one of the three tables. Smokey started right up talking to Berta in Spanish, asking her about lodging in the area. She allowed there was a room upstairs if we didn't mind sharing the outhouse with a white man. What's a white man doing down here? I asked. Berta sat down and told us all about him, a fellow named Jim, who was hiding out from some bad hombres, but a polite man, and handy too. Handy with what, I asked. "Todo!" she said. "He fix la estufa, el eléctrico, el baño! El baño es muy bueno." I made an arrangement with Berta and we moved upstairs. By then it was showtime. Smokey invited Berta to the Lanes, but she said they didn't allow Mexicans where dancing and bowling was going on simultaneously.

I couldn't keep my mind off the boardinghouse trailer idea.

After work, I tried to sketch it out. I could hear the bedsprings squeaking and creaking upstairs, but it didn't bother me. The trailer dealer had told me a custom job as I described it would probably cost five thousand dollars. I decided to keep the cost down to under four thousand dollars if possible. I'd have to sleep and feed enough boarders to make payments plus a profit. Eight boarders at sixteen to twenty-five dollars a week would pay the bills and fatten my bank account. Each boarder would need a bunk, a locker, and there'd have to be enough room so guys wouldn't be falling over one another. Two washbasins. What had seemed like a simple job at first was becoming a matter of logistics.

The slats in the bed upstairs went blametyblam, crash! and Berta screamed. Then the floor got to squeaking in rhythm. A radio played boleros. Somebody was smoking outside. I followed the smoke, and it was a little man sitting in a metal chair in the backyard, in the moonlight. "Buenas noches," I said.

"Five to one, I know why you're here," the man answered in a soft voice.

"My partner and I just hit town. We're musicians," I said.

"I lose. Smoke?" He put his tin can ashtray down and held out the pack. I took one, and he lit it and used the light to study me. I got a look at him — older and scrawny the way a hobo looks, but with the watchful eyes of a smart man.

"Thanks. I'm Al Maphis. Gambling man?"

"Jim McGee. I have been, off and on. Ended up here, somehow. I like Mexicans, they don't push."

"You were expecting somebody else?"

"Always, ever since my last bad hand. Up in Joplin, it was. I saw that Buick of yours out front. That's an interesting vehicle. You could go straight across the country without ever stopping."

"We have, on occasion."

"What's in the big box over top, if I may ask?"

"Water tank, and the instruments ride up there. String bass and drum set. I'm the drummer, Ray's the bass. We're appearing nightly here in town." McGee seemed to relax a little. He leaned back in his chair and looked up at the black sky streaked with clouds.

"I never saw a night sky like you get out here," he said. "Ever been in Joplin?"

"Never worked up there. This is a crap town. Arizona is a crap state and very nonswinging unless you like to sit and watch clouds."

"I can still get my kicks. All I need is a stake."

I let the line out a little. "Berta tells me you're quite the mechanic."

"Master machinist, first grade. I was head tool and die maker at Martin-Marietta in the war."

"That a fact? I wonder if you could help me. I got a money-making idea, but I need expertise. See, Jim, music is a two-bit racket. You can't get ahead unless you make records and the mob controls that, so what's a drummer supposed to do? But I been around out here in the West, and I found out one main thing. This road building and oil drilling and increased population since the war, it depends on housing. Housing is the key. You can't have workers on the job if they can't afford to live. Then they can spend the rest of their money on music and girls and booze."

"On crooked cards and loaded dice and horses," McGee said.

"I'd sure like to show you my ideas. I bet a trained man like you could figure everything out to the nickel."

"Try me."

"See you tomorrow." I left him there in his chair with his smokes and his clouds.

I woke up smelling lard and thought I was back in Tulsa. Ask any Mexican about his earliest memory and you will get the same answer: frying lard. My daddy was a white man and a peace officer, but he couldn't control the situation at home and it broke him down. I saw it happen. Mamma was a Mexican firebrand. She was dark and different from Dad as day is from night. She lived for dancing. Cain's Ballroom was her real home, and she could be found there any night of the week, dancing with every man in the place. Blood was shed on a routine basis over who'd be next in line. One night, my dad walked in there and told her we were moving to California. A big man, probably some oil field roustabout, told Daddy to get out of Dodge. Dad was in uniform, and he drew his service revolver and told the man to step aside in the name of the law. The man grabbed the gun and beat my daddy over the head with it, and he beat him down to the floor while the crowd watched. That was the end of my parents' marriage and my dad's career in law enforcement. He drifted off and we never saw him again, only heard tell. Mamma died of a busted liver five years later. I got the news of her death in Catoosa, Oklahoma, while I was onstage. A man in the audience passed a note up. I played on, what else could I do? Mamma loved rhythm. One thing I learned in Tulsa was that things go better if you can front as a white man, daddy's example notwithstanding. Doesn't always work, but that's my theory. I told Smokey when we started traveling together: let me do the talking. "No problema, mi jefe," he said.

I washed up and went downstairs. Smokey was there with his nose in a bowl of tripe soup, the Mexican cure for hangover. "Too much pussy," he said.

"Forget it. We got a real chance here. It's going to fit together, it's going to work."

"No tengo that much jam, jefecito." Smokey ate his tripe soup with a worried look.

Harry Spivak said there was a group from the high school for the matinee and we had better act like gentlemen. Pianist Billy Tipton had just got into town. That was supposed to be hot, a personal appearance by a known celebrity in a hick burg like Kingman. I had worked a previous engagement with Billy in the Dallas–Fort Worth area, so we were acquainted. Billy had a career in show business that was unusual. She had been pulling it off working as a man for years. She wore her hair cut short and styled tailored gabardine suits with a bow tie, her trademark. A regular tie would stick out, you dig. Billy dug women — like who doesn't? — and the word was she got more ass than a toilet seat. She had the hicks fooled but good. So Billy says, "Ladies and gentlemen, especially you ladies! Right about now, for your dancing and listening pleasure, the Billy Tipton Orchestra is pleased to offer you a rendition of a little number titled, 'I Didn't Know What Time It Was.' Take it away, Al Maphis!"

I took it. Billy was actually a very swinging piano man. "Falling in Love Again" was a special number featuring a vocal by Billy: "Love is my game, I play it how I may. Guess I was made that way, I can't help it." The high school girls were intrigued. Billy sat at the piano and signed autographs. That's a square hustle, in my opinion. People think they want a memento to take away; then they forget all about it and lose the paper in the parking lot. The girls crowded around the piano and seemed to go wild for her. Him, I should say. They were just ordinary white kids; they didn't know what time it was.

Billy was suave, I checked her out. I loitered nearby. She picked up on two girls in particular, a blond and her friend, a plump little brunette. Two friends together, that's good trolling. They feel safe with each other, and you can cut them out of the pack. Billy says, "I'm having a little party back at the hotel. Some friends of mine from town. How 'bout you girls ride with me in the limbo?" Billy had a husky voice for a woman.

"What's a limbo, Mr. Tipton?" asked the blond girlie.

"I meant limo, that's just musician talk, you know how it is with entertainers, how we like to kid around, you're gonna know everyone at the party, we'll have a ball!"

The brunette said, "Well, I don't know about going to a hotel."

"Oh, sure, that's the fun part," said the blond, "I've never been. Wait 'til Maxine hears!"

"Wait 'til your friends hear about who you got to meet. Hey, Al Maphis, tell them who's going to be there!" Billy gave me the look. I took it.

"Girls, pick up on this. There is a VIP here in town to see Billy about a very big deal. I'm sure I can rely on you to keep it under you hat."

"Mum's the word!" said the blond, getting excited.

"His name is Johnny Dollar, and he is a top gambler in Los Angeles. When he meets a person for the first time, he gives them a silver dollar just to remember him by, and that goes for you, me and the lamppost. Johnny digs people, he wants everybody to have a blast when he's around."

"A gambler?" asked the brunette. Her resistance was fading. Free drinks and food were winning out.

"Johnny's the man with the action-packed expense account," Billy said. "You never can tell. Everything will be in the line of hilarity." She put her arm around the blond and gave her a squeeze. Deal closed, I could smell it.

Hick-town hotels are a real pain in the ass, as you know. No coloreds, no unescorted women, no drinking, no gambling. Billy had a suite on the top floor, the fourth. The management was not with it. It was "Right this way, Mr. Tipton. A pleasure to see you again, Mr. Tipton," et cetera. I rode up with Billy and the two girls.

Billy sent the bellhop out for liquor and sandwiches. The girls checked out the suite. They dug the king-size bed; they bounced up and down on it, laughing and carrying on. Billy sat there and watched. The blond, her name was Betty Newlands, had nice juicy little legs, and she could really bounce. "Betty's a cheerleader at school," Joyce, the brunette, explained. Betty really bounced. She lifted her dress up like cheerleaders do, showing off her underpants. "Betty, put your dress *down!*" Joyce said. Suddenly I was back in Oklahoma. I saw the white sheets, the burning cross, I felt the heat.

"Al, why don't you take Joyce over to the sitting room and get her something to eat and drink?" Billy told me. Billy had eyes, she was juked.

I steered Joyce out and closed the bedroom door. "Let's see. There's ham, cheese, ham and cheese, and some of these little cocktail tamales, Joyce, honey. Here's scotch, bourbon, and ginger ale. Bet you're ready for a plate and a drink. I'm feeling a little warm, how 'bout a tall cool one? How's that going to be? Let's play the radio. Look, we're all the way up on the fourth floor, look out there." Two blocks past the hotel, Kingman quit trying. The desert stretched out for a hundred miles, maybe more.

Joyce got a tamale plate. "I never tried these before," she said. I fixed her a weak highball and made myself a stiff one.

"Those are Mexican tamales. Pork on the inside, corn on the outside." *Just like you, honey.* I was getting a bad feeling, like when the sax player solos in the wrong key and there's nothing you can do about it. *Schoolgirl held captive. Public demands justice.*

"My daddy told us to always stay away from Mexicans."

"That's good advice. Drink your drink, honey."

"Where is everybody? When does the party start?" Joyce asked. In the bedroom, it was quiet. The party had started. Right on cue, there was a knock at the door of the suite. I knew it was a bad mistake, but I opened it. There was a man in a Western-cut sharkskin suit, polished black cowboy boots, and a Stetson city brim like gamblers wear. His clothes cost more than I make in six months of steady work. Six-feet-four, narrow and hard like a telephone pole. *Just kill me, por favor,* I thought.

"I heard Billy Tipton was here," he said.

"You heard absolutely right. Come on in, have a drink, Jackson. There ain't nobody here but us chickens." I said, trying to act breezy, like the joint was jumping.

"Who are you, friend? Where's Billy?" he said.

"I'm Al Maphis. Mind if I call you Hurley Jim Bowling?" It was a crazy thing to say, but I hadn't eaten all day except the highball.

"Why should you?"

"Because that's your name. Joyce, meet Hurley Jim, a well known man in certain circles. I told you the party was going to pick up steam."

"I don't get your drift," he said, quietlike. "What's the set-up? You look Mex to me."

"No offense meant. I play drums for Billy. How many drummers does it take to screw in a lightbulb? Three: one to screw, one to count off."

"Maybe you better take the air, Pancho. Take the kid out of here, they got laws in this state."

"We were just leaving. Joyce, Hurley Jim has got a point. Shall we vamonos por some nice quiet place?"

"What about Betty? I can't leave without Betty?" Joyce said.

"Who's Betty?"

"Another good friend of Billy's. Ever been in Joplin?"

"Just came from there. Anything to it?"

"Nothing at all. Never made it that far north. Never did." I steered Joyce into the hall and hustled her down the back stairs.

Night was coming on. The wind blew fine-grained dust off the hills and down the main drag, which was empty of people and cars at that time of day. Everyone was hunkered down with their chicken-fried steaks and mashed potatoes. We walked in the direction of the bowling alley. The sky went from orange to red to purple, and the dust and paper trash swirled around our feet. "That wasn't a very good party," Joyce said.

"What'd you have in mind?"

"I thought Mr. Billy Tipton was going to be a nicer man. I thought we were going to have fun and meet people."

"You did."

"Ugh, I didn't like that man. Why did he say you look like a Mexican, are you? You've been very white to me." She put her hand up to her mouth. "Oops, I'm sorry."

"No offense. Hurley Jim Bowling isn't a likeable man, I admit. He's a big-time gambler, and this is a small town. I don't know what he's doing here, but I'm going to try to stay out of his way."

"Betty Newlands is always playing tricks on me. We go places together and then she finds someone and takes off without telling me. I'm never around at the finish."

"Tell her you don't like it."

"Oh, no. Betty's a very pretty girl, it's different for her."

"Why? You're pretty nice looking."

"You don't have to say that, I know I'm fat."

"So get some exercise, go dancing."

"I like bowling. Fat people are good at bowling. Do you like bowling?"

"Never tried it."

"I could teach you! Betty doesn't try, she doesn't care what I like."

"That's mighty kind of you, but I'm in the band and the management, they don't want to see us on the other side of the stand, understand?" I told Joyce adios and I beat it back to Spic Town.

Jim McGee had papers spread out all over Berta's back table. I got a beer and sat down across from him. He'd been working. "Eight men can live comfortably on two hundred square feet of floor space. Most states say ninety-six inches is maximum width for trailers on their highways. A majority of states specify thirty-five-foot overall length as maximum.

"If you want to travel through all the states, you got to comply with the maximums. Besides, if your mobile boarding house is going to poke around in the backcountry, the narrower and shorter the better. So to get the required two hundred square feet and yet stay within the legal limits, I suggest making the trailer eighty-nine inches wide and twenty-seven feet long. That gives you 202.5 square feet.

"It takes about twenty minutes to wash, brush your teeth, and shave — on the double. Statistically speaking, two washbasins and a shower would keep three men busy simultaneously and turn out all eight boarders, washed, shaved, and in their Sunday best within forty-five minutes. A thirty-gallon water tank, electrically heated, will give you all the hot water you can use. Each of the lockers contains fourteen cubic feet. That's enough for clothes and working gear, if your boarders are day workers. The outside toilet would have to work anywhere. An automatic pressure flusher draining through a two-inch hose seems to be the answer.

"You ought to use extra-heavy channel iron for the frame, six-inch stuff instead of the usual four-inch. From two to four inches of spun glass and rock wool insulation between the trailer walls. Open up an account at the liquor store for the duration. Two dozen cartons of Chesterfield cigarettes. Cash — an even thousand to start. It'll take me a month if I don't have to stop for anything. Any questions?"

"Just one. What's a man like you doing in the desert?" McGee put his cigarette out in the tin can and lit another. Across the street, the El Otro Lado cantina was pumping, the jukebox trying its best to be heard over the din. "Ingrato Amor," it sobbed.

"I got no complaints," he said softly. "I did somebody wrong. If I do this work for you, then I got a stake. If I can run it up and square myself with some characters, then I can go on about my business, maybe even get back with my wife and kid."

"Some characters in Joplin?"

"That's the size of it."

"Okay, it's a deal. I'll get you what you need, somehow." We shook. McGee had little hands and he felt weak, but he had a big brain up there. You know what they say about drummers and lightbulbs.

Harry Spivak called us together on the stand. "Boys, I've extended the contract two weeks. Billy has informed me he is staying with us for the duration."

"Did I hear you say 'raise'?" I said.

"I want to see clean shirts and pressed pants. If it says six o'clock downbeat, I want you here at 5:45, with a good attitude. Leave your shit off the stand, and I'm talking to you, Maphis."

"We want five dollars a week raise, a fifteen-minute intermission, and access to the facilities." I said.

"I got pains in the kidneys, I got to piss a lot." said Junior Tommy McClennan, our little guitar man.

"Maphis, I expect some gratitude. I run a strictly no coloreds in front of house place, you just keep that in mind." Spivak said. Right then, Billy walked in through the front door — Hurley Jim on the left, Betty Newlands on the right, in tight and solid.

"A friendly discussion with the boys," Harry said to Billy, but he didn't pull it off.

"We are standing down until we take a vote," I said. "We know our rights." I turned to the band. "All in favor?" The ayes had it.

"What do you need, Al?" Billy asked me.

"We're opening the talks at eight dollars a week increase in pay and decent working conditions. They expect us to piss in the alley."

"Maphis, you're fired." Spivak snarled.

Hurley Jim took a step toward Spivak. "Raise 'em ten dollars a week. Toilets. Maphis stays."

"Who the hell are you, giving orders? This is my goddamn place, I'm Harry Spivak."

"I'm Billy's manager. You'll take it and like it."

Smokey took Berta shopping at the Western wear store up on 66. He got a new Stetson and a fancy gabardine cowboy shirt with arrows and rhinestones. "Gives a man elegancia," Berta said. She got a pair of fancy suede Indian moccasins with buffalo nickel buttons and a shawl embroidered with la Virgen. She looked real cute, saucy. We went across the street to the Otro Lado to celebrate our new money. Jim McGee had his nose in his trailer schematic, but Berta made him come along. "All work y no plays, el señor!"

I asked McGee about Hurley Jim Bowling. He said, Bowling was there, in Joplin. He ran the game. Hurley Jim is here, in Kingman, I told McGee. He said, Kingman is going to get hot.

We played the jukebox: Lalo Guerrero, Beto Villa, Chelo Silva, Lola Beltran. I danced with Berta, Smokey danced with Berta, Jim danced with Berta. Jim was a very smooth dancer. "Muy guapo!" said Berta. Nobody called me a Commie or a lousy Mex all night.

The labor dispute was settled. Hurley Jim looked like a winner, Harry Spivak looked old. The real story, though, was Billy Tipton and Betty Newlands. Frank Napolitano, the first trumpet, was desperate for information. He says, "Al, you're tight with Billy. I got a little camera like the divorce dicks use. Look at this. You could get some shots, Al! Please!" The guys pooled their money and offered it to me. I said, "No chance. Hurley Jim Bowling is in the picture now. A Mexican likes his life, such as it is." Frank begged and pleaded: "Does the chick *realize*?" "I don't know nothing," I said.

Hurley Jim had the suite right next to Billy's at the Hotel Kingman. He'd drop Billy off at the Lanes in his Cadillac, then take off for a while and check in later. He said we could bowl free of charge, and that meant a lot to the fellas. He always drove Billy and the girl home.

Spivak took it all without saying a word. Why? I asked Billy. Play the drums, she told me. I suggested she might not want to be seen around with a high school girl in a hick town like Kingman. Shut up and count off, she said.

Berta said they ran illegal Mexican booze into the Lanes, then rebottled and shipped it to Los Angeles. It was common knowledge on the south side. "Es un troquero, mi hermano, he knows," Berta said. Smokey said it was verdad, he saw it being loaded. You saw them take the cases? I was taking a piss. What are you doing pissing in the parking lot, we fought for toilet rights? I saw what I saw, mi jefe.

One night, Billy asked me to drive Betty home. She lived on the north side. "How does all this rate with your family?" I asked her.

"All what?"

"Late nights, hotels, Cadillacs. Some people don't like musicians, they got a bad rep."

"Billy is helping me with my singing. He says I got natural ability. He's going to let me sing with the band as soon as I'm ready. My mom thinks he's a perfect gentleman."

"How bout Hurley Jim? Does Mom like him too?"

"Oh, yes. He's going to help invest my dad's life insurance money."

"Where's Dad?"

"He died last year. Heart attack."

"Sorry." *He'd have keeled over anyway.*

"Here's our house. Thanks, Al."

"Hasta mañana, Betty."

"When do I start?" Jim McGee asked me. "I can't hang around here much longer. Bowling's in town, my ulcer is kicking up. Your buddy Ramon keeps me awake, he sings, he screws the broad. So what'll it be?"

"There's money in Kingman," I said. "I can smell it."

We had Monday nights off. I was drinking beer in the Otro Lado. Billy came in, looking all around. She located me and sat down in the booth. "Welcome to the dark side, Billy," I said, "may I suggest the pork enchiladas with the green sauce?" I was a little drunk.

"Drive me to Los Angeles."

"You look nervous. Why are you whispering? You don't have to whisper, we're Mexicans here, but we're all friends just the same. How 'bout a beer, I'm buying."

"Shut up, Al. Listen to what I'm telling you. I'll pay you good money."

"I can always use it. What's the matter with Kingman?"

"Don't ask."

"Who's going with us, I'd like to get the car washed."

"Betty."

"They'll stick the Mann Act up in you and break it off. You can't do hard time, Billy."

"A thousand dollars."

"They'll hang me from the chandelier. No more 'Take it away, Al Maphis.'"

"Fifteen hundred."

"When?"

"Right now. Betty's had some trouble, we got to get her out of the state."

"Two thousand, in advance." We shook on it. Billy had strong hands for a woman.

Billy gave me the cash, it cleaned her out. I took a few dollars for expenses and left the rest with Berta. "Take care of Smokey," I told her, "regreso en la mañana."

"Vaya con dios," she said.

If I make it, I'm going back to the Church, I thought, remembering Father Bernalillo, my first drum teacher. He taught me to sit straight and hold the sticks out front. I learned music from an alcoholic dwarf named Ray Diker. Gene Krupa was the man back then, all the drummers in town were crazy about him. Ray told me, "Forget Krupa. He plays with his hands up around his face like he's eating chop suey. If you're going to eat, eat. If you're going to play the drums, keep your hands down." Ray died of a burst appendix backstage at Cain's Ballroom. The guys in the band laid him out on two chairs, that's how short he was. My mother cried, she dug his rhythm the most. *I'm coming back, but I don't know when, Padrecito.*

At 2:00 a.m., we hit the highway. Billy went to sleep in the back, Betty rode up front. I found a radio station that played swing music. Driving through the desert at night, you feel like you got all the time in the world.

Something was wrong with Betty, she was dead quiet. I had a bad feeling, like the Klan posse was saddling up. The Buick was old and slow — just a stock model, no armor on it.

"Say, Betty, if you reach under the seat, there's a bottle. Have a drink."

"I don't like liquor."

"No? I do, sometimes. We got a bit of driving to do, so I think I'll have a snort, if you don't mind." I took the bottle.

"I don't care if you do."

"Thanks. Maybe you'd like some coffee, maybe you're hungry. When did you eat last?"

"I had a sandwich."

"I like sandwiches. What kind of sandwich?"

"It was strange. Pink. Salty."

"Pink and salty? That is strange, where was that?"

"I'm not supposed to say."

"Okay, but I'm interested in this sandwich. Was it meat or chicken? Salami?"

"Nothing like that."

"What did they call it?"

"I forget, who cares."

"Lox, maybe? That ring a bell?"

"Yes, lox. He called it lox. It came on this weird round bread. It was hard to chew. I asked for regular bread."

"What else? What about salad?"

"Chopped up lettuce and pickles. I don't like pickles. He put his hands on me. I don't like anybody to do that except Billy. He laughed at me and called me a 'shiksa.' I didn't like that, whatever it is."

"That wasn't very nice, I agree with you. Lots of people don't like pickles. What did you do then?"

"I shot him."

My fingers were so tightly clenched around the steering wheel I wasn't sure if I'd be able do anything ever again but drive. I managed to take hold of the bottle and drink.

"One time, two times?"

"I forget. It kept going off."

"That must have been loud, there in the hotel room."

"I'm not saying."

"Did Hurley Jim have lunch with you?"

"He was in the bedroom. He didn't have lunch."

"Why not?"

"Because he was dead, that's why."

"Of course. You know that for a fact. No mistake about it."

"There's no mistake, don't talk to me like that, I saw it!"

"I'm with you, Betty, a hundred and ten percent. But, now, how about this, because I'm wondering, did you shoot Hurley Jim?"

"No, I didn't, don't say that! Your friend did. He's your friend, not mine, I don't like him."

"If you don't like him, I don't like him. Who is he?"

"I told you! Why do you keep asking?"

"The man you shot."

"Yes. Harry Spivak."

The lights were on inside the Cool Springs Bar and Grill, a nice little roadside place, built out of stones. I needed to be where ordinary people were living their lives, maybe even enjoying themselves. I pulled up.

"I'm going in there and get us some cheeseburgers. You like cheeseburgers. Wait for me, don't leave the car."

"I'm cold, I'm going to sleep." Betty said. She closed her eyes. I covered her with her wool coat.

"One thing more, Betty. Where was Billy?"

"I don't know. He came later."

I went inside. The empty dining room was very cozy, all done up in knotty pine. That's a nice look, friendly. There was a fire in the fireplace at one end, burning low. I sat at the counter and studied the pies in the case. Apple, cherry, berry, and rhubarb. "Rhubarb, that's the ticket," I said out loud. A man came out wearing a white apron that said "Floyd" in blue thread. "I was just taking a nap. Not much trade at 3:00 a.m. What can I get for you?" he said.

"Three deluxe cheeseburgers, fries, one slice of rhubarb pie."

"Just one?"

"The wife and kid, they don't like pie. Fries, that's what they like. The pie's for me."

An Arizona Highway Patrol car pulled up out front. Two officers in green uniforms came in and sat in a booth. I watched them in the mirror.

"Hey, Bernie, Dan. Usual?" Floyd said.

"Sure, Floyd. Take your time." One cop put money in the jukebox and went back and sat down. They talked to each other in low cop tones. Glen Miller came on, medium loud. Floyd brought my order out. "That'll be $8.50." I gave him a ten and told him to keep the change.

"Thanks!" he called out over the music.

The radio was on in the patrol car. I could hear it as I walked by with the cheeseburgers. "Be on the lookout for a man traveling with a female companion. Last seen, Kingman. Man is medium height, wavy blond hair, gray suit. Age, forty. AKA Billy Tipton, entertainer. The female is AKA Elizabeth Newlands, a minor, five-five, hair blond in color. Believed to be headed in the direction of the state line. Destination unknown. May be armed, approach with caution." I watched the two cops through the window for a minute. They were yakking with Floyd, they didn't hear the broadcast. Billy was awake. I passed the food back.

"We're hot, we're on the air. You feel like you can lose the suit? They're not looking for a woman." I pulled out. Billy ate her burger, Betty slept. "If not, it's five to one we don't make the state line. Betty told me the whole story about Hurley Jim and Spivak. You didn't tell me about Harry. That's trouble. That means the bright boys are out there looking for you besides the cops. Harry was connected. We don't have time to get fancy."

"We'll make it. I've got friends in Hollywood."

"I'm telling you we won't. I won't. I don't have friends in Hollywood, or anywhere, except Mexicans and a broken-down airplane mechanic in Kingman. You can fake it. Use the kid's makeup and coat, you'll look terrific. There's a light and a mirror back there."

"I haven't worn chick threads in twenty-five years. What if Betty sees me?"

"Fuck Betty! Vamos!" I got my point across. Billy went to work. She fixed herself up real nice. We kept rolling, good old Buick. Bernie and Dan caught up to us just outside Oatman.

I pulled over. "What's the trouble, officer? Was I speeding?"

"Identification, please," he flashed his light around on the inside.

"My wife's asleep. My stepdaughter's asleep. They ate all those French fries, it must have knocked them out."

"All right, go ahead." He didn't like it, but there it was. *A man and his wife and kid. They looked like Mexicans.*

We crossed the state line at 4:00 a.m. I pulled up at Essex, on the California side. It was just a wide spot on the highway — a gas station, general store, and four empty tourist cabins. It was cold and totally silent and still, like the dark side of the moon. I parked behind one of the cabins.

"What are you stopping for?" said Billy.

"I want to talk a little, and I want to watch the road for a while," I said. Billy got her clothes and went behind one of the cabins. When she came back to the car, she had the suit and tie on again, like Clark Kent in reverse. "You look super, Billy," I said. "So let's work backwards. Betty was there in the hotel. Hurley Jim was with her, and Harry was there. But you were out. Harry shot Hurley Jim, or Betty thinks he did. Then he made a move on Betty and she got hold of the gun, or had a gun, and she shot Harry, or thinks she did. The way she told it, some things were missing. She's got a loose wig, what the hell did you leave her alone for? Tell me that."

"I had definite business. Betty was there with Hurley Jim, I didn't know Harry was going there."

"Hurley Jim would never keep a teenage girl in his hotel room, I happen to know it and you know it. That's a bad rap in Arizona, hard to beat."

"I was gone for a half hour, no more."

"Gone where, doing what?"

"That's personal."

"We don't want a little thing like a double murder to get in the way of the personal."

"Nobody knows Betty was there. Two business rivals argued, they fought. It's a well-known fact that Harry Spivak hated Hurley Jim Bowling, resented Bowling's muscling in on his business interests in Kingman."

"Then why am I driving you all the way to Los Angeles?"

"I got a sudden offer from Hollywood. An audition with Capitol Records."

"Is that bullshit or is it true?"

"It's perfectly true, it's all set up."

"Are the guns where they should be? All set up and perfectly true? The cops like to know."

"I did the best I could, I had to get her out of the hotel. I had to find you." Betty woke up. She got out of the car and started walking away from the road, into the desert. We both watched her. "What are you going to do?" I asked Billy.

"I don't know. She wants to get married in Los Angeles; she wants to sing at the Hollywood Bowl. I got a possible two weeks with a trio at the Embers, in Santa Monica. After that, it's Spokane, Washington. Hurley Jim was going to get me into Reno. That's out now."

"Que pena. What about the mother?"

"Hurley Jim paid her. She drinks, she doesn't know nothing."

"You can send her a card from Spokane." I said. Betty finished her business and came walking back.

"I'm cold. Are we going to Los Angeles or aren't we?" she said.

"We're going, honey," Billy said. I hit the starter and the Buick came to life, like an old horse. The clouds were turning ten shades of pink. It was going to be a beautiful day in the desert.

"WHERE TO? THE ocean's right over there, we can't go much further," I said. It was raining hard in Santa Monica.

"Third Street. The Embers is next door to the Dan-Dee shoe factory. Earl's got a place for us to stay," Billy said.

"What's the line on Betty?" Betty was still asleep in the back, had been since San Bernardino.

"Betty's my niece. She's out here for a screen test."

"Solid. Vaya con dios, you'll need him."

"Where are you gong?"

"Kingman. I'm going to start a Mexican boardinghouse. There aren't any, you know."

"I paid you two thousand dollars."

"I earned it." I pulled into the alley behind the Embers. Betty woke up. "Are we in Hollywood?" she asked.

The Embers had a back door, and two cops came out of it. They hurried to their car and didn't look up. The black Ford sedan backed out and took off up the alley.

I drove around the block and found a pay phone. Billy talked for a few minutes.

"I'm hungry," Betty said.

"Shut up, Betty."

Billy came back. "Earl said don't come near the place. I had two weeks' work. Now what?"

"Don't tell me to shut up," Betty said. "I'm hungry and I want to go to Hollywood. I think you better take me there. I've got a story for the cops and they'd be very interested. You think I been asleep all this time. I'm seventeen years old. They'll mop the floor with you, *Mister* Billy Tipton."

I drove east on Santa Monica Boulevard. The windshield wipers did the best they could but there was a leak in the vacuum tube. Betty started talking to an imaginary policeman. "See, officer, they gave me a drink that tasted funny. When I woke up, my dress was up around my head and Harry Spivak was on top of me. He hurt me. Billy left me there, they made her leave. Did you hear me, officer? They made *her* leave. Billy was scared of them, she let them take turns on me. That was the deal." I watched Billy. I watched Betty in the rearview mirror. Ever seen a bad wreck on the highway and you can't stop looking? "I want a big steak dinner, with a baked potato and sour cream. I want some new clothes. I want to see famous people and have fun," she said.

"That's a bunch of crap, Al," Billy said. "Never happened. Nothing like that happened to Betty, you've got to believe me."

"You know what Harry Spivak said right before he shot Hurley Jim? 'A piano-playing dyke is shtupping a little shiksa in my place? Plus I got you giving me the high hard one?'" Betty made a face like an angry monkey. She looked just like Harry.

"What I'm telling you is perfectly true from my stand-point," Billy said again.

"Billy, I'll take you to a cheap place I know. You'll be safe there," I said. "What happens later isn't my goddamn problem."

"Oh really, is that so," Betty said. " 'Officer, Billy Tipton paid this man to bring me here from Arizona in his car. He pretends to be white but he's a Mexican. He gave me liquor; he took advantage while I was asleep. Mexicans do dirty things to girls. I'm so ashamed.'"

Billy looked over at me. "What's all that about, Al?"

"Fuck you both," I said.

I headed for downtown. Destination: Bunker Hill, home of no questions asked. Once, Ray and I put up in the Clover Trailer Park on Court Street. The trailers were not bad and you could rent by the week. You can stand anything for a week.

The office was in the old house next door. A little bald guy in a sleeveless undershirt answered my knock. He was carrying a ukulele.

"I'm looking for the manager," I said

"You're talking to him."

"Where's Hector?"

"Hector's dead, two, three years."

"We want to rent a trailer."

"When and for how long?"

"Now, and I don't know."

"Ten dollars a week."

"It'll break our backs, but I think we can swing it."

"All right, follow me."

"What are we, the poor relations?" Betty said when she saw trailer number eight. "What about some of those places back there?" The nicer ones had little awnings and geraniums in boxes, but they all looked sad in the rain.

"This is all I got left. Take it or leave it, ten bucks a week." I gave him my last ten-dollar bill. I went out to get the bags, and the manager followed me. "I don't want any trouble in this camp," he said.

"Then don't start any."

"Any business with the girl, I touch half."

"You're a smooth operator. Half, it is."

The trailer looked lived in, but by what. No hot water, no stove, just a sink and a hot plate and three narrow bunks. You had to walk across the muddy yard and down the wooden stairs to get to the bathrooms. "What's for dinner?" Betty asked.

"Steak, baked potato, string beans, apple pie," I said.

"I don't smell anything. Where is it?"

"Grocery store. Get it yourself." I left them there and walked down the hill to Temple Street. I needed to get away from white people.

The rain had stopped and it was nice to walk. I passed the City Hall at Main, then Los Angeles Street and San Pedro Street. The cafes on Temple were getting crowded for dinner. I smelled cheeseburgers, spaghetti, pork, and undesignated. I had about two dollars, so I kept walking. I walked south on Central Avenue, past three liquor stores, an all-night secondhand clothing store, a Chinese herb shop, and a penny arcade. Up ahead, I heard a saxophone, a tenor, blowing a one-note riff, like ba-ba-bada, over and over. I caught up to the sound — a pachuco in a purple zoot suit walking in rhythm as he played, followed by two drunk sailors with a midget hooker in between them, another Filipino with too much snap in the brim and too much point in the shoes, and a Fifth Street wino in an overcoat tagging along with the party. The sax player turned into a bar called the Club Rendezvous, and the party went in with him. The wino came stumbling out a moment later and fell in the gutter. I gave him a hand up, and he thanked me politely and went on his way. I went in.

The place was narrow in front with a bar along one wall. The customers were mostly Filipino, drinking beer and talking in Spanish and Pinoy. It opened up in back with tables and a stage and a little dance floor. A five-piece band was trying to maintain a three-chord progression behind the saxophone riff. Piano, bass, drums, guitar, and trumpet. They were about to keel over, like it had been going on for a week. The sax player tagged it, and the tune, such as it was, stopped. The two sailors clapped. The band shuffled off the stand.

The sax man put his horn on the bar and sat on a stool. I walked over. "Gimme five, Johnny," I said. Recognition seeped through. "Al Maphis! Que pasó, carnal!" We hugged.

"Good to see you, Johnny," I said. "What's with the horn, you're a singer." I knew Johnny from the old days. He called himself "Johnny Dolor and the Five Pains," and his thing was crying on stage. He sobbed, he moaned, he collapsed on the floor and kicked his feet. Women, a certain kind, dug him, but he had never made it off Central Avenue.

"This is my new act. I play only the B-flat. The cats play the changes. They sing 'I want pussy.' I answer back 'ba-ba-bada.' Dig this. I started walking around in the joint with the horn, just for a gag. I sat at the tables and blew. You got to get the women, Al. Then, I went out on the sidewalk. I took a street-car, rode two blocks, got off and came back, blowing. The band stayed with it, and I was right on the tip! Twenty people followed me! I says, 'Who wants pussy?' They go, 'We want pussy!' It's a hit, Al!"

"Got to give the public what they want, Johnny," I said.

One of the sailors passed out, and the hooker was trying to keep his buddy from falling out of his chair. The band was nowhere around.

"Well, it's a little slow right now, the rain scares people off, you dig," Johnny said.

"I'm traveling with Billy Tipton," I said.

"Very uptown, Al."

"Let me pull your coat to something interesting. Our last engagement was in Kingman, Arizona. A girl came down to the gig. She wanted to sit in. You know, sing."

"All the chicks think they can get a drink and do it like Anita."

"That's right. But Billy is kind, so she let this girl get up. Now, I'm going to be straight with you. She isn't great. But she has an act. I want you to pick up on it. I can't do anything with her, but you have the perfect setup here."

"Lay it on me!" Johnny's big eyes were wet.

"She's athletic, and she has a routine that just won't stop. She bounces. While she sings, mi carnal. On this little springy platform that lets her get altitude. In a place with high ceilings like this, she could really bounce. But here's the payoff, Johnny. This will kill you. She features this Little BoPeep dress, and she don't wear no panties."

"Simón, ese! This is la verdad? Tits?"

"I swear to you. The tits come out."

"Órale! Man, where is she, bring her right over here!"

"She's resting now. How about tomorrow?" We hugged. The Filipino with the sharp clothes drifted by the bar and Johnny gave him the handshake. "Eyes?" he said. I shook my head. "See you tomorrow," I said. Johnny eased off the stool and drifted out the back. I drifted out the front. Step one.

Step two was a ten-cent phone call to Ramildo of Holly-wood. Ramildo ran a little custom tailor's shop across the L.A.

River in Boyle Heights. He was always available, since musicians keep odd hours.

"Speak," he answered.

"Al Maphis. How's my credit?"

"Your credit is good, Al, but I got Jorge Negrete opening at the Million Dollar in three days. Ten full-dress charro suits. Solid gold buttons, silver thread, matching hats. It's a big order for me, I had to bring in an extra seamstress."

"I got a chick that needs a trick outfit for a dirty act with Johnny Dolor. The tits have to pop on cue."

"Twelve noon, sharp. Don't be late."

Betty was subdued after a night in the trailer. "Don't make me go back there," she said.

"Maybe you won't have to. I got a little thing going, but you got to cooperate. Bandleader friend of mine is looking for a girl singer. He agreed to give you an audition. We're going to see a tailor friend of mine. He designs clothes for all the big acts in town. He's booked up, but he'll see you as a favor to me. You got to get outfitted."

"What am I going to sing? Billy said I wasn't ready."

"Johnny is going to be the judge of that. Forget about Billy."

"I suggest gold lamé, it is very sympathetic, very *chaise-lounges*," Ramildo said, turning Betty this way and that, sizing her up.

"What about one like that?" Betty said, pointing to Jorge Negrete's charro suits hanging everywhere. "I like black."

"That's a Mexican ranchera singer's type of thing, Betty," I said. "You don't want to look like a Mexican, do you?"

Ramildo held up his hand. "*Au contraire.* I think she has *la inspiracion.* I think it could be most . . . *interesting.*" Pat, the butch-looking seamstress, nodded and smiled.

"Meet me at the Club Rendezvous, on Central." I said. "Six o'clock."

"She'll be there," Pat said.

I drove over to Central. I found a pay phone in a second-floor boxing gym that was quiet at that time of day. I put in a dollar's worth of nickels. Berta's Pollo Encantado didn't have a phone, the Otro Lado didn't have a phone, but the Kingman Championship Lanes had one. Hazel the cashier answered. I disguised my voice as best I could and asked if an overweight brunette named Joyce was in the place. There was a pause, then Joyce came on the line. "Mom?" she said.

"Al Maphis. Say, 'Oh, it's you, Dad.' Say it."

"Hi, Dad," she said.

"Memorize this number. Go to a pay phone and call me back. Say, 'See you later, Dad.'" I gave her the number of the pay phone in the gym. I hung up and waited five minutes. The phone rang.

"This is Joyce. What happened to you, where are you? Where's Betty? Where's Billy Tipton?"

"Joyce, listen. We had to leave in a hurry. Betty's all right now, she's staying with friends. I want to know if the cops have been around there."

"Well, I'll say! The police talked to everyone, they were looking for Mr. Tipton. I didn't know anything, so I didn't say anything."

"That's good, Joyce. Did they ask about me?"

"No. All your friends disappeared right after you did. Mr. Spivak and Mr. Bowling are dead, they were gangsters, did you know? The police wanted to close the bowling lanes, but everyone made such a fuss, they left it open, as long as there isn't any more dancing. When is Betty coming back? Is she there, can I talk to her?"

"She told me to tell you she's going to write you very soon."

"Where is she? Where are you?"

"Hasta la vista, Joyce. Don't worry about Betty."

I was back at the rendezvous by five. I took a seat at the bar and watched the door. At six o'clock sharp, Betty walked in and the Pinoy chatter at the bar came to a dead stop. She was wearing her new outfit: black boots with four-inch heels, a black brocaded sombrero and a gun fighter's belt, with bullets. The bolero jacket was cut very short and open to the waist, and she was naked underneath. The pants fit low and tight and made her ass stick out like a bullfighter's. She was carrying a horsewhip.

"Where'd you get that?" I asked.

"Pat gave it to me," she said.

"Sammy," I said to the Chinese bartender, "say hello to your new star, Miss Bunny Rae."

"Haryew, Bunnylay?" he said. Betty set the whip down on the bar.

"I want a Coke."

I introduced Johnny to Betty. He was suave, Latin-esque. He huddled with Betty in a booth, making diagrams in the air with his hands: I go from here, you come from there. They went onstage and did some steps. Johnny spun her around. He threw her down and picked her up. Betty was a cheerleader, she got it. He counted off "Hernando's Hideaway" — a pop tango for straight-life moms and pops. Johnny gave it the twist — a domestic scene from the dark side of town. The man is aroused, the woman is coy. He slaps her around a little just to get a mood going. He preens, checks his attitude. They embrace, they dance, she stabs him in the crotch with a big prop knife. Olé, thank you ladies and gentlemen, especially you, ladies.

A man walked in. He stood and watched the stage. He was a black man, five-feet-five in elevator shoes, wearing a green sharkskin suit and a green snap-brim. He meant business and he wasn't drunk. Johnny waved his arms for applause. The Filipinos banged their glasses on the tables.

The man turned to me. "That girl belong to you?" His voice was deep and menacing and seemed out of place in his small body; but his face was bland and his eyes, which were hooded, seemed amused.

"I'm her manager," I said.

"I'll give you five hundred." He reached in his pocket and pulled out a wad of money like a hay bale.

"She's not for sale."

"Everything got a price tag," he said. Betty walked up.

"Bunny, this man wants to *buy* you. What do you think of that?"

"How much?" Betty said.

"I'm John Lee Hooker. I got the number-one record in *De-troit* right now. I'm a stranger in yo' town. Jus' because I'm a stranger, everybody wants to dog me 'round. I need somebody to tell my troubles to." He peeled off five hundred more. "Got a big 'un," he said to Betty.

"Bunny Rae is appearing with Johnny Dolor and the Five Pains, nightly and indefinitely," I said.

"That's one too many Johnnys," Hooker said. He went up onstage. The cats were lounging around, smoking. "Hey, mister guitar man," he said, "let me have it for a little while. I won't do you no harm."

He took the guitar and sat in a chair. He brought the vocal microphone down and spoke to the audience.

"Right about now, I'm goin' to do a solid number that is hit bound, and I want you to dig it and pick up on it, and it's called 'Too Many Johnnys.'"

He cranked up the knob on the guitar. He grooved in the key of E: Chunk-chunk-a-chunk-a-chunk, tapping both feet in straight-four time. "Need somebody to help me on the drum! Take it!" he hollered. I took it. I went up on the stand and set a little blues shuffle behind him. Doo-cha-doo-cha-doo-cha doo-cha. His voice sounded like trouble, and it made you listen:

Too many Johnnys, 'bout to drive me out of my mind
Yes, too many Johnnys, 'bout to drive me out of my mind
It have wrecked my life, an' ruint my happy home

When I first got in town, I was walkin' down Central Avenue
I heard people talkin' about the Club Rendezvous
I decided to drop in there that night, and when I got there
I said yes, people, man they was really havin' a ball, yes I know!
Boogie!

The Filipinos stopped yakking and started paying attention. Sammy came down to the end of the bar and watched. Betty watched.

I might cut you, I might shoot you, I jus' don' know
Yes, Johnny, I might cut you, I might shoot you, but I jus' don'
    know
Gonna break up this signifyin',
'Cause somebody got to bottle up and go

He tagged it on the guitar: ka-chunk-ka-chunk-ka-chunk-ka-chunk-doo-*daaa*, said, "Thank you," put the guitar down, and left the stage. First time I ever heard "thank you" sound like a reprieve. The Filipinos banged their glasses harder this time, I thought.

Hooker strolled up to the bar and put a twenty down. "Bartender, I want one scotch, one bourbon, and one beer."

Sammy looked at me. "He mean, at same time?"

"Line 'em up," Hooker said. "I want all my friends to drink. Long as I got money, I got friends almos' every day." The Filipinos ran for the bar. The wino in the overcoat had been standing in the door, and he looked over. Hooker pointed at him. "Give him as much as he wants to drink, I'll pay fo' it. Give him the whole jug, I don' mind. I have *been* down, and a good friend was hard to find."

Johnny smiled. "That was good, man. Very suavecito. I dug it the most. Entonces, we gonna try something I trust you will enjoy."

The band followed him onstage. He adjusted the microphone. "Es una canción muy sencilla, and it's been berry good to us here. "Loco Amor." One, two, threes, quatro." Clink-clink-clink-*clink*-clink-clink, went the piano. To-to-to-*ta*-to-to went the drums, a slow-dance bag. Six over four in a minor key. The place got quiet.

> *Este, este, loco amor. En la sangre, me hierve*
> *No puedo estar, no puedo estar sin tu amor*
>
> *Este, este loco amor. El amor de mi vida*
> *No puedo estar, no puedo estar sin tu amor*
>
> *Es loco amor, lo que en mi corazón, siento por ti*
> *Toma, toma, todo mi amor, amorcito querido,*
> *No puedo estar, no puedo estar sin tu amor*
>
> *Loco amoooor, loooocoooo amooor*

Crazy love. It's in the blood. I'm going crazy, I can't make it without your crazy love. Johnny got on the title phrase and wouldn't stop: "Loco, loco, loco, loco por tu amor." He started crying, he pulled his hair. He fell on his knees clutching the microphone stand in both hands. He was doubled up in pain. He gasped, he shook. "Loco, loco, loco, tan loco . . ." He raised his head. Tears of grief rolled down his face. The band pushed at him, they worked him. The out-of-tune piano pounded, the spacey guitar jangled. The Filipinos banged their glasses down hard and whistled.

Then Betty made her move. She strolled across the stage and stood over Johnny, brandishing the horsewhip. He looked up and whimpered, "Loca?" and she brought the whip down. He screamed, "Loco!" and the whip came down again and again. The bolero jacket came apart each time and her tits popped. The Filipinos went mad. They rushed the stage, they threw money — bills, change, whatever they had that they weren't going to need later.

Hooker turned to me. "I can't top that," he said. He walked down the bar and out the door. The wino followed him. Winner: Johnny Dolor and the Five Pains, hands down.

"Titties, oh boy!" Sammy said.

Johnny came and sat at the bar. "She doesn't hit you with that thing?" I asked.

"No, no, vato. I told her, pa' el *lado*, chica, *behind* me! You think it looks good?"

"Very good. You got something there, Johnny."

"Gracias por todo, you are a great friend, Al. Where is the man of the blues?"

"He had to cut out. Told me to tell you you're the man on Central Avenue now. By the way, I moved Betty in with Ramildo's seamstress, over in Boyle Heights."

"The dyke? Betty does not object?"

"No, she's used to it. She doesn't want to live with colored people. Work is something else. Nothing personal, I think she likes you. There's just one thing. Betty can be, let's say, temperamental, if she doesn't get what she wants. I've seen it."

"Do not be concerned. In me, she has found a man able to *control* her temper. Already, we are understanding one another, I think." Johnny Dolor, a sax-playing clown? Not on your life, cabrón. "And you, amigo?" he asked.

"I got to move on," I said.

"You are the Lone Ranger."

"Just a drummer from Tulsa." We hugged. Johnny gave me the handshake and there was money in it. The Filipinos crowded around Betty, laughing and drinking. She signed autographs — a square hustle, in my opinion. I left. Step three.

I saw the glow of Billy's cigarette outside the trailer. "Pack up," I said.

"Where to?" she asked.

"Spokane. I'll take you to Union Station."

"What's the setup?"

"You're off the hook; I'm off the hook."

"I don't have enough money for train fare to the city limits."

"I promoted a little something for expenses."

"So where's Betty?"

"Betty is among friends who appreciate her. Forget about Betty."

"She was juicy. Girls cluster round me like moths to a flame. If they get their wings burned, am I to blame, Al?"

We left in the Buick. I had a refund coming, but I figured the next trailer park I live in, it's going to belong to me.

"I hear Spokane is a friendly town," Billy said, "I sure could use you up there, it might turn out to be a long-running engagement."

"Thanks, but I'm looking for something smooth. I might even leave the business."

"Citizen Al Maphis? Don't try and kid Billy Tipton."

"Never kid a kidder, right Billy?" I said. She took her suitcase and walked into Union Station. And that's the last time I ever saw her. Him, I should say.

I got gas in San Bernardino. The California trip had been rough, but there I was, back on the same old road with the moon and stars. East of Barstow, I pulled over to rest my eyes and stretch my legs, and I saw what looked like an automobile over in the soft sand. It was a prewar Chevy, smashed up like it had rolled a few times. That's a bad stretch through there, known for terrible wrecks. There was clothing scattered on the ground and a small accordion, the kind the border Mexicans play. Two or three phonograph records. I picked them up, and that's when I saw the body. It looked like a small man, but it was hard to tell, the coyotes had got to him and there wasn't much left. Just a brother on his way to a gig somewhere. Vaya con dios, amigo, hasta la tumba final, I said to him. I got back in the car and pulled out. The Buick was old and slow, but I wasn't in any particular hurry this time. The Harry James Orchestra was on the radio, live from Hollywood. Good tone, for a straight-ahead white man. It seemed to me I was somewhere in between Harry James and the dead accordion player, and it was a pretty good place to be.

End of the line

1954

—m—

Please Note: The Baker Boy Confection Roll people have NOT seen this script. It doesn't seem to offer a very positive message about the American home. I predict they may strongly object to the idea that women steal from their employers and drink. The ending is morally ambiguous. Baker Boy has warned us about this in the past, let me remind everyone. Thanks for getting Baker Boy product into the story, it may help!

(Music, Truman Bradley lead-in, actor voice-over, sound effects.)

WHEN I GOT to work, the yard crew was shoving 606 through the washrack. "What's the big idea?" I asked Kappy, the yardmaster.

"Orders," he said.

"You don't wash a car when it's scheduled out — you know it and I know it. Nobody wants to ride in a wet car," I said. Kappy handed me a work order and a pink slip, both signed by the super. The pink slip had my name on it: "You are hereby notified and advised," et cetera, et cetera. I stood there, and Kappy stood there.

"Sorry, Ed. It's a tough way to get the news," Kappy said.

I went across the street to the coffee shop the motormen use, called the Roundhouse, and sat at the counter. The waitress came over.

"Evenin', Ed. Coffee?"

"I got time, this time, Lydia. What's on the dinner?"

"Pot roast and carrots."

"I'll have it."

"The dinner ain't ready yet. I can give you ham and eggs, bacon and eggs, but the dinner ain't ready."

"I can wait," I said.

"Well, Ed, I never know'd you to wait for dinner in fifteen years," she said.

"That's right, Lydia, you got a good memory. Me and 606 are retired from service as of right now. It's the end of the Playa del Rey line."

"What! How the people gonna get out to the beach? How'm I gonna see my sister in Venice?"

"No idea. It would take you all day on foot, and too darn much money by cab," I said.

The counter got busy. I read the paper and ate the dinner. I kept an eye on the carbarn. The maintenance boys finished up and left for the day. I finished eating and left some money on the counter. I bought a pint of Old Stagg bourbon and a package of Baker Boy Confection Rolls for dessert at the liquor store on the corner and walked across the street.

It's a hell of a way to get fired out of a job you had for fifteen years. Fifteen good years. I'm a better motorman now than at any time previous, but I'm not a motorman anymore, I thought. To me, trolleys have a face, like people. Two big eyes — that's the front windows. The cowcatcher along the bottom front looks like a mouth, and the lights make a shape like a nose. 606 looked puzzled, as if she was looking all around for me.

There was nobody there to see, so I climbed aboard and sat in the motorman's chair like so many times before. Just me and 606. She was a Saint Louis car, built by the Saint Louis Car Company in 1907. Other than a new coat of yellow and green paint in 1947, she was totally original and totally fit for service. In fifteen years on the job, 606 had been my car for the last eight. That's a long time, when you break it down into hours. I was married once, but Mom didn't like her. Mom passed away before I got assigned to 606, so as you can see, it's been real steady. Except for Lydia, I don't even know any living person as long as I been knowing car 606, and I been knowing her good.

Now, let me tell you what I did then. I raised the trolley pole to the overhead wire, rolled the dash sign to "Not in Service," and notched the controller to move 606 out. It's about a twenty-mile run from downtown to the beach on Jefferson Boulevard. First you pass through the downtown residential area. West of Crenshaw, Jefferson is no-man's-land until you get to the Hughes Aircraft sheds off to the left. Then you start to smell the ocean and the Ballona Creek marsh. Downtown L.A. smells pretty bad, unless it's raining.

You take the Culver Boulevard cutoff and the track dead-heads where Culver runs out. After that, it's just sand, a few beach cottages, and the ocean. Playa del Rey was some promoter's seaside development scheme, but it didn't work out. The beach-bound riders say, "Who'd ever want to live all the way out here? There's nobody around, there's nothing to do," but the idea appealed to me. I had some hope of making a down payment on a cottage, but you need a steady job. I don't know how to be anything but a motorman. I always figured people and trolleys naturally go together, why change it?

It was midnight by the time I got to the end of the line. I switched off the lights and sat there with the door open listening to the surf. You can hear the ocean at night, but you can't see it. Sometimes you see little lights out there on the black water. Boats, moving around in the dark. A boat and a trolley are pretty similar, I thought. I had a drink from the bottle. After a while, I thought I heard the sound of shoes, a woman's highheeled shoes, tap-tapping along. At that time of night, it stuck out. Then I saw her, carrying a suitcase and wearing a long coat, walking up from the beach side. She crossed the street and came over to the car.

"Evening, miss," I said.

"Are you just going to sit here all night?" she said in an abrupt tone.

"Sorry, ma'am, I'm out of service," I said. A motorman is always courteous.

"Don't kid me. If you're out of service, what are you doing here? What did you do, steal it?"

"This is my regular run, ma'am. I didn't steal anything."

"Then let's get moving." She climbed aboard.

"I can't take riders when I'm out of service. That's the rules."

"Don't kid me about rules. I need to get back to town, and you're going to take me or there's going to be trouble, because I think you're up to something." She was what Mom used to call a "mean-business woman." She gave me a funny feeling. I thought it might be a good idea to get away from there, just to quiet her down, so I said, "All right, I guess we can get started." I walked back to change ends, but she blocked me.

"What do you think you're doing?" Now she was getting furious.

"Look, miss, I got to change the pole if we're going," I explained.

"You bet we're going. You just try something and watch what happens."

In order to change ends, the motorman has to crank down the trolley pole on one end and raise the one on the other end to the overhead power line. Finally, the woman sat down. "Why don't you relax and enjoy the ride," I said. "What are you doing all the way out here, anyway? The cars don't run out here at this time of night. Suppose I hadn't come along? What were you going to do at this time of night?"

"You try any tricks, I'll start hollering 'copper,' then we'll see!" she shrieked. There wasn't a cop around for miles, but the idea bothered me just the same.

I released the air brakes, pulled the controller out a few notches, and we got moving. The girl sat in the front bench and stared straight ahead. I watched her sort of on the sly. She was young and nice looking, I guess, if you like 'em on the thin side. She had a hat pulled down low across her face, but I could see she was a little banged up. That accounted for the nerves, I thought. She caught me looking. "You watch what you're doing!" She had an all-of-a-sudden way of talking.

"No offense meant. Perhaps you had a car accident back there?"

"I didn't have any car accident! I fell down. I tripped on something in the dark."

"Maybe you could use a drink." I handed her the bottle. She grabbed it and drained about half. "Better take it easy there," I said. "Have a Baker Boy, it's my personal favorite."

"Thanks, mister. I guess I'm sorry for yelling at you. I didn't know what you were going to do, I thought I was stuck back there." She handed back the bottle.

"My name's Ed Breen," I said.

"Ida Jenkins." That seemed to make a difference, her telling me her name.

"So, Ida, do you like the beach? I think it's very relaxing. Some people fall asleep on the sand, they lose track of the time."

"I never saw it. It was dark when we, when I got there. Dark and loud and cold. You ever been to Saint Joe?"

"Never heard of it."

"Good for you. I tried to get away from there for so long. I thought this was going to be it, finally." I waited, but she didn't say another word.

I eased 606 back into the carbarn at 2:00 a.m. sharp. There wasn't nobody around except Pop Cord, the night man, and he was asleep as usual. Ida had fallen asleep back there around Western Avenue. She came awake with a scared look, but I told her everything was all right, I was going to introduce her to a friend who might put her up.

The Roundhouse coffee shop is on the ground floor of the brick building across the street. Upstairs is a row of two-room apartments where Lydia has a place. Not a nice place, as Lydia would say, but it's hard to get a nice place. She was just closing up at the restaurant when I walked in.

"Lydia, you'll never guess what happened," I started off. She spied Ida out on the sidewalk, and said, "Bad news first."

"I took 606 and rode out to the beach one last time. See that girl? She was stranded out there, all alone. What could I do?"

"Two days is all I can handle. Three at the most."

"Thanks, Lydia. I got a good feeling about it, somehow."

That was Thursday. I dropped by the Roundhouse on Saturday. "How's it working out with Ida?" I asked Lydia when she had a moment.

"There is one thing, Ed. There was a gun in her purse. I don't suppose you caught sight of it before bringing her to me."

"What sort of gun?"

"Well, Ed, it's a Smith and Wesson .32 snub nose. It's little, but it has been fired. What were you thinkin'?"

"I'm not sure. A gun changes things."

"Ida is not a whole lot different lookin' than your ex."

"You got a good memory, Lydia."

"I sure hope you do." Some of the fellas from the day shift came in and Lydia got busy. Charlie, the Edgeware Road shuttleman, sat down next to me and banged his coffee cup on the counter until Lydia hurried over with the pot. "Ed, it's a crying shame," he said. "Look at you, a no-accident record nobody can top. Look at me; I hit three Cadillacs in two months! I'm demoted down to a lousy shuttle! They might have given you something in the traffic office, Ed. It's a god-awful way to treat a man just because he takes a drink once and a while." Charlie had had a few. His eyes teared up.

"No, Charlie, I'm a man for the road. I got to feel the car move over the rails and smell the electricity. If I can't do that, then I'm gone. I'll be seeing you." It was a good exit line.

An item in the city section of the paper had caught my eye, and I wanted to get away from Charlie and study it. "Mystery Man in Surf," it read. "Police are searching for the identity of a man found in the surf near Playa del Rey. The man is described as being of medium height, medium weight, and wearing a heavy overcoat. Detective Sergeant Duncan Mahoney confided to this reporter that the man 'bears an interesting resemblance to one Earl McDonnell, a bright boy from the Midwest, and not the kind of man we're happy to have with us here in Los Angeles. McDonnell had several known associates in the area, and we'll be talking to them.'"

I went back inside the Roundhouse. "Take a look at this," I said to Lydia. She read the story and then put the paper away, out of sight. She opened the cash register and showed me the gun and a set of car keys on a key ring with a Lincoln medallion.

"I'm going to have a talk with her, I think," I said, taking the keys and the gun.

"You take in mind what I said about Ida and your ex. The crack still goes, as the fella says," Lydia said. She never liked my ex-wife, most people didn't. I went upstairs and knocked at number three. No answer. "It's me, Ed," I said softly.

Ida opened the door against the chain and looked out. "Where you been at?" she said.

"Nice to see you looking rested, Ida," I said. She took the chain off and opened the door. The place was greasy with cigarette smoke. "Lydia won't like it," I said.

"You got me all cooped up."

"You're not cooped up, you're on you own."

"I didn't come out here for my health."

"You said you needed a place to stay. I think you needed to get off the street. Start with the gun," I said.

"You spied on me when I was asleep!"

"Lydia wasn't born yesterday, or the day before. See, I'm in between jobs, and I love a story. Let's hear it." I passed her the bottle of Old Stagg, it had worked before. She drained what was left in it.

"My boyfriend gave me the gun. He says Los Angeles is a dangerous place."

Ever since you got here, I thought. "Tell him to come and get you."

"I came out by myself."

"How did you get here?"

"What's it to you. You're just bluffing."

"I'm interested, that's the way I am."

"I took a bus as far as Tulsa, then I met a guy with a car. He rode me the rest of the way. Gave me a ride, I mean. In his car, for crissakes. When we got here, he wanted to go to the beach; he said he'd never been there. He said he wanted to go swimming. We were drinking and he passed out. I left something back there. You could help me if you wanted to. I thought you liked me, maybe I was wrong."

"Help you how?"

"Maybe you're the kind of man that takes advantage when a girl is in a tight spot and can't perfect herself." Ida stuck out her chest like a girl in a tight spot.

"A man like me might get into a real tight spot nosing around a Lincoln belonging to Earl McDonnell. Earl being the kind of man who likes to go swimming in his overcoat." I shook the car keys at her.

She shot out of the chair like she had a firecracker go off in her pants, and came right at me. "Give me those goddamn keys!" she hissed. I pushed her back down in the chair. She sat there glaring at me, ready to pounce again.

"I'll give you a full report, Ida." I left. She didn't try to follow me. She was mad, but more scared than mad. It was all very familiar, somehow. Lydia was right, there was a certain resemblance.

(Baker Boy message, Truman Bradley lead-in.)

Before I was married, I didn't know too much about the retail clothing business, or women. I bought one pair of shoes a year, shirts every six months, and a new suit every three years. The railway provided the cap and badge. I've never been much for dressing, but at the same time, I'm not hard on clothes like some fellas.

When I met my future ex-wife, she was working at Grayson's department store on Spring Street. She was in women's blouses, on the second floor, and the sister of a fellow motorman named Fred Keller. Her name was Inez. Fred introduced us one night at the Roundhouse. He was going off shift and I was coming on. Inez was meeting him for dinner. Looking back, I think she was there specifically to meet me. I was living with my mother on Hoover, and had just started as a motorman with the Los Angeles Railway Company.

We started going out together on my off nights — movies, bars, dancing now and then. Inez liked to go out and drink, and she liked to talk. We'd get in a place and sit down and she'd start talking about her job at Grayson's. She was really hipped on the subject. One night, after we'd been seeing each other for about a month, she told me a story.

"See, Ed, the higher up in floors you go, the more things cost. All the cheap stuff, like costume jewelry and makeup, is on the street level. Second floor is sportswear, like blouses and handbags. That's my floor. Third floor is women's suits and shoes and better accessories. But the fourth floor is the good stuff — fur coats and real jewels and watches, and that. There's a floorwalker on each floor to keep an eye on things, but there's two floorwalkers on the fourth. They lock everything up at the end of the day and unlock it in the morning. Everything on the fourth has a serial number and a catalog number. They watch you like a hawk up there."

"That's very interesting, Inez. You know a lot about it."

"You bet I do, I made a study of it."

"Why?"

"Look, Ed, you and I are getting along pretty good, wouldn't you say? So, you won't be surprised if I tell you that I got a system figured out to make some pretty good money."

"Don't they pay you well enough?"

"Are you kidding? A salesgirl doesn't make enough to live on and never will. I want things, Ed. Nice things like they got up on the fourth. Don't you want me to have nice things? Don't you want me to be happy?"

"Well, sure I do, but what can I do about it? You know I make a motorman's wage. It's nothing fancy. If I didn't live with Mom, I couldn't even afford a little house like we have."

"That's just what I'm talking about, Ed. If you want things like I do, then if you help me, we can get the things we both want. I think you like me just that much, don't you Ed?"

"Maybe you had better tell me what you want to do, if we're going to do something together."

Inez laid it all out for me that night. She had gotten started by stealing blouses, one at a time. The trick was to take them right after an inventory of stock was done. Every salesgirl was afraid of the inventory, afraid to get blamed if something was wrong. But there was always what they called "shrinkage." The inventory, which was supposed to account for stock and sales receipts and actual cash, never came out quite right, so they called the discrepancy a "shrinkage" and wrote it off. The trick was to know how much shrinkage they would accept. If it was more than usual in some department, they got suspicious. Inez knew where shrinkage was typical and where it wasn't. Apparently, shoes was a shrinkage-free department; also, the luxury goods on the fourth floor. Shrinkage was not acceptable up there.

I listened. Inez looked at me to see how I was reacting so far. "So, you take a blouse here and there," I said.

"We all take little things. I can't afford clothes from that store, even with the employee discount."

"So, what's your plan?" I asked. We'd had a few drinks in this place she knew about, and it made me kind of unconcerned.

"It's this. The store manager's name is Guy Richard Cummings. He's a big, fat man that acts superior to all the girls. All high-and-mighty. He eats Sen-Sens all the time because he sits up in his corner office on his fat ass and drinks and talks on the phone all day. But I found out about Mr. Guy, and this is what it is: We take cheap little blouses, but he takes the store's money. He steals money from the accounts. He fixes it so he can show the money is disappearing from ten different places. Very hard to trace. Then, he charges it back to the head office. Then, the head office accountants pay back the loss, but they pay it directly to him, in cash. It's normal, because the store uses a lot of cash every day. But he puts the extra money in his pocket! That's some trick, wouldn't you say?"

I realized then that Inez Keller was nobody to fool with. "Are you going to turn him in?" I asked.

"Are you kidding? I got his fat ass right where I want it. He's going to help you and me steal a mink coat, maybe two or three."

"Wait a minute. How did you find all this out?"

"He called me up to his office. He said the ledger showed I was short three blouses, and he was going to dock my pay. He accused me of stealing. Unless, of course, I was willing to be reasonable. 'Reasonable,' you get it, Ed?" Inez made a circle with one thumb and forefinger, and pumped the other forefinger in and out. "So I said, 'Mr. Cummings, you accuse me with three blouses, but I know you are bluffing, because I only took one. You already put in a receipt for the cash value of three; then you put the extra money in your pocket. Am I right, *Guy?*' He turned white in the face. I was sitting in his lap at the time, and I saw it up close. He said, 'You got balls.' I said, 'That's not all I got.' It was the happiest day of my life."

"What's wrong with the head office that you know all this and they don't?" I asked.

"I don't know that," she said. "I think someone there is shielding him, but I don't care. I want that mink coat. I've got it picked out; I know which one it is. I want that coat more than anything in this world. Except for you, of course. Do you want me like I want you, Eddy?"

We were married on her lunch hour, one month later. She moved her stuff in with Mom and me in the little house down on Washington and Hoover. Mom and Inez never got along, they argued about everything. She said she needed me to help with the coats. We were going to be a team. Cummings was on the hook, he was the inside man. It was going to be a three-way split. I stalled her. I said I had to think it over. Finally, an accounts investigator discovered the cash rake-off, and they arrested Cummings. He had been under suspicion for some time. Then the police showed up at our house one morning after Inez had left for work. I was asleep since I had the night shift at the railway. They told Mom that a mink coat was missing from the store and that Cummings revealed he had given it to Mrs. Inez Breen, and that she was blackmailing him. He claimed the whole embezzlement scheme was her idea. She denied the charge, but the officers found the coat in the garage. Being the husband, I couldn't testify in her defense. Inez made a deal for a petty larceny charge and drew a five-year sentence, which she is still serving, as far as I know. Cummings was the big fish they were after. "Your mother turned me in, how about them apples? See you sometime, Eddy," was all she said. Mom got the marriage annulled on a technicality.

(Baker Boy message, Truman Bradley lead-in.)

In the daylight, Playa del Rey looked like a dump. There was a small neighborhood of older houses up along the bluffs to the south; then you had the marsh and the half-dozen beach cottages built on the dirt levee along the creek. Will Build to Suit signs sprouted here and there, and a fish and chips stand that was closed for the winter. I walked down the sandy dirt road leading to the cottages. The first four looked lived in, but the fifth and sixth had realty signs posted. Of the two, one garage was locked, and one was not, so I took a look.

The Lincoln was tucked away in there, all nice and neat. It was a Continental convertible, just the kind of flashy car a bright boy would choose for a trip out west. The registration was missing. There was a lot of loose junk on the floor, like someone had been looking for something. The little trunk lid was open: nothing in there and nothing in the backseat. I raised the hood. A Lincoln twelve-cylinder, ready for the road. What about that air cleaner? Big as a saucepan. I unscrewed it and lifted it off the carburetor. I removed the filter unit and felt something like a small package in the bottom of the metal container. I put the filter back inside and tried to get the clumsy thing back on the carburetor. It was dark in the garage, and hot, and I couldn't see what I was doing. I got dizzy, and then I got scared. They'll notice somebody's been handling it, I thought. I went out and looked around. There wasn't one person anywhere, just the wind and the sound of the surf, which was about a hundred yards away: How did you get Earl down there? A woman couldn't drag a man that far, you must have lured him down to the water somehow. In the dark? In the overcoat?

My hands were oily. There was just enough water in the creek to get most of the oil off, but it worried me. There was a man's hat lying in the creek bed. I picked it up. It had a Tulsa haberdasher's name on the hatband and the initials "EMD" stamped in gold. So you and Earl went shopping, I thought. You wanted to see how much cash he had.

I put the oilskin bag under my shirt, in back. I had a jacket on and it felt like it was covered up good enough to get going. I walked up Culver, then north through Venice, as far as Washington Boulevard. It took a long time. I kept thinking someone was following me, but nothing happened. I caught the Washington car and rode downtown.

I didn't recognize the motorman. Normally, I would have talked to him, like hey buddy this and hey buddy that, but I was so tired and hungry I almost passed out. Then I saw the Pup Café up ahead on the right. You can't miss it, it's made to look like a big dog sitting there by the sidewalk. You walk inside through his stomach. He looks worried, as if he missed his lunch. I had a cheeseburger with onions and tomatoes and pickles. Then I ordered another. The counterman said, "Seein' you wolf down your food reminds me of somethin' happened here last week. You want to hear what happened?"

"Sure," I said between mouthfuls.

"It was quittin' time, nine o'clock. A colored man comes in, kind of a large man, and says: 'Five cheeseburgers, with everything, to go.' Just like that, just as bold."

The counterman waited for me to make a comment, but I kept eating, so he continued. "Well, I says, 'We're closed.' And you know what? He reaches in his pocket and pulls out a fistful of money like you ain't seen before and shows me a hundred-

dollar bill! And he says, 'Make it six, with pie, and step lively!'"
The counterman waited for a reply, so I said, "All right, so you
made six cheeseburgers."

"Well, you're darned right. No colored man in my experience ever had a roll like that unless he's a gangster or a dope
fiend or some desperate character. I made up the order, and he
gives me the hundred dollars! And then he says, 'You ought to
mind your manners, Bub, you never know who's coming through
the door. I'm Charlie Parker. You ought to keep that hundred-
dollar bill; it might be worth something someday. Tell your little
ofay grandkids.' And he left. Got in a great big Cadillac and
took off! Can you tie that? The things I seen here — I could
write a book."

"How 'bout a slice of apricot pie," I said. You can have all
the cheeseburgers and pie you want when you have twenty-five
thousand dollars.

I showed Lydia the money first. "I say we split it up three
ways. Ida gets one third, and you and me can take the rest. What
about it, Lydia?" I was all excited.

Lydia shook her head. "You kill me, Ed. You been a motorman in this town for fifteen years, but you never got the hang of
it. You can't see what's going on outside of that trolley car. It's just
ding-ding, smile, fares please, and thank-you-laze-and-jellmen."

"Wait a minute, what's so wrong with that? It always
worked for me. I made a lot of nice friends that way, including
you. This is the only chance a guy like me is ever going to get."

"Ed, I wouldn't give you a nickel for that money. If Ida
Jenkins doesn't get what she thinks she's got coming, then I
wouldn't give a nickel for your chances. You got away lucky with
Inez. For Ida Jenkins, I just wouldn't give a nickel." Lydia went
back to the counter. I walked upstairs and knocked.

Ida just sat there watching me. I told her an even split
was better than no future with Earl. I laid it all out, I had it all

wrapped up. I counted out $12,500 in hundred dollar bills. She took it. She got her coat and hat and suitcase. "I thought you were afraid to go out," I said.

"Maybe you're the kind of man that would sell a girl out just to make a lousy buck."

"There you go again. Sell a girl to who, exactly?"

"Maybe you'll find out. Then you won't act so goddamn cute. Adios, Eddy. Maybe I'll see you sometime."

I sold the house on Hoover for twenty-five hundred dollars in cash. I bought a beach shack on a lot in Playa del Rey for a thousand dollars and moved in. One day I saw an article in the paper saying that the Los Angeles Railway Company had made a deal to sell retired trolley cars to Argentina. I went straight down there and told them I wanted to buy car 606, that I would double what Argentina was paying. In cash, on the spot. They went for it, why wouldn't they. It was just scrap lumber and metal as far as the railway was concerned. I paid eighteen hundred dollars.

They towed 606 behind Big Bertha, the service car, right down Jefferson, all the way to the beach. Bertha was set up with a lift crane, and they jockeyed 606 around so that she was sitting sideways on my lot, up by the sidewalk. The converter had been removed for shipment to Argentina, but otherwise, the car was in perfect shape for what I had in mind.

It was the Pup Café that gave me the idea to convert 606 into a lunch counter. I hired a local carpenter to do the hard work, but it was not a bad job to rearrange the benches and set up the little tables. We partitioned off the back third of the car for the kitchen, with a window for the cook to hand orders up to the server. The fish and chips man sold me his kitchen equipment cheap. He was going to move to Yuma, Arizona, and get into the candy business. Said the salt air gave him lung trouble. I asked Lydia to come in with me as a full partner, but she wouldn't have it. "The Roundhouse is my home since I got off the sauce. They'll probably bury me under the floorboards," she said. The carpentry, plumbing, and electrical set me back three thousand dollars in time and materials. I paid the city twelve hundred dollars for the license.

I called it the "606 Café — Featuring the World Famous Trolley Burger." I borrowed the idea of six o'clock dinner specials from Lydia. I hired the cook from the fish and chips joint, a cheerful Japanese fellow named Mats, and we opened up just in time for the summer. Things were a little slow at first but trade picked up since 606 was the only lunch counter at the beach for miles around.

I started fooling around with plans for a deck with tables and umbrellas. People seemed to prefer sitting on that side, they were willing to wait just to get a glimpse of the sand and the water while they ate their Trolley Burgers. I liked being my own boss. No strings out there — my mother was gone, Inez was gone, and I never expected to see Ida again. On that score, I was wrong.

(Baker Boy message, Truman Bradley lead-in.)

It was Friday evening, a little before six. The place was still empty. We were starting to pick up trade for dinner on Friday— folks said they liked driving out to the beach at sunset and sitting down to a nice meal. They usually came in around six thirty, seven o'clock. I was organizing the cash register when I saw a big black sedan pull up out front. It was a seven-passenger Caddy, not your typical family car. Two guys got out and walked over. One was heavyset, the other was built regular. They both had on hats and overcoats. They came in and sat at the counter. They kept their hats and coats on.

"Evening, jellmen. What can I get for you?"

"What do you want to eat, Al?"

"I don't know what I want."

"I'll take the pork chops and applesauce."

"Pork chops is on the dinner. The dinner isn't ready, won't be ready until six o'clock. I can give you any kind of sandwich, bacon and eggs, ham and eggs, but the dinner won't be ready until six o'clock."

"I'll take the chicken croquettes with the mashed potatoes."

"Chicken croquettes is on the dinner."

"So everything we want is on the dinner. That's how you work it?"

"What do you call this dump?"

"Playa del Rey."

"It's a dump. Where's everybody?"

"Right now, it's just me and the cook."

"You think you're a pretty bright boy, don't you?"

"Bright enough."

"Well, you're not."

"Okay, I'm not. Customer's always right."

"What's your name, bright boy?"

"Ed Breen."

"We got a friend of yours out in the car. Her name's Ida. You remember Ida, bright boy."

"I'm not sure, a lot of people come in here."

"Ida remembered you. Not right away, but later on. Later on, she remembered real good, right, Al? She told us all about you."

"All about you and the money. Twelve-and-a-half thousand bucks that belongs to us. What were you going to say?"

"Nothing. I was just thinking of something. I wanted to write it down before I forgot."

"Hey Al, bright boy is a thinker. Ideas come to him."

"You got anything to drink, bright boy?"

"I got a bottle of Old Stagg under the counter."

"Let's have a drink, I think you need one. Then you're going to tell us a story all about our money. We love a story." Earl McDonnell's Smith and Wesson .32 was right there under the counter. The fat man looked around for one second, and that was one less pair of eyes.

I brought the gun up and stepped behind the big National cash register. I pumped two slugs at point blank range into the fat man's stomach. He spun around on the stool and hit the floor. That knocked Al off balance. He pulled a .45 and fired at me, but his aim was off and he hit the cash register. One hundred pounds of solid brass, a good business investment. My lucky shot nailed him in the throat. His head hit the counter and he didn't move.

I ran outside. It was Ida, all right. She was tied up in the backseat of the Cadillac. Her head was over to one side at a funny angle. Her eyes were half closed, and she was dead. They had really done a job on Ida. The inside of the car smelled like blood. That's something you don't realize when you see the pictures in the paper. In eight years, I had blood in 606 twice only, both Filipinos, but it didn't smell anything like that Caddy.

I went back inside. I had written Lydia's name on the outside of an envelope while the bright boys were going through their tough-guy routine. I put a nickel inside the envelope and sealed it; then I called the cops. Al and his fat buddy were real tough guys, but they talked so much. If you're going to make a move, make it, as my stepfather used to say. Don't sit there all night yakking about it, somebody might get the drop on you and get you hurt. That's the last thing Daddy Rice said to me before he died. He was sitting in the living room, listening to *Amos 'n' Andy* at the time.

I heard sirens headed down Culver: "Dinner's ready," Mats called out.

Announcer: "And now, here's Truman Bradley to tell you about next week's story."

TB: "Next week, a Filipino stabs a man in a movie theatre, but a Mexican gets blamed for it. Or is it the other way around? Join us, won't you, for I Love A Story.*"*

(Theme music up, actor credits, producer/director credits, Truman Bradley closes for Baker Boy.)

My telephone keeps ringin'

1956

—₥—

SANTA MONICA IS Douglas Aircraft and Douglas Aircraft is Santa Monica. Three shifts a day, seven days a week means prosperity for all.

Douglas has contracted with the Fritz Burns Company to build low-cost tract housing for the workers and their families in the south end of town between Ocean Park Boulevard and West Pico. They call it "Sunset Park," a nice place to live and work. Always a fresh breeze off the ocean, which you can almost see just over the hills of Ocean Park.

Sunset Park is a plateau, so the air is dry and the light is good, in a lower-middle-class sort of way. There are three grammar schools, two junior highs, and a high school, called Samohi. You can walk to three or four good-sized grocery stores that feature the modern shopping carts for your convenience, as well as drugstores (Airport Rexall), a movie theater (The Aero), liquor stores, coffee shops, and bars — especially the ones up on Ocean Park Boulevard that stay open twenty-four hours a day on account of the strategic work that's going on at Douglas Aircraft twenty-four hours a day.

Over on Thirty-first Street and Pico Boulevard is the Gresham Building, headquarters of the Gresham Detective Agency. It's a two-story stucco job with the entrance on the diagonal at the corner. Kind of ugly and squat looking. Here comes George Gresham in his 1950 Oldsmobile. George recently purchased the car from Ned Hillael at Hillael's Used Cars, corner of Thirtieth and Pico, one block over. Paid four hundred fifty dollars in cash, which is a lot of money for a used car in 1956, but George thinks he really put it over on Ned with the cash offer. Got Ned to come down seventy-five dollars. George handled it just right; he's on top this year. Got the building with his name on it, and he's doing some bill collecting and credit checking just to get things going in a business way.

Ned is the only used car dealer in the airport vicinity, and he does good business with Douglas employees and the occasional professional like George Gresham. Finally got rid of that Olds — goddamn cracked block wouldn't hold oil. Ned himself drives a late-model Cadillac Sedan DeVille. And there's Herb Saunders, a mechanic, a colored man, who works for Ned. Ned gets these cars from repo auctions and police impound sales, and Herb doctors them up so they run for six months. All sales final at Ned Hillael's.

Herb himself drives a Muntz Jet, a weird little sports car marketed unsuccessfully by Earl "Madman" Muntz, the king of cheap TV sets. It has a Cadillac motor and an orchid-pink paint job, and it runs and looks sharp. Herb lives in the little black and Mexican neighborhood over by Woodlawn Cemetery, down around Sixteenth and Michigan, in a 1900-era cottage on a deep lot, and he grows his own vegetables right alongside the garage where he works on bad cars for Ned.

The aircraft workers are doing good, and they want things nowadays, so Ned is doing good and therefore Herb is doing good. He trades vegetables for eggs with the Mexican woman next door, Andrena Ruelas, who keeps a few laying hens in her backyard. Andrena and Herb are about the same age, forty, forty-three, or thereabouts. Andrena's husband was killed in the war, and she lives alone.

It's eight in the morning, and Herb is on the lot getting the week's work together.

Ned is sitting at his desk inside the little kiosk at the back of the lot. "Studebaker's gone," he tells Herb without looking up from his stack of sales receipts and credit reports.

"That's a bad car. I couldn't get the brakes to set up right. I put glue on the linings, but that won't hold too long," says Herb.

"I know all about that. The guy paid three hundred dollars down from three hundred twenty-five dollars," Ned replies.

"Traveling man, I hope."

"Address in Venice. A machinist." Ned checks the paperwork. "Douglas man."

"Should have known better."

"His wife liked the color."

"Got anything for me?"

"'48 Chrysler Windsor, two-door."

Herb drives south on Pico, getting an impression of the car. Compared to his Muntz Jet, the Chrysler feels like a bathtub on wheels. Sluggish off the lights. Fluid drive, a transmission for church ladies, Herb thinks. He pulls into the alley behind his property and unlocks the gate. He drives the car up onto a pair of streetcar tracks and scoots underneath the car on his mechanic's dolly. "Fluid drive needs fluid," he says to his little dog, Scrubby. Scrubby sits on her pillow in the sun and watches Herb work. He replaces the transmission fluid, spark plugs, and fan belt. The engine oil looks good and the brake linings look fair. "Do the minimum" is Ned's motto. Ned pays Herb time and materials, but you better be right: "That radiator hose looks fine to me, put it back on"; "That oil was definitely clean, Herb." Ned knows where his next dollar is coming from, you can't fool him.

After lunch, Herb drives the Chrysler back to the lot. An unmarked police cruiser is out in front, a Ford, dark blue in color. Herb pulls around to the back alley and waits. After a while, the sound of voices coming from the kiosk tells him the officers are on their way out. He waits a minute more and then walks around to the office.

"What's up?"

"Studebaker."

"What happened?"

"Guy crashed into a bus and fled the scene this morning. I'm still the owner of record."

"Told you that's a bad car."

"I know all about that."

"The Chrysler's okay, needed trans fluid and plugs."

"See you later."

Herb walks down Pico toward the cemetery. He thinks, Ned's a worried man today, got a worried tone, like a bad main bearing. Didn't even argue about the plugs.

Spring evenings in Santa Monica have a softness, a gentleness on account of the marine air that builds up toward the close of day. Down around the cemetery, it's just right for having your dinner outside, which is what Herb and Andrena are doing. Herb has fixed up a nice outdoor barbecue for her, using bricks from the reject pile over at the brick factory. Andrena has made cabrito with garden tomatoes and guacamole on the side, cilantro for sabor, and beer. On the radio, "It's time for *The Hunter Hancock Show*, with your host, Old H.H., and Margie too, bringing you the finest Negro singers and entertainers! Swing to sweet, and blues to boogie! But first, *This Is Progress*. And progress has no ending, but it does have a beginning." Right in the middle of *This Is Progress*, Herb's telephone starts ringing. He hates the sound, it's always been bad news. He walks through the gap in the rose hedge and into his house to pick up the call.

"Herb, Ned."

"Yeah, Ned."

"Job for you."

"Night job?"

"Yeah. Need you to take the Chrysler over to a customer."

"Now?"

"Yes, now."

"Where?"

"Venice."

"Special sort of customer?

"Yeah."

"Why can't he come get it himself?"

"Car's right out front, address and keys on the seat."

Herb goes back next door and explains. "I watch Scrubby," Andrena says.

The Chrysler is out front and the keys are right there on the seat. Herb heads south on Seventeenth, then west on Pico Boulevard, toward the beach. It's 8:30 and getting dark. A '50 Oldsmobile pulls around the corner and follows along two car lengths behind. Here we have George Gresham joining the party, Herb thinks.

Aside from Watts, Venice Beach is the most overlooked place in Southern California. It's a jumble of beach shacks and old wooden apartment houses built in the teens or even before: dive bars, dope addicts, beach bums, jazz musicians, and a little community of concentration camp survivors. These people fit right in simply because Venice is not "family" and the old Jews don't have families anymore, just each other. They sit around the boardwalk speaking Yiddish in low tones and soaking up the sun.

Herb is looking for an address in the canal zone, where the oil derricks are. The unpaved streets wind around the derricks, and it's hard to find house numbers or even street signs. Dudley Court turns out to be a cluster of five bungalows in very bad shape. There is no sign of life around except for the sound of a radio coming from the back somewhere. "Crazy Arms," Ray Price. This must be it — Jewish folks don't much care for Ray Price, and they don't usually require sudden nighttime vehicle deliveries. He leaves the keys on the seat and walks back up Neilson Way toward Ocean Park. The oil rigs make a groaning, whining sound — "watch out, bad break, watch out" — a chorus of old men nodding their heads up and down, like trouble is one thing they've seen plenty of.

Crossing Washington Boulevard, Herb spots the Oldsmobile parked in a gas station. In the darkness, George Gresham is just a fat shape in the front seat. So, the machinist's wife liked the color, did she now, Ned, old buddy? Detective George Gresham on stakeout? Herb shakes his head. Clowns, definitely.

Herb walked as far as Main and Rose, the boundary line between Venice and Ocean Park. The delivery had caused him to miss dinner, and he was hungry. At 9:30 on a Monday night, Olivia's Soul Food Café, on Main, was empty except for Olivia.

"Herb Saunders, what a pleasure."

"How are you, Olivia?"

"In the pink, Herb, in the pink! What can I get for you?"

"I believe I'll try the short ribs, with greens and sowbelly. Been eatin' too clean lately."

"Why don't you play something on the box for us? Something of yours? Seeing you puts me in the mood." Herb went over to the big old Wurlitzer in the corner, the one with the 78 records, left over from when the place was a wartime dance joint. He selected "My Telephone Keeps Ringin'" by "Atomic Bomb" Saunders, on the Imperial label.

> *My telephone keeps ringin', sound like a long-distance call*
> *Yes, my telephone keeps on ringin', must be a long-distance call*
> *Sayin', don't look for me in Heerosheema,*
> *Ain't nothin' left down there at all.*

Well, I'm goin' to Nagasaky, see if my good gal is down there
Tell yuh, I'm goin' to Nagasaky, see if my good gal is down there
Well, if she ain't in Nagasaky,
Must be down on Central Avenue somewhere.

"You felt that one, Herb, I can see it still." Olivia brought Herb his food.

"I had a handle on it. Maxwell Davis had a great band, top notch." Herb said. The record turned itself over and the flip side played, a jitterbug number with a crazy fast tempo.

Here comes Robert Oppenheimer, got his finger on the timer,
Droppin' by to let you know, we ain't got long to go!
Two minutes to bomb time,
Two minutes to boom time,
Two minutes to bust time, got two minutes to go!

Two minutes to shake time,
Two minutes to bake time,
He's gonna hit the switch and let it blow!
Got a minute to pray, Oh Lordy! Got a minute to say, Oh Baby!
Got a minute to pray, a minute to say, and two minutes to go!
Got a minute to spend my money! Got a minute to call me
*   honey!*
Got a minute to spend and a minute to blend, and two min-
*   utes to go!*

J. Robert just wants to let you know,
Only got two minutes to go! Baby!

"Solid, Herb. I remember that one. You nailed it."

"That one nailed it down tight. They wouldn't play it, even on KGFJ. Said it was subversive. Said I was duped into it. The man from the record company put another cover picture on it —

a white girl in a nightgown holding a tomato-soup can — and called it *Rock and Roll Bomb Shelter*."

"You wasn't rock, Herb, just ahead of the times."

"You know something, Olivia? I don't regret leaving the business, it's a bad old road. I'm a happier man today. This guy I work for now, he's a little tricky, but those record guys had tricks nobody could see. This little used car man here, seems like he's always about to trick mostly just himself."

George Gresham was getting hungry. He was thinking about a plate of spareribs and greens like you get at the colored joint in Ocean Park. Tailing the colored man down to the canals made him think of it. It'd be a big plate, with pie. There was sweet potato, pecan, and rhubarb. What do I want? Try all three, that's the ticket.

George almost missed the light at Ocean. The Chrysler turned right and headed up Broadway. He ran the light and made the turn, but a guy trying to cross the street had to jump back fast, and he yelled at George. That was bad, he hoped the quarry in the Chrysler hadn't noticed. George didn't do tail jobs as a rule, but Ned Hillael had mentioned a good-sized fee. Follow the colored guy, he'll lead you to the white guy, tail him and find out where he's going, who he talks to, call it in. No contact, no rough stuff. George was the man to find out just what it was Ned was up to, but that would come later. He was too hungry for any kind of thinking like that.

The Chrysler pulled into the parking lot behind the DanDee shoe factory at Third and Broadway. Downtown Santa Monica was deserted except for a few cars parked around the back door of the Embers cocktail lounge, a popular spot on Third Street. George parked the Olds and watched the little man in the hat get out of the Chrysler and go into the bar. Next door to the Embers was The Huddle coffee shop. A man on a tail job has got to have coffee, George thought, got to have it. A man better stay on the job, Ned told him. Patty melt with fries sure would go good.

Locate your man, call it in. The patty melt won out, like always. George locked up the Olds and walked in through the back entrance. The place was cheerful and kaleidoscopic: gold metal-flake lamps shaped like beehives, flashy linoleum tiles that sparkled, and blond waitresses in orange shorts. George sat at the counter and one came right over. "Double patty melt, double fries, coffee, apple pie. Double pie," he told her. They had one of the little countertop jukeboxes. George hit Patty Page: *If you like the taste of a lobster stew, served by a window with an ocean view, you're sure to fall in love with Old Cape Cod.* The waitress came by with more coffee. "Looks like you really enjoyed your patty melt," she said.

George felt good after his meal and ready for some detective work. He checked his watch: 11:00 p.m. Out in the parking lot, the fog was coming in and the Chrysler hadn't moved. He was unlocking the Olds when he heard a soft sound behind his right ear, something like a whisper. If George had been a real detective instead of an overweight bill collector, he'd have recognized it for sure. But as it was, he just crumpled to the pavement and sat there with one hand on the door handle and the other on the wet ground, the back of his head sapped wide open. His brain popped a fuse and he died in about two minutes.

Herb reached the corner of Third and Broadway at eleven thirty. He'd walked the five miles from the canals to downtown Santa Monica and he was getting tired. He decided to catch the number 7 bus, up Pico Boulevard. Herb liked how the fog made the lights glow and sputter, especially the Dan-Dee shoe factory sign. It was a fancy neon affair with pink letters and little pink shoes that seemed to be walking forward along the side of the building. He sat on the wet bus bench and watched the shoes until the bus came.

A dark blue Ford sedan pulled up in front the next morning. Herb saw it, and he knew just who it was. He turned off the water and stopped the flow to the plants. Herb had installed a system of half pipes set into the ground that ran throughout the yard. When the water was turned on at the outdoor sink in the back, the open drain fed the pipes and the water was carried to the tomatoes, the onions, the chives, the lettuces, the squash, the eggplants, and the lemon tree. Herb could water the whole yard in a few minutes. He walked out to the front and stood on the porch and waited.

"Morning, gentlemen."

"Herbert Saunders?"

"Check."

"Yes or no."

"That's my name."

"All right. You work for Ned Hillael."

"Yes."

"Doing what?"

"Mechanic work."

"Regular employee?"

"Freelance."

"A 'freelance' colored man."

"That's how it is."

"When did you see him last?"

"Mr. Hillael?"

"I'm waiting."

"On the lot yesterday."

"What'd you do there?"

"I picked up a car."

"Just tell it."

"I did the work here and drove it back."

"Then what?"

"I walked home."

"Then what?"

"Ate dinner with my neighbor."

"Where's he now?"

"She."

"Let's go there." Andrena was hanging clothes out.

"You know this man?"

"My neighbor."

"See him last night?"

"We had our dinner."

"What time was that?"

"Sunset time. We played the radio."

"What radio?"

"Hunter Hancock."

"Don't leave town."

"Say, just a minute." The second man hadn't asked any questions, but now he had a look. "Are you 'Atomic Bomb' Saunders?"

"I was."

"My kid brother had your records. He liked that spade music. He was killed in the war."

"Sorry to hear it. So was mine."

"Don't leave town."

The two policemen left in their Ford. "A spade and a Mex woman?" said the younger officer, shaking his head.

"I live in South Gate, we keep it clean. Those two don't know nothing."

Andrena and Herb sat for a moment. "Thanks," Herb said. "De nada, amigo," Andena said. Talking to the police was nerve racking but driving always calmed him down, so he got the Muntz Jet out of the garage. Scrubby jumped in the passenger seat, ready for the road.

The Cadillac motor purred, steady and deep. In a car as lightweight as the Muntz, it was the bomb. They drove east on Pico Boulevard: a pink Muntz, a black man, and a white dog like an old rag mop.

"Ned's lot is closed up tight, the Gresham Building is closed up tight," Herb said to the dog. "Ned's gone and George is off somewhere. George knows I made that delivery last night. George had the canal man staked out, but he's no stakeout man. Ned is doing some business with the canal man, but he's not rough, he just sells bad cars. Truth is, Ned and George are a couple of squares from Santa Monica, the little city of squares." Scrubby sat straight up in the seat, fur blown back, eyes fixed dead ahead, listening to the steady rhythm of Herb's voice as he thought out loud. "What do the cops want with Ned? You can rob the working man blind, they don't care about that. 'Don't leave town,' the standard line. I'm not going anywhere, I like it here in square town. It's pretty easy on a man. I got an agreement with Andrena. She's going to bury me in her backyard, and I'll do the same for her, whoever goes first. Woodlawn Cemetery is strictly for white folks. No fun allowed, no barbecues, no Hunter Hancock. Lucky for us we got a little something put by under the mattress, right, Scrubby?"

"Ralph!" Scrubby agreed.

Tuesday morning was foggy and cool down by the pier, but Ned Hillael was starting to sweat. His hands were clammy, and the steering wheel was getting damp. His mind was starting to wander to more pleasant things, like the luxury of his Cadillac's air conditioning, new this year. Cadillac, the standard of the world.

"Hey, you listening to me? Doesn't this interest you?" Lonny Tipton was sitting in the passenger seat, his .38 resting on his knee.

"Definitely, Lonny, most emphatically."

"The money just went up. My knees hurt on account of your shit car."

"Right, and you are going to get your money, I'm happy to say."

"What about a doctor, you said you knew the right one for me. That was the deal."

"You are going to be taken care of 110 percent."

"See, a guy tailed me last night. He picked me up down in the canals and tailed me over to Santa Monica. A big fat guy. Tell me what you know about that, Ned."

"Nothing, not a thing. That Chrysler is clean and sharp, I checked it out personally."

"You are the one that knows where I been at, and the fat guy knew right where I was at. Was that a little something of yours, Ned? Friend of yours? Don't you trust me?"

"My partner and I are very happy with your work. What if I say, same time next Tuesday? The money, the doctor?"

"What if I use this gun right now? Gut shoot, that's what I'm thinking about. I'm gonna do it slow, nice and slow. Here, and here . . . you want to listen to the radio while you bleed to death in the Cadillac?"

"My word is my bond."

"I'm not feeling so good, I don't like being followed. You get me a doctor, or you are going to need a doctor worse than me."

"I'll be calling you, we've got definite business. I'm known as a pretty big man in Santa Monica."

"Big, legitimate man. How would a big, legitimate man like you feel about two slugs in the belly? Just a teeny little push?"

Lonny got out of the car and walked down the hill to the pier.

The fog was burning off and it was going to be a nice spring day in Santa Monica. Breezy, about sixty-five degrees, light chop, good visibility. From where he was parked up on Ocean Avenue, Ned could see the KTLA broadcasting truck. Ten or twelve cars were lined up diagonally, and the television announcer was getting started with the broadcast, which consisted of selling used cars on live TV. The announcer had a way of introducing each car in the animated style of a talk-show host. The cars tended to be flashy and bright colored, the kind celebrities might drive. Ned gave the finger to the TV crew. "Bastards! Trying to undercut a local man, jacking down the price on television, like I don't have expenses!" he shouted.

Ned drove up Ocean Park Boulevard and parked in front of the Airport Center on the corner of Eighteenth Street, across from the Douglas plant. It was a new arcade-style complex of offices and shops catering to the needs of the working man: doctors, dentists, lawyers, and the office of Airport Equity Home Loans, upstairs in the back. "I want to see Bill O'Leary," Ned told the receptionist.

"Mr. O'Leary is in the field all day, sir."

"Well, find him in the field and tell him it's Ned Hillael, and I'm going to sit right here." There was a large map of Santa Monica on the wall behind the receptionist with the Sunset Park development outlined in red: "Airport Equity is Airport Friendly." Ned sat there, aware of his stomach trying to crawl out of his body backwards. "Where's the bathroom?" he asked the girl.

"Down the hall, right, then right again, third door on the left."

Ned went left when he should have gone right. By the time he found the restroom, he was sick. He made it to a stall and threw up all his bacon and egg breakfast and part of his prime-rib dinner. He was hanging on to one of the sinks trying to clean up when Bill O'Leary walked in.

"Ned, where you been at, you look terrible."

"Bill, I'm sick. Lonny Tipton is crazy, he's going to kill us."

"Kill us? Well, I don't think that's quite right, Ned."

"Yes it is, goddamn it. He wants money and doctors. This is all your doing, your idea. 'Home equity foreclosures, real American money,' you kept saying. George Gresham's gone, I don't know where."

"That was your mistake, Ned, not mine. First you told me you had Lonny Tipton under control, then you told me you didn't and you needed the detective to watch him, and then the detective wanted in. Now you tell me your man is out there going crazy. Your mess, you clean it up."

Ned's mind was starting to work a little. "Oh no, Bill. You told me, 'Find a Douglas man who wants something bad enough, and then make him get you the employee credit records.' If we don't get this doctor for him I definitely think he'll stop at nothing."

"Not we, Ned. You. I'm a respected member of the Santa Monica business community. You are barely legal, a loan-sharking used car dealer under a cloud of suspicion, so I hear. I'll deny all this, Ned. I never met him; don't even know what he looks like. Don't come here again. I get in touch with you." Bill O'Leary turned and walked out of the restroom.

Ned wiped his face and stood there looking at his reflection in the mirror. Not good, he thought. The new suit from Desmond's looked terrible. He walked down the stairs and out to the sidewalk. His Cadillac sat waiting at the curb: emerald green and gold two-tone, with green leather seats, factory air, and AM/FM WonderBar radio, both exciting new options. "Shmuck! Putz! Goddamn Irish pig!" he shouted. That made him feel a little better, but he knew it didn't solve anything, so he went next door to the Skywatcher's Lounge and sat at the bar.

"Ned, what'll it be?" said the bartender.

"Whiskey sour. And bring me the phone, I've got definite business."

"Sure, Ned, sure," said the bartender. Ned dialed and waited.

"Herb, Ned. Got a job for you. Never mind where I've been. I'll be at your house in twenty minutes." A girl walked up and sat at the bar next to Ned. A big blond, on the heavy side.

"Well, Ned."

"Charmaine."

"Well, buy me something," she said.

"Whiskey sour," Ned called out to the bartender.

"I don't like whiskey sours," said the blond. "Make it a Ramos gin fizz."

"Ramos gin fizz, coming up," said the bartender.

"Where you been at, Ned?"

"I been very busy, Charmaine, and I'm very busy right now."

"Busy Ned, screwing the poor working man."

"Maybe you ought to try it sometime."

"Screwing?"

"Working."

"You call it what you want, Neddy."

Ned's eyes went from slack to hate in two seconds. "Don't call me Neddy," he said through his teeth.

The girl slid off the stool and walked toward the restrooms in the back. "So don't call him Neddy," she said over her shoulder. The bartender came over to Ned, wiping down the bar. "My opinion? One of these days that stool is gonna stick to her ass like a continental kit," he said. Ned put some bills on the bar and walked out to the street. It was lunchtime on Ocean Park Boulevard. Workers in overalls and Red Wing boots were drifting across the street to the hamburger stands, and the office types in cheap suits were headed for the cocktail joints. "Don't call me Neddy," Ned Hillael said again as he drove away in the Cadillac, a standout car in Sunset Park.

In the early part of the century they built wide front porches on little frame houses in poor districts, as if a working man was entitled to some relaxation and comfort. But Herb wasn't taking any comfort from his porch, not just now. Ned Hillael had been hiding out, and now he was on his way over. It sounded like a long-distance call for sure this time. The Cadillac pulled up in front. Ned got out and walked up the steps to the porch and sat down.

"So, Herb, we got a problem."

"Stop right there, Ned. Anything you need me for, it's a new deal."

"This is going to take a very smart man."

"Just tell it," Herb said.

"It's like this, Herb. I have a deal going with this friend in real estate, a close friend, a partner. We've put loans together for folks over at Douglas, some friends up there. Home loans. I'm getting into some business here in town, not just the car line. Things are definitely moving forward. This other friend helped us meet clients up at Douglas. His name is Lonny, a very good man to know, very helpful. But he has a medical problem we didn't know about. We could have taken a closer look, but things were moving rapidly. So now, we feel responsible. He helped us, we should help him! It's the right thing. Let me put it in this way. He says being a man is not working out for him. He wants to change over and be a woman. He needs a doctor that can do the job right, and I need to find this doctor or there might be some trouble." Ned sat there, out of breath.

"Why come to me, Ned? Tell me, this I got to hear," Herb said.

"Herb, you know and I know that you know people. You've been around, an entertainer like yourself, in the nightlife. I'm just a business man from Santa Monica."

"And I'm just a black man out there on the fringe where the freaks are. Matter of fact, I do know. But, now, why should I help you? The cops are after you, I don't know why. I have had all the trouble with cops a man can stand, but that's past and gone."

"You will help me because you are with me. If the police ask, tell them I am the boss and I back you up, 110 percent."

"I am not 'with' you, Ned. I do jobs for you on the car lot, but I am not at all 'with' you. I'm a car mechanic, not an errand boy for trouble. What is this man holding on you?"

"This is a problem I got to take care of. A problem for me is a problem for you."

The two men sat quietly. Here is a fork in the road, Herb thought. The sign points two ways: "shortest" and "best." No second chances in the land of a thousand dances, the valley of ten million insanities.

"I can take care of Lonny, but I want something, too, Ned. Somebody in Santa Monica owns this house and Andrena's house next door. Who, I don't know. We pay rent to a company up on Ocean Park, called Airport Equity. I want the deeds signed over to us, free and clear. Easy for a smart man like you. Little old properties like these aren't worth anything compared to getting this guy off your back, I expect. Deal?"

"You have a deal, very definitely."

"Every time you say that, I get nervous."

"I am being perfectly truthful."

"Well, that's all right, then. Where's our man?"

"He's waiting down on the pier at the far end. Little guy, sandy colored hair, tan jacket, hat."

"Where's George Gresham?"

"I am very worried about George. He was working on a job for me. I don't know where he is."

"Man, this is going to cost you. It isn't just a case of new points, plugs, and condenser."

"Please sit down, in the light. Let me look. You know, I am an *especialiste*, Herb has told you. But, in the way to the man, that is my work. Actors who must look strong in the tight pants! Ha ha, yes, I have done well, I think. But you, you desire the opposite, no? That is more difficult, more . . . more . . . como se dice? . . . *complex*, like the woman. Well, we will see."

"Don't give me any of that 'we will see' shit, I'm telling you — " Lonny started to say.

"Stop! Do not raise you voice to me! Do not make threats, my friend. You know, there is nothing so terrible as a bad job in this work, eh? You remember Tony, Herb? Tony, he threatened me, he put his hands to me. What did the boys call him afterward? Needle Dick! Ha ha, yes, needle dick, the chicken fucker.

So you see, you must remain calm. You have good eyes to be a woman, I think. And a good mouth. These are the important attributes, no? What do you say, Herb? Will I make the success?"

"You know what you're doing, Doc. Esquerita was good work."

"Oh yes, and he went on to do great things. I was happy for that. *Pianiste*. So, I accept, I will do!"

"Doc, I got a good place for him to recover. My neighbor. She's always home, works at home. She can take care of him. Her."

"Your name is Lonny, so we will say *Lonnie* and change only the spelling. Ha, that bodes well, no, Herb?"

"Sure, Doc, it can't miss."

Herb made arrangements with the doctor. He would pick Lonny up in three days. Payment due on delivery. Recovery time two weeks. Herb walked down the old wooden stairs. A sign over the front door read "The Edwin Apartments, 1914."

"Not much of a front," Lonny had observed. "What's this guy do, scrapes?"

"Exactly," Herb told him, "but he's got a sideline. He did some work on a friend of mine a few years back, did a great job."

"What's his name, Dr. Frankenstein?"

"Doctor Mario."

"Mex?"

"Cuban, but don't be put off, you'll walk out of here a free woman."

Herb explained the deal to Andrena. "This isn't work for hire, this is an exchange. The deeds would mean security for us. You can't throw a homeowner out of his home, that's what America is all about."

"Yes. But either way, I am happy here. When Arturo was killed, I thought God had turned his back on me. Now, I feel He has opened a new door." They were sitting in the tiny living room where Andrena did her sewing. Day and night, she worked at the machine, creating the marvelous designs that made the women of Brentwood and Beverly Hills so happy.

Lonnie slept in the bedroom, Andrena slept in the living room. Doctor Mario sent along a powder to be taken with meals. Light meals. "Do not tax the body. Do not contact me unless it is very bad, I must insist. I am an artiste, but my art is concealed. A secret! Ha, the *Edwin*. You see, I am disguise."

Ned brought a satchel full of money. The handle was wet. "Four grand. It makes me sweat, I can't help it," Ned said.

"I told you five, Ned. Four for the doc, one for Andrena to take care of Lonny," Herb said.

"See you in two weeks, Herb," Ned said.

Doctor Mario's timetable was right on the money. Lonnie was up and around after about ten days. "She is helping me with the work," Andrena told Herb, "She has good hands." Herb stayed on his side of the hedge, at first. He was reluctant to intrude on the two women, on their rapport. There was no word from Ned Hillael. Herb spent more time in his vegetable garden trying out new things, like Kentucky red runner beans and giant tomatoes new on the market. He felt like he was on vacation not having Ned call five times a day. Lonnie was looking better. Her hair was growing out and her face had started to soften a little.

Herb thought they should have a barbecue. Cabrito, squash, guacamole, beer, and short ribs, Scrubby's favorite. "I want to tell you a story," Lonnie began, after dinner. "I love a story," said Herb. He was in a good mood, the best in a long time.

"Four years ago, I got a job at Douglas Aircraft. They needed skilled machinists for the new interceptor guided missile design project. I had the background up at Lockheed in San Josey, so I was hired on as machinist, first class. That's a good-paying job, even if Douglas is nonunion. The machinist's union threatened to expose me as a scab, but I said, who knows if the defense work will keep going, it's already ten years after the war. I moved down here, I got no family. But I had nervous problems, and it got worse after I moved. You understand now.

"Then, one day, I met Ned Hillael in a bar up on Ocean Park. He acted friendly and bought drinks, and we talked. He was interested in my problem and he said he could help me, but he wanted something. I said, we all want something. He was interested in the employee credit union at Douglas, as in, who was solvent, who was in debt, and how bad. I had security clearance from the missile job, I told him. He got very interested. Could I use the clearance to check out employee records in the credit bureau? I guess so, I said. So he said, if I could bring him the credit records, he would use his influence as a successful businessman to find me a doctor so I could have an operation. He said I would definitely make a really cute girl, and he was already attracted to me. Security at Douglas is pretty loose. Your security guards spend a lot of time in the Skywatcher's Lounge. Now, listen to this. Workers are always living beyond their means, that's nothing new. They start buying things like cars and get into debt and can't pay their mortgage loan. Then, Ned and his partner foreclose and take possession and sell the house and split the money with the bank. Ned has a friend at this particular bank, the Airport Equity Home Loans. A nice little setup. But I found out something else, something I never told Ned. Douglas Aircraft is going out of business. They're going to close the plant, because they've lost the Defense Department's missile contract to Hughes. Everything else they make is obsolete, so they stand to make more money by closing the plant and selling off the real estate. Nobody knows this. Not Ned, not the bank, not anyone."

"And what becomes of the workers?" Andrena asked.

"Out of a job and not earning a dime," said Lonnie with a shrug.

"Well, and all the people who sell them things. In Santa Monica, todo el mundo."

"When is this supposed to happen?" Herb asked.

"In about two years, tops."

"Who's Ned's partner?" Herb asked.

"I never saw him, but Ned calls him Bill."

Herb and Scrubby walked through the hedge to Andrena's the next morning. Scrubby was tired from their big morning walk through the cemetery. She drank some water and lay down by the side door to keep an eye on things. Andrena was at her sewing machine, listening to *The Guiding Light*, followed by *The Romance of Helen Trent*. She never missed a morning with her soap operas.

"Where's Lonnie?" Herb asked.

"I'm worried," Andrena said, looking worried.

"Why, what'd she do?"

"It's Helen's novio, the doctor. He's not a good man, I knew he wasn't."

"I thought you meant Lonnie."

"She went out before I got up."

"It's two weeks, today. I got a bad feeling about Ned. I don't think he's going to hold up his end of the deal."

"I'm afraid Helen finds out the doctor is bad."

"I'm afraid Ned is worse!"

The radio announcer was speaking in an emotional tone: "I'm Truman Bradley, and this is the program that asks the question, can a woman find romance after thirty-five? But first, this message. You know, constipation is something people don't talk about much. If you are experiencing problems with your normal regularity, take Ex-Lax, the tiny, chocolated laxative that won't disturb your sleep or your money back! Be sure to ask your druggist for chocolated Ex-Lax today, and don't get the laxative habit!"

Andrena's sewing machine hummed and whined. She moved the cloth around and around without stopping, almost in a trance. "Lonnie is two people. The colors are still drying," she said.

Herb shook his head. "I don't know. Something is ticking like a stuck valve. I don't like it. Think I'll go out and look around."

On the radio, a jazzy female trio sang: "If your whites aren't white and your colors aren't bright, switch to White King D! White Kinnngggg!"

Herb drove south past Washington into the canal district. The canals smelled like oil and garbage mixed with the cleaner scent of saltwater blowing in from the beach two blocks away. In the afternoon sun, Dudley Court looked just as abandoned as before. Herb knocked at the house closest to the street. A woman came to the screen door. "Yeah?" she asked.

"Sorry to bother you," Herb said. "I'm supposed to meet someone in the court here, but I don't know which place. It's a woman, short, blond, about thirty."

"Nobody like that!" the woman laughed. "I'm the only one left. My toilet is broken again. What should I do, go in the dirt?"

"Landlords are all the same," Herb said. "That's how I got to be a mechanic. You want something done, better do it yourself."

"I can't," said the woman.

"I could take a look at it for you."

"I would be grateful. Please come in."

Herb followed the woman into the tiny house. There were photographs everywhere, smiling faces from another life, another time, another world.

"In here." She stood aside for Herb to enter the tiny bathroom.

Herb lifted the tank top. The stopper chain was broken, as usual.

"Got any wire?" he asked.

"I don't know."

"I could use the wire from the photographs."

"Take what you need."

Herb removed the wire from the back of one of the large pictures, a portrait of a young woman with soft eyes and a look of amusement. "That's me, in Berlin, before the war," she said.

Herb adjusted the wire and tried the handle. The ancient toilet flushed with a groan. "It'll be all right for a while," he said.

"Thank you. Please come and sit down. I'm wondering about something," she said.

"Shoot," Herb said.

"There aren't any blond girls in this neighborhood. I'm curious why you came to this court, if you don't mind. I'm worried about what they are going to do. It's been empty for a year now, except for the man in the back, and now he's gone, I think."

"Sure, I understand what you mean. I'm not from any real estate outfit, and I'm not a bill collector or a cop, believe me. I'm a renter, like you. But, now, here's the thing. You say you saw the man in the back house. I'm interested in how he got here and who brought him."

"That I can tell you. The landlord brought him at night. Since the war, I can't sleep at night. This is a poor place to live, but it's quiet, so I can sleep in the day. If I have to move, where can I go?"

"What's the landlord's name?"

"That's Mr. Hillael. He comes for the rent every first Monday, but he's late. He missed yesterday and I thought you might be him. I don't have visitors. What's your name, please?"

"Herb Saunders."

"Sadie is my name. Very nice to meet you, such a nice man."

"Yeah, I'm a real dinger," said Herb.

"Dinger?"

"That's someone who can't put two and two together."

"I'm sure you will, Herb," Sadie said.

Herb told Sadie he'd let her know if he heard anything.

She thanked him again and disappeared behind the screen door. Dudley Court went back to sleep.

Lonnie waited in the front office of Airport Equity for the receptionist to finish her call. "Can I help you?" the girl asked.

"I'm answering the ad for an office assistant." Lonnie showed the girl the ad.

"Mr. O'Leary needs someone to help him with his seminars. Why don't you sit down and wait for him, he'll be back soon." Ten minutes later Bill O'Leary came hustling in, waving his fat briefcase around.

"Who's this?" he said.

"She's here about the ad."

Lonnie followed Bill into his office. "This is going to be a big event around here, and I'm going to be very, very busy," he said. There was another wall map in Bill's office covered with clusters of little red pins.

"What hours?" Lonnie asked.

"If I need something, I need it when I need it. I have to promote, promote, promote. You have to take care of the applicants. Spreadsheets! Sales figures! I want everything front and center!"

"What are you paying?"

"The real estate business is a fabulous business, and people who aren't making money at it, it's their own fault."

"Okay," said Lonnie.

"Mary will fix you up, get you started. What's your name?"

"Judy Smith."

"Good. Airport Equity is a Christian organization." He stuffed some papers into his briefcase and marched out of the office, slamming the door behind him.

Mary showed Lonnie where everything was and what the filing system was all about. "Mr. O'Leary has his real estate work and his new seminar work. It's too much for one person. I hope you like it here." Mary drank Nehi orange soda continuously. "I don't like Coca-Cola," she said. She was short like Lonnie, but fat and pear shaped.

"What's he like to work for?"

"He's all right. Always rushing around."

"Married?"

"No. He goes out at night on business. He's part owner of a bar down in Venice, the Los Amigos. I think he does a lot of business at night."

"What are all those pins for?"

"The pins show his rental properties. That's another thing he does," Mary said. Lonnie stood and looked at the map. Most of the pins were concentrated in the area around Pico Boulevard. She followed the trail of pins around the cemetery and found Sixteenth Street. Herb's block was all red.

"He owns all these houses?"

"Owns them or manages them for other people."

"That's a lot of houses."

"Oh, yes. Mr. O'Leary says one day soon it will all be brand-new apartments. He's getting ready for that. He's got plans all drawn up."

"Then what happens to the people living there?"

"They're out. The houses come down, the apartments go up. Mr. O'Leary says one day soon, Santa Monica will be all apartments. He's got friends in city hall. He's very connected."

"How can aircraft workers afford to live in fancy new apartments?"

"Mr. O'Leary says there's going to be some big changes. Progress is coming soon, he always says."

"Where is the Los Amigos?"

"Way down on Mildred, in Venice. I don't like it there — I generally go to the Skywatcher's. They have a television and you can watch *Supermaket Sweepstakes*. I try to watch every night. The way it works is the contestants line up with their shopping carts and when the whistle blows, they run around and put as much as they can in the carts. Then the whistle blows again and they add up everything in the carts. The one with the highest total amount wins."

"Wins what?"

"Whatever they put in their cart. It's very exciting. There's so much you could do, if you're smart. I would start in the meat department. Whole chickens, steaks, oh my God. I don't like liver. Then fruits and vegetables. I don't like grapefruit or lima beans. The trick is to memorize where the most expensive things are ahead of time. Mr. O'Leary always says, if you fail to prepare, you're prepared to fail."

"I'm going to keep that in mind," said Lonnie.

It was five o'clock at the Skywatcher's. Mary sat at the bar in front of the TV set. Lonnie and Bill sat in a booth. Bill had had a few drinks, and he was starting to loosen up. "You have to understand the territory. The territory means knowing your man on the street. Talk to them, get interested. 'What's your job? Where do you live? What church do you go to? What do you want?' That sort of thing. We don't want colored, Mexican, or hillbilly. No use wasting time if they haven't got ambition. Women, that's where you come in. Talk to them about self-betterment, the family, money. Nobody wants to be an aircraft worker, they want to get up in the world, they want things. What do you want?"

"But everyone around here is an aircraft worker," Lonnie said.

"That's going to change."

"Why?"

"Because I know a thing or two, why do you think I'm successful? Once the plant closes down, the property value around here will take off. You stick with me, you just watch."

Lonnie's eyes got big. "I just don't believe it, Mr. O'Leary, the plant closing down. Where did you hear that?"

"Never mind where Bill O'Leary heard it." Bill realized he was getting careless and he tried to change the subject. "What do you want," he asked her again.

"Nothing."

"Everyone wants something. What makes you any different? Don't try and kid Bill O'Leary."

"Oh my God, the fat girl won!" Mary screamed and clapped her hands. The television announcer had his arm around the winning contestant:

> "And the grand prize winner is Daylene Batters! She totals out at seventy-four dollars and eighty-seven cents! How did it feel out there, Daylene?"
>
> "In the beginning, I was nervous. I'm a little heavy on my feet, but I had a plan, and I stuck with it."
>
> "And it paid off! Can you tell the folks just what was your plan, Daylene?"
>
> "Prime rib. It's the most expensive thing in the market, so I just filled up my basket with that."
>
> "Now, folks, in addition to her groceries, Daylene takes home a brand new 'Kold King' home freezer! How does it feel to be the proud owner of all that prime rib?"
>
> "Prayer changes things."

"If that was me, I wouldn't be crying," said Mary.

"She knows what she wants," said Bill. "They like it when you cry on TV. Then they know they got a winter. Winner."

Summer had arrived. It was warm at night and there was no fog. Herb and Andrena and Scrubby drove down to the pier for a seafood dinner. There was a regular population on the pier, people you might see all year regardless of the weather: Japanese fishermen, winos, body builders, and the rollerskate addicts who hung around the skating rink. Herb and Andrena bought fried squid on paper plates and sat at one of the little tables just outside the guardrail that ran around the big wooden floor. The building was open across the front and the saltwater-and-cooking-oil bouquet blended nicely with the dance-hall tang of floor wax and sweat. Herb thought for sheer entertainment, you couldn't beat spending an evening watching the skaters. There was one in particular, a lanky, Western-dressed cowboy dude who came every night of the week and had an eccentric skating style that Herb enjoyed. Herb called him Tex. "There he is," Herb said to Andrena. "Keep your eye on him."

The skaters went round and round, counterclockwise, while an organ played a perpetual waltz. Herb didn't see the instrument anywhere, and he couldn't tell if it was live or recorded. The music was meant to have a calming effect, but there was always a lot of interesting drama on the floor. Loudspeakers were mounted in the vaulted ceiling rafters, and if a skater got too far out of line, a voice would cut in: "Skater in the red shirt, change direction. Speed skater, slow down, last warning. Skater in the cowboy hat, keep moving."

"See," said Herb, "Tex stopped again. Look at his face, he's somewhere else."

"Now he goes," said Andrena. "He heard the voice." There was a scuffle on the floor. Two men collided and went crashing into the guardrail. They shouted at each other. A short, stocky man on skates appeared and hustled the pair off the floor with surprising speed and power. "If they take you off the floor three times, you can't come back," Herb explained.

Tex drifted by with a shuffling step, his long arms swinging loose like Buddy Ebsen. The organ began to play "I'm An Old Cowhand" right in time with him. Tex finished the song with a backwards flourish and a tip of the hat. Andrena and Herb applauded. The aimless waltz resumed. "So the man is playing somewhere, and he can see the floor," said Herb. "That's a great job to have."

"It's a woman," said an old timer with a broom.

"Where is she?" Herb asked.

"Up there, behind the glass." The man pointed to an opaque glass panel at the far end of the rink. "She's in a little room, just high enough to see the floor. Name's Mary Dee, ten years on the job. I'm the janitor. My name's Ray Diker. You're 'Atomic Bomb' Saunders."

"Well, that's right, I was. This is my friend Andrena Ruelas. I've been coming around here for a long time, but I never understood the setup."

"I seen you around before, knew it was you. I was a drummer in country western before I got lung trouble. Don't you folks want to skate? It's not that crowded. I'll watch your dog."

"I will if you will," Andrena said to Herb. The janitor told the floor man they were friends of his. Herb and Andrena got skates and skate shoes. The floor man had them wait until a space opened up. "Skate to the left. Stay on the inside. Don't try anything fancy." They took tiny steps and began to move, hanging on to each other. The crowd went flying by. Tex came up alongside and took Andrena by her outside arm and skated off, towing her. Andrena hung on to Tex, and Herb hung on to Andrena. They managed to stay on their feet. Falling was the thing to avoid, you could cause a pileup and get run over. Herb felt like he was going sixty miles an hour, and it was shocking and exhilarating. Once they got in step with the pack, Tex let go of Andrena and they were on their own. They made it through the turns and stayed on their feet. After a while, the voice called out, "Clear the floor." The skaters pulled up to the gate and waited while the floor man skated around, mopping up sweat. When he was finished, he picked up his microphone and said, "Skate!" the crowd went back to work and the pace picked up instantly. Herb and Andrena took off their skates and put their street shoes back on. "Dios mio, it's hard." said Andrena, out of breath.

"You did all right," Ray Diker said. "Some folks just can't

ever get the hang of it. Can't afford to let 'em get hurt. Some of the regulars are pretty tough."

"The floor man is good," Herb said.

"Ex-professional, like me," said Ray.

"Like us," Herb said. "Music was a hard old road."

"I traded my left lung for it. What kind of work do you do now?"

"I'm sort of a part-time car mechanic."

"I had a car, but I left it somewheres. Most of the folks you meet on the pier, we live right here. I got a room around back, goes with the job. Sea air is good for my lungs, or lung, I should say. Got a little hot plate and icebox in there. Radio. I haven't been off the pier in years, no need to." Ray laughed, showing what teeth he still had. Herb and Andrena thanked him and walked to the end of the pier.

Out on the water, a few lights bobbed up and down in the darkness. "Some people with boats live aboard," Herb said. "But that's too lonely. At least Ray Diker has Mary Dee for company."

"I wonder if she ever comes down," Andrena said. They walked back. The skating rink had closed for the night, and Ray Diker was sweeping up out in front. "Say hello to Mary," he said.

A woman was drinking coffee from a thermos at one of the tables. She had thin features, a wide mouth, and eyes that sparkled. "Howdy, folks, I'm Mary Dee. I saw you earlier. Ray says you're a singer, a well-known man?"

"I was. This is Andrena Ruelas. We sure enjoyed your playing."

"Thanks. Yes, it's always interesting, always different. I try to play things that compliment the skaters, like the fellow in the cowboy hat. Most folks wouldn't understand, but I think it's better than movies."

"Well, sure! In movies, you already know everything," said Ray. "I ain't been to a movie in ten years. No reason."

"How did you get started here?" Herb asked Mary.

"I was a church organist in Pasadena, but I just couldn't keep my mind on it. The religious part, I mean. I liked music, but I wasn't so interested in Jesus and heaven and that. I tried, but it wasn't any use. After three churches, I ended up down here. It was while I was skating, one night, when the organ stopped. They asked for a doctor, and then they brought the organist down. Heart attack. I told the floor man I could play and I needed a job. He hired me on the spot."

"Where do you live?" Andrena asked.

"Upstairs at the merry-go-round, on the top floor. It's beautiful — the ocean, the birds, the people. It's like I have all these friends and they come to visit me every day. I love every day."

"Me too." Ray said. "I'm satisfied. No sense kickin'! Plus, you'd be surprised what you can find, cleaning up around here." He went on with his sweeping. Herb, Andrena, and Scrubby walked with Mary Dee toward the promenade. She said good night and climbed the wooden stairs to her room in the carousel building. Scrubby fell asleep as soon as they got in the car. At eleven o'clock, the parking lot was empty except for cars belonging to tenants of the apartments along the boardwalk. Pickup trucks, mostly, and a few rundown prewar models. "I think I see a Cadillac. I think I know that car," Herb told Andrena. It looked sinister and out of place, like a shark in a goldfish pond. Herb looked inside the driver's window and then got back in the Muntz and drove up the hill to Ocean Avenue.

"That's Ned's car, for sure," he said.

"What's he doing here?"

"Hiding out."

"Maybe he has a novia, maybe it's Mary Dee."

"Not our boy Ned. He doesn't like music, he told me so himself."

It was a muggy night in Santa Monica, and Ned Hillael was having a nightmare. Hot weather gave him bad dreams, but this was worse than usual. There was an auditorium. Bill O'Leary was standing at a lectern speaking to a large crowd. "Santa Monica High School" was cast into the plaster molding around the proscenium arch above the stage. Men and women in business attire sat motionless in their seats, watching Bill. A cloth banner proclaimed "The William O'Leary Seminar: The Right Activity at the Wrong Time." Bill looked strange. His eyes were black-rimmed and his voice was deep and harsh. He waved his arms about in spastic motions and spoke in a zombie cadence, accompanied by organ music that was random and dissonant:

I know you're not sleeping, and you ain't going nowhere
You're watching television, and sitting in your chair
It's three o'clock in the morning, and there ain't no way out
So you better call this number, I'm the only friend you got

Yesterday they told you your little job is gone
How you going to tell your little wife at home?
She thinks everything is going to be all right
But she's over there asleep, and you're smoking cigarettes all night

You used to think you had the whole world swingin' by the tail
Now you'll be lucky if I can keep you out of jail
Just look who's swingin' now, what's that sound you hear?
Must be the wind, whistling past your ears

Saying, 'Time, time, time is all you got. . . .'

The people began to get up out of their seats and spin around like tops, hollow-eyed graduates of the Seminar for Lost Souls. Bill O'Leary stood on the stage, his eyes fixed on Ned. "Time, time, time is all you got," he rasped as the organ music twisted itself around and around in a frenzy. Ned forced himself to wake up. He was soaking wet. "Goddamn Catholics and their god-damn organs," he muttered. The clock said 11:30. He got dressed and walked down the stairs to the parking lot. The Cadillac was wet from the sea air. He thought he might head over to the Sky-watcher's Lounge, but then he realized Charmaine would be there. "Bitch," he muttered. He drove to Third Street and parked behind the Embers and went in through the back. The bartend-er greeted him. "Evening, Mr. Hillael, nice to see you. Whiskey sour?" The Embers was a nice place, not like the Skywatcher's. It was air conditioned, and Ned began to relax. Just the heat, he told himself, and the strain of having to duck the police just because some of the cars didn't have good pink slips. He noticed a neat-looking blond woman alone at the bar, a few stools down. She was wearing a light blue coat and white gloves. Sharp, my type, he thought. "So, how are you this evening?" Ned started right in.

"How am I?"

"As in, how about a drink?" asked Ned. He was feeling loose after being cooped up in the Carousel Apartments. "Hey Mac, two more, over here." He steered the girl toward a booth in the back, amazed at how smooth and easy it was. "Now, I'm Ned, and you are who?"

"Judy."

"Terrific." The waitress brought drinks and set them down. "You're definitely new around here, that I know."

"You're right, I'm new. This is a nice place."

"It's very nice, and you are pretty nice yourself." Sudden-ly, Ned liked his life, things were clicking. "So Judy, tell me all about you!"

"Nothing much to tell. I had a job up at Douglas in the accounting department, but I got laid off. I had an apartment on Thirty-fourth and Pearl Street, but I had to move. I live in Venice now."

"What do you drive?"

"Oh, I can't afford a car, Ned. I take the bus everywhere."

"Well, this is amazing, because I am in a very good position to help you. I have been working closely with Douglas people to help them in financial matters, such as cars."

"Is that so?"

"Cars are a specialty of mine. We'll talk more about that later." Ned looked up and saw Charmaine coming through the street door. She stopped at the bar and started talking loud to the bartender. Ned panicked. "Say, Judy, this place is getting on my nerves, let's us take a little ride."

"Suits me, Ned." She got up and followed him down the hall and through the back door to the parking lot. "Here's my Cadillac, right here. Now, let's just see." Ned turned onto Broadway. "Now, let's see," he said again. "There's a lot of nice places . . ."

"I know one. It's called the Los Amigos, in Venice. Ever been there, Ned?" the girl asked.

"The Los Amigos! Let's go!" Ned was a little light headed from the drinks and the narrow escape from Charmaine and the blond girl in the seat next to him. He drove down Nielson, through Ocean Park, and into Venice. "Turn right on Mildred, park in the back," said the girl. The place was just a storefront on the boardwalk, with no sign or address. Not my style, Ned thought, but the girl had him by the arm, and he realized she was strong like an athlete. Inside the place was very dark and damp and thick with dancing bodies. There was a tiny stage and a four-piece combo trying to play jazz. A man in a ruffled shirt was singing: "I get no kick from cocaine, but I get a kick—" "*Whoa!*" the crowd screamed on the bass drum accent — "Out of youuuu." Ned was having trouble seeing in the dark. "It's all just men, I think," he said. A waiter in a black leotard and lipstick came over. Bad acne showed through his makeup. "Now, tell Tonette what you want," the waiter said with a lisp.

"Hi, Tonette. Whiskey sours," Judy said.

"Honey, you are stepping out tonight."

"What's that supposed to mean?" Ned asked the girl.

"I've been here a few times."

"I don't like this place," said Ned.

"Why not? I do. For a girl on her own, it's friendly. Nobody bothers me, nobody even notices me."

Ned wiped his face. "I'm getting nervous in here, it's too hot." A voice made Ned jerk his head around because it sounded like Bill O'Leary. Peering through the dark, Ned saw Bill in the corner, in a booth. He was sitting with a younger man, and they were kissing and laughing and touching each other.

Ned ducked his head back down. "I got to get out of here," he whispered urgently.

"Where do you want to go, Ned?" asked the girl.

"I got to get to my car, right now. Get me out of here." The girl steered Ned through the crowd and out the door. His legs started to wobble and she had to work to hold him up. Once behind the wheel, Ned's eyes began to focus a little.

"That's the worst goddamn place I ever saw. A queer joint. The chairman of the Santa Monica Christian Business Men's Association is a dirty queer. 'No Jews in breakfast meetings,' he tells me. Bastards! Goy shitheads!"

"You done?" the girl asked.

"What?" Ned turned sideways to the girl with a surprised look, as if he was seeing her for the first time.

"Forgot about me, Ned?" She had a gun now, a nasty little .32 snub nose in her gloved hand resting on her knee.

Suddenly, Ned didn't like his life so well. "What's that for? What do you want?"

"Nothing. I have everything I want. Look at me, Ned. Take a good look."

"Look at what? I don't have any money."

"I'm not Judy, I'm Lonnie. Look at me." Ned tried to look. The light in the parking lot was bad and his head hurt from the Los Amigos. Things weren't making sense.

"Lonnie?"

"Doctor Mario did a good job. I can feel a pussy whenever I want. Mine. You lied to me, you jerked me around, you promised me money and cars. I could have died in that Studebaker, you ever think of that, Ned? Getting those files was not easy. O'Leary tried to put the cops on me for that job, but there isn't any Lonny Tipton anymore. I know all about you and O'Leary. Him, I don't like. I'm going to fix him good and you're going to help me do it."

Ned's tongue felt like it was a mile wide. He could barely talk. "Help? How?"

"You're going to sit here and die, that's how. This is O'Leary's gun. They call it a belly gun. I followed him and his little friend the other night. They played games with it over at the Edwin Apartments, and I watched them, I found out what Mr. Bill wants. Then they left and I went in and took the gun. Didn't you ever wonder what happened to me, Ned? Let me fill you in. I live in a crummy little room over at the Edwin, and I work for Bill O'Leary. How do you like me now? Look at the gun. This gun is dirty. Bill O'Leary is dirty, he's a nasty man. The gas room is all ready for Mr. Bill. Remember what I said before? Just a teeny little push. Adios, Ned."

The gun snapped twice, low to Ned's beltline. At point-blank range, his upper body slammed back into the seat like a roller coaster. He gasped and clutched at his stomach with both hands. Lonnie turned on the big WonderBar radio. She got out of the car and walked toward the beach. Ned sat there, unable to move, blood oozing from between his fingers. A radio announcer spoke softly, reverently: "Ladies and gentlemen, it's time once again for *Your Rosary Hour*." "Hail Mary, full of grace . . ." the voices began. "Goddamn Catholics," Ned whispered through his teeth. After a while, he passed out.

Herb was dreaming about his old friend, Johnny Ace. Johnny stood at the foot of the bed and turned his head from side to side, displaying the bullet hole in his temple. The piano intro from his hit, "Pledging My Love," filled Herb's bedroom with its mournful sound. Johnny regarded Herb with sad eyes. "Tell me, Herb, why would a man with a number-one record play Russian roulette with a loaded gun?"

Herb answered, "Johnny, I know you didn't do it. I'm sorry."

"Herb," the voice echoed, "I got a message from Ned. He says blonds have more fun."

"Where's Ned, Johnny?" Herb asked, but Johnny was fading out.

"Good-bye, Herb, my telephone is ringin'. . . ." The plink-plink-plink-plink of the piano drifted away.

Herb woke up. Scrubby was hiding under the bed and wouldn't come out. "It's all right," he told her. "Johnny had to deliver a message. He's gone back now."

Herb finished dressing and walked over to Andrena's. "Ned's dead and gone, can't be any doubt about it."

"What now?" asked Andrena.

"Nothing to be done. Someone's gone and killed poor Ned, that's all. We'll just have to wait right here and see. But Johnny Ace brought me the news, and that only means one thing. Whatever they say about Ned, it's going to be dead wrong. The message was blonds have more fun."

Andrena looked up from her sewing. "Is it true?"

It was Tuesday, and that meant that the Christian Business Men's Association of Santa Monica was having their monthly breakfast in the Moose Hall up on Ocean Park and Sixteenth. Chairman Bill O'Leary had just dismissed the meeting with a friendly reminder to register for his Investment Seminar that was getting underway very soon. A twenty-dollar package, lunch included. Exciting opportunities in home equity foreclosures, don't miss it. My colleague, Miss Judy Smith, will answer all your questions.

Two men had arrived toward the end of the breakfast. They

sat in the back and declined the offer of pancakes and coffee. When the meeting broke up, they stood and waited by the door. Bill O'Leary came walking up the center aisle, back slapping and shaking hands and grinning like a Cheshire cat. He saw the two men, the policemen, which was what they were. "Mr. O'Leary, may we speak to you, sir?"

"I'm Bill O'Leary," said Bill.

"I'm Detective Sergeant Donald McClure, and this is Detective Charles Stahl. Would you like to step this way, sir?"

"Step what way?" asked Bill, his Cheshire-cat grin fading.

"Sir, we are here on police business."

"Jellmen, what can I do for you, perhaps this is inconvenient."

"I'm going to ask you to accompany us down to police headquarters."

"I am the chairman of the Christian Business Men's Association of Santa Monica. I want to help in any way I can."

"Mr. O'Leary, do you own a .32 caliber Smith and Wesson detective's special?"

"I'm a leader in this community, you realize."

"William O'Leary, I'm placing you under arrest for the murder of Nedwin Hillael. Anything you say can and will be held against you. Put the cuffs on him, Chuck."

State your full name.
William O'Leary.
Occupation?
Real estate broker.
Address?
3162 Ocean Park Boulevard.
Is this your gun?
I gave the gun to a friend. We met in a bar.
What bar?
The Los Amigos.
What do you do there?

I go there to meet friends.

You go to the bar to meet men to perform obscene acts?

Larry said he needed a gun.

Did you engage in lewd acts with Larry?

We had some drinks, we went to his place.

Where was that?

In Venice, on Mildred.

Did you give him the gun there?

Yes.

Did you perform obscene acts with the gun?

He wanted to use the gun to scare a friend.

What did you do then?

We left the apartment, we went to the beach.

At night, you went to the beach at night?

Yes. We left the gun in his place. When we got back, it was gone.

When was this?

About two weeks ago.

Where was this?

It's called the Edwin apartments. On Mildred.

All right, Bill. I like you for pandering and soliciting, the murder of Ned Hillael, and the murder of George Gresham. I also like you for the break in at the Douglas Aircraft Business office, and that interests me. I don't care about the fag stuff, that's for the newspapers. I look for motive. Point number one: Hillael was weak and you knew he'd crack eventually and expose this scheme of yours to defraud employees of Douglas Aircraft.

We questioned a waiter from the Los Amigos. He stated that Hillael was there on the night he was shot, in the company of a blond woman. The waiter said he was definitely a straight john, not a regular. I suggest that the blond woman was employed by you to steer Hillael to the Los Amigos bar. She set him up, and you followed him out to the parking lot and shot him as he sat in his car. No signs of a struggle, he knew his assailant. The radio was on. That was a nice touch, Bill.

I didn't kill anybody. You can't prove a thing. I don't know any blond woman. The gun was stolen, like I said. I didn't steal the documents. Ned Hillael's man Lonny Tipton stole the documents.

What's this Tipton look like?

I don't know. I never saw him.

We got an anonymous tip about that. We checked it out. Douglas shows a "Lon Tipton," machinist, discharged six months ago. We got him on the Teletype, but he's gone, no forwarding, no police record. Nothing there, in my opinion. Ned Hillael had a colored man working for him. We checked him out. He has a weird background. Used to be a singer of jive music, recorded some so-called subversive material. Nothing for us there, this is nonpolitical. There's no "Larry" living at the Edwin Apartments on Mildred, we checked the place out. Old Jews on pensions and one Cuban who says he's a retired barber. What we got is Bill O'Leary. Now, let's back up a little. Point number two: Ned Hillael hired George Gresham to spy on you because he thought you were going to double cross him. I suggest that Gresham threatened you with exposure, so you sapped him down in the parking lot behind the Embers.

You got no evidence, no proof, nothing.

A transient on the beach in Venice found a gun and turned it in. A .32 short barrel, registered to Mary Miller at 3162 Ocean Park Boulevard. Your secretary, your office. The lab found prints all over it, two sets. One is yours, the other is not on file. They found blood, Gresham's blood type, and that's good enough for me. You killed both men in their cars. They're going to call you "The Carhop Killer." I like it already. See, Bill, they just gassed Caryl Chessman up at Quentin. The room's all yours.

Lonnie walked into the Airport Equity office for the last time at about four o'clock the next afternoon. Mary was sitting at her desk, crying.

"What's wrong?" Lonnie asked.

"Mr. O'Leary's in jail."

"What for?"

"They're saying he killed somebody."

"Who?"

"I don't know. What happens now?"

"Did you talk to him?"

"He said, go right ahead, like it was nothing. He says it's all a mistake and he'll be back soon."

Maybe in twenty years, maybe never, Lonnie thought. She went into Bill's office and sat behind his desk. There was a large notepad headed, "From the office of William O'Leary." She tossed it into the wastebasket.

"I don't like this job anymore," Mary wailed from the front room. "I need a drink." She left the office.

Lonnie went to a filing cabinet. She pulled out the folder marked "Titles/Deeds."

She used Bill's typewriter to make out two title transfer forms, for 334 and 336 Sixteenth Street. The forms stated that the legal ownership of the two properties was being transferred to Andrena Ruelas and Herbert Saunders, respectively, and that Airport Equity Home Loans was acting with power of attorney for the current owner, listed as one Nedwin Hillael, of Santa Monica. Lonnie typed steadily for about one hour, then she took the new titles, along with Mary's notary kit, and went next door to the Skywatcher's. "I Fall To Pieces" was playing on the juke-box. Patsy Cline was a favorite with the daytime drinkers on Ocean Park Boulevard.

Mary was sitting in a booth. Lonnie put the paperwork down in front of her. "Sign these papers and put your notary stamp on them. Now."

"Wha—?" Mary was practically unconscious from drinking and crying. "Documens?"

"These documents."

"Wassa hurry, wassa point? Wha' 'bout Misser O'Leary?" She began to cry again.

"I'm telling you now," Lonnie said in a harsh whisper. "Bill won't be interested anymore, he's got other things to think about." Mary signed the papers, but she wouldn't touch the notary stamp. Lonnie grabbed her wrist and forced her hand with the stamp in it down on the papers. Then she put the papers in a large manila envelope addressed to Herbert Saunders, and walked out onto the street.

Lonnie dropped the envelope in the blue mailbox on the corner and went back upstairs to the office. She replaced Mary's notary book and stamp in the drawer. She left by the back stairs, crossed the street, and caught the number 10 bus, eastbound for downtown Los Angeles.

Herb had Ned cremated at Malinow Silverman funeral directors, out on Fairfax, and took Ned's ashes home in a little jar with Hebrew writing on it. He tried putting it up on the mantle in his living room, but Scrubby wouldn't come in the room afterwards, so he took the jar down.

"What's the best thing to do here?" Herb asked Andrena.

"We always make a little shrine in the yard, with flowers," she said. Andrena seemed to know how to go about it. She had Herb set up a five-tiered brick pyramid, about four feet high, in a corner of the yard on his side. She decorated it with saints' pictures, an assortment of silver milagros, electric Christmas tree lights, pink geraniums, and a large plaster stature of the Virgin of Guadalupe. She placed Ned's urn behind the statue. Herb thought the shrine looked like a Mexican wedding cake.

The deed package arrived. Herb showed the papers to Andrena and explained what they meant. "This seems to be all legal and proper. Here's yours, and here's mine."

"You keep mine for me," Andrena told Herb. Herb went down to the corner and bought a bottle of champagne.

"It's Lonnie's way of saying gracias, I suppose," Andrena said, when Herb finished telling her as much of the story as he knew or wanted to know. "Maybe we can be safe for a while, now."

"For a while. Bill O'Leary had a plan to develop this neighborhood. The cops are saying he had something to do with poor Ned's getting killed, so he's out of the picture. But there's going to be others. Only thing is, most people with money wouldn't care to live next door to the cemetery."

"Pero, it's muy tranquilo," Andrena said.

A nice little corner in the city of squares, Herb thought. "Ned owned these places the whole time and never let on, never said a word." They were sitting outside in Andrena's barbecue patio. Herb turned in his chair and raised his champagne glass to Ned's corner shrine. "Gone be all right, Ned. You can stay here with us. Definitely."

Gun shop boogie

1958

—⚡—

AT TEN O'CLOCK at night, the Sierra Highway was dead quiet. Mike Brown heard the car coming; he heard the motor working through straight pipes. *About a mile away*, he thought. *They got the cutout open, they think they're smart.* Mike dumped the day's load of cigarette butts and ashes out in the parking lot in front of the shop and stood there watching for the car to come around the bend just below the little rundown shopping center. The sound got louder. *They got a cam in it*, he thought. *Probably got a crummy J. C. Whitney cam, and they think they own the road.* Headlights swung around the corner. The car slowed and pulled up to the curb. Mike stood where he was, holding the empty Folgers coffee can. "Hey kid," somebody hollered out. "Got a dollar? We're out of gas."

"No."

"Sure you do, you can get a dollar." Mike walked up to the car, a purple '49 Ford convertible with lake pipes and Hollywood Spinner hubcaps. The ragtop was patched with gaffer's tape. *They cut the springs too low, they can't hold it in the road. Can't go past forty miles an hour with the springs cut like that.* Mike looked inside the front seat. There were two guys with a girl in between them. The girl was about Mike's age, with an unhappy look. The guy on the passenger side had his arm around her in a proprietary way and a quart bottle of Southern Comfort between his legs. The inside of the car smelled like whiskey. The driver said, "Listen, we got Lorrie Collins in here. Didn't you ever see the Collins Kids on television?"

Mike heard the gun shop door open behind him. "Who's that out there?" Dolly called out.

"They want a dollar, and there's a girl here," Mike said over his shoulder. Dolly walked across the parking lot, his cane in one hand and a sawed-off, double-barrel twelve-gauge shotgun in the other. He never left the gun shop at night without it.

Dolly stooped over to get a good look. "Well, boys, it's your choice," he said. "You let her out and you get a dollar and go on your way. Or, I'm goin' to blow the doors off this vehicle, starting right here." Dolly pointed at the passenger door with his cane. The driver leaned over. "Look, pops, we're just asking for a dollar so we can get down the road here to someplace where we can show Lorrie Collins a little bit of a good time. Go mind your own damn business."

"What you want me to do, count three like they do in the movies?" Dolly brought the gun up, pulled the trigger and blew the front fender clean off the car. Out there on the empty highway, the shotgun reverberated like a field howitzer. The fender banged down on the sidewalk and lay there rocking back and forth. "You see the kick in this gun? I cain't always hold it steady, I cain't be sure!" Dolly said, waving the shotgun all around.

"Shit!" the driver shouted. "Get out, Johnny, get her out!" Johnny jumped out and pulled the girl with him. The Southern Comfort bottle rolled out and hit the curb. He scrambled back in and the Ford took off up the highway, sort of at an angle.

A sidewinder. They went into the turn too fast and barely made it around the corner. You could hear the pipes echoing in the low hills as they went. The two-lane highway got quiet again. "Let's get inside," Dolly said. "Nobody's got any sense anymore." Mike Brown picked the fender up off the sidewalk and followed Dolly and the girl back inside. *Thanks a lot, you crazy old man. They didn't know me before, but they do now.*

They walked through the clutter of tools and gun parts to the T-Bird lounge, a room in the back where Dolly did his drinking and porno reading. There was a cot, two chairs, and a small icebox with a "Get the US out of the UN" bumper sticker on the door. The girl sat down on the cot. Mike stood.

"I guess I have to thank you, sir," the girl said. "I was getting pretty scared with those boys. We just kept on driving and driving. I have no idea where I am."

"Terry and Johnny Poncey. What the hell is a young girl doing with trash like that?" Dolly opened a fresh pack of Pall Malls, the third one of the day.

Mike spoke up, "She's a singer, Dolly. From television, I think."

"I met them at a party. They said they wanted to take me to where my brother was. I think they wanted to get me drunk."

"Did they make you drink?"

"Do the police have to hear about this? The record company will have a fit. I'm supposed to be home in bed. They didn't hurt me."

"Where's your folks, honey?" Dolly asked, trying to be nice.

"They're back visiting in Oklahoma. My brother and I are staying with friends."

"Where's your friends now?"

"That's Joe and Rose Lee Maphis. Joe's out somewhere with my little brother, Larry."

"Joe Maphis?"

"Yes."

"Hell, I know Joe, I been knowin' him good. Call him, tell him to come and get you."

The girl dialed and waited. "Mister B's. It's a dance club in Lancaster," she told Dolly. Someone came on the line. Mike could hear the noise coming out of the receiver from where he was standing. "Hello, this is Lorrie Collins. Can I please speak to Joe Maphis?" She waited. "They're saying he's onstage with Larry now." She handed Dolly the phone and he barked into the receiver, "You tell Joe to call Dolly Carney." He read off the number twice and hung up.

"I got to lie down," the girl said.

"Why shore," said Dolly. "We'll wait for Cousin Joe to call."

Dolly and Mike went up front. "Who's Joe Maphis?" Mike asked.

"The fastest guitar alive," replied Dolly. "The fastest, not the best. I did some work on his guns in Bakersfield about ten years ago."

"What about the girl," Mike asked. "You going to keep her here?"

"Course not. Got to get her back to her people. Joe can take care of it."

"I thought you might try and keep her here, like the other one."

"You shut up about that." The shop phone rang. Dolly picked it up. "Dolly's Guns and Swords. This is Dolly. Joe? It's me. You better get over here and get Lorrie Collins. I don't want any trouble, I'm livin' right. Sierra Highway, two miles below the Half-Way Café. We'll be waiting."

"You better get on home, Mike," Dolly said. "You done enough for one day. Go on." Mike got up and left the shop, closing the front door behind him. *You want me out of the way. You don't care where I go or who's around when I get there.* It was cold outside, the way the desert gets cold late at night. Mike buttoned up his Levi jacket and walked up the road in the direction the Ford had gone, but he didn't go far. He circled back around through the oak trees behind the shop and stood there watching. It was dark inside, but after a while Mike saw something move. He duckwalked up to the window without making a sound and looked in. The girl was asleep on the cot and Dolly was standing there looking down at her. He reached down and lifted the hem of her dress up a little. She stirred, and Dolly stopped lifting and waited. Then he lifted the dress up some more. He stood there looking at the sleeping girl's legs for a while, then he put the dress back down and walked out of the room and closed the door. Mike took a breath. He felt a little better about leaving the girl alone with Dolly Carney.

Mike Brown got off the school bus at 4:30 the next day. He bought a bag of fried donuts and walked across the parking lot to the gun shop. Dolly wasn't in front, but Mike could see he'd been working. There was a trigger-receiver section from a Winchester .30-.30 in the vise, and the engraving tools were out. Mike looked through the magnifying glass. In an area hardly bigger than a matchbox was a tiny world: trees, a foreground, and a big buck deer looking proud. Mike could see the idea was good. He'd heard Dolly mention about engraving like he knew all about it, and sometimes people would stop by to talk guns and ask Dolly for custom work, but the answer was always the same: "I'm just an old cowboy that cain't do it no more." There were photographs on the wall above the workbench of Dolly as a younger man holding fancy guns and trophies, but he never did any real work in the shop except for light repairs and a sale once in a while. Mostly, Dolly drank T-Bird and looked at pictures of guns and naked girls.

"Dolly," Mike called out. Getting no reply, he went to the back and opened the door. Dolly was lying on the cot and he looked bad, worse than usual. Mike saw immediately that something had happened. Dolly's eyes were closed, and he didn't seem to be breathing. *He's dead, get used to it.* "Dolly," he said again.

"I'm here." Dolly opened his eyes.

"What's wrong?"

"Ticker blew. Too much excitement."

"Where's Lorrie Collins?"

"Joe came, finally."

"What do you want me to do?"

"Nothing. It'll be all right after a while, or it won't."

Mike thought he should say something positive. "You got a good start on that Winchester."

"I felt like trying. Just cain't manage the line anymore."

"Looks good to me, Dolly."

"I'm gonna close my eyes and rest a while," Dolly said. His breath was shallow and irregular. Mike dozed off, and when he woke up, Dolly was watching him. "If you're just going to sit there, light me one."

"Maybe it's a good time to cut back," Mike offered.

"Your point being what?"

Mike lit up a Pall Mall and passed it over. Dolly took a deep drag and started to talk. "Frank Pachmayr offered to sponsor me at gun shows and get me on the circuit. He offered to talk to Winchester about me. I told him I wasn't trying to get famous, I just wanted to get good, and that was enough. Frank said that's not the way it works. They want something and you got to show them you care about what that is. I said, I don't care what they think or want. After that, Frank called me a loser, but I never thought I was anything like a loser, even in prison. I always had a good time in life, right up until about two hours ago. Light me another one, will you? Why don't you eat something? Have a donut."

A FORD RANCHERO with its lights out pulled around back of Dolly's Guns and Swords, and two men stepped out. At that hour, there was no traffic out front and no lights on in the gun shop, which had been closed up since the death of Dolly Carney. The driver went to work on the back door. One minute later he had the lock picked and the door open. He switched on his chest-mounted flashlight and the two men commenced to tear up Dolly's T-Bird lounge. Not finding anything, they moved on to the front room. They started with the workbench, then moved to the shelves and the cardboard boxes. "Where the hell's it all at?" the driver said to the other man. A police car cruised by out on the road, and they ducked down behind the workbench. "There's shit in here that I want. It's got to be here."

"Day late, Woof. Day late, dollar short," the other man said with a chuckle in his pea-gravel voice.

With Dolly gone, Mike Brown needed a new job. The owner of the donut shop saw an opportunity to cheat a high school kid out of the minimum wage. The niece had started working there, hoping to get into the business as a family member, but Uncle Ralph said, "I can't afford you no more, and that's it." "Well, I'm not going back to the hot dog on a stick thing, I can't stand that," she told him. "Aunt Louise won't like for you to fire me, and I need to earn some money." Her aunt and uncle had a side business with a hot dog event trailer, and they traveled out on weekends to rodeos and drag races and swap meets. "Why not let me manage the store, and you can stay out with the hot dog trailer. Mike Brown can work alongside me in here. What's wrong with that?" Uncle Ralph had to admit it was feasible. He preferred moving around to being stuck on Sierra Highway, no telling what a man might come across out there. He told Aunt Louise he had a great idea on how to revitalize their business affairs. Whatever Sheree wants, said Louise, who had no children of her own.

Mike asked for a tall locker at school instead of the square one he'd had for three years. Only one month left, why bother, the coach in charge of lockers wanted to know. "I got a job after school. I need to change clothes. My mom's sick and can't work," Mike said. "Good for you, Brown," said Coach Nunez. The high school administration knew about Mike Brown, knew the situation at home — father locked down somewhere, alcoholic mother, all that. His transcript read, "Scholastic aptitude: poor. Social skills: very poor." The line about "expectations" was blank.

The problem was the big lockers were in plain view outside the showers, and there was something about locker rooms that made people get nosy. But it was better than trying to hide Dolly's stuff at home. You couldn't leave a thing like Dolly's pornographic Winchester lying around where people might stumble onto it.

Mike had gathered from the old man's rambling, T-Bird-inflected discourse there were a few things that needed taking care of when the end came. Like his engraving tools, which had a history of some kind, and the trophies. Dolly often spoke about guns he'd worked on that had slipped away over the years, but then there was the Winchester. "That's the one they'll come after. Get it out of here after I'm gone. Don't never tell nobody, there's people out there you do not want on your trail." That was the time Mike asked to see it. Dolly pulled up a loose floorboard and took out an oblong wooden gun box. Inside was a Winchester model 1895, a commemorative reissue that Dolly had covered with minute and highly detailed engraved studies of a naked girl in various explicit poses. Customers were always after Dolly to decorate their guns with curlicues or scenes from nature featuring wild animals and trees, but this gun was hyper-realistic in a way Mike had never imagined. Dolly had even inlaid the wood stock with silver and ivory carved into tiny full-body images. Mike saw that it was not some generic female, but the same girl over and over, rendered from every angle — front, back, top, and bottom. Mike thought she was young, possibly a teenager: "Is this what got you in trouble?" he asked Dolly.

"They never saw this, how do you think I have it still?" Dolly said. "A man worked for me in Bakersfield. I think he found some pencil drawings and he started a rumor, and the rumor took on a life of its own. There's a type of person that wants something nobody else has got, regardless. They'll stop at nothing. Stay away from them, and maybe you'll be all right."

The paramedics took Dolly away at four o'clock on a Friday afternoon. They asked Mike if he wanted to ride along, but he declined, saying he had some things to take care of in the shop. When he was sure they weren't coming back, he pried up the loose board and pulled out the wooden box. He wrapped the gun in a blanket and put the engraving tools in a paper bag. He replaced the box and the floorboard. Then he remembered that Dolly kept some money in the back room. He found the envelope inside a gun magazine featuring pictures of trap shooting with nude fat women. There was a hundred and forty dollars in cash plus a personal check made out to Dolly for $28.50, signed by Merle Travis.

Mike dismantled the Winchester, making it easier to take to school. He put the parts and the engraving tools in a canvas duffel bag and stowed the bag in his new locker. He locked it with a regular combination gym lock, but one that he bought at the True Value hardware store. The gym office issued all locks and had a master list of combinations, but Mike figured there was no chance anyone was going to start checking lockers for dope or booze with school over in a month. He changed clothes every day after school for his donut job and nobody paid any attention, since Mike Brown was the kind of kid nobody paid attention to.

Sierra Vue Donuts opened every day except Sunday at 6:00 a.m. Sheree worked alone until Mike arrived after school. She usually went home for dinner at seven and returned to work until closing time at ten. Mike worked alone in the back making up the next day's batch until eleven at night. Sometimes he was so tired he would fall asleep in the kitchen on the cot that he had retrieved from the gun shop.

When Woof Daco and Indian Charlie Smallhouse broke into the gun shop, Mike heard it. The donut shop was two doors down, and the store in between was empty. Mike knew just what it was about. He watched them leave empty handed, and he saw the car, a Ford Ranchero with a fiberglass shell over the back. He didn't recognize the car or the two men.

Mike got up a little before six the next morning and fired up the oven. He mopped the floor in front and wiped the tables down. He was bringing out the donut trays when Sheree arrived.

"Are they going to let you graduate, Mike?" she asked.

"I don't know."

"I sure hope you can stay on here."

Mike got the bus to school out on the highway. He was at his locker when Coach Frazer came around the corner from the showers. "Where you been, Brown? They want you in the office. I don't like to waste my time looking for you nonathletes." Coach Frazer had it in for him, but Mike never knew why. He once made him get inside a metal trash can and then sat on the lid while he took roll. *Bastard.*

The administration building was full of kids laughing and talking about what they were doing and where they were going. Especially the girls, Mike thought. *They all look good. Why?* Mr. Potts stood in the doorway, glaring at him. Mr. Potts' glare was one for the books. He had a nervous tic of baring his lower teeth and then leaving his mouth open in an absentminded way, like Charlton Heston.

"You haven't *done* very well, Mike," Mr. Potts looked over the top of his glasses and rattled some papers. "You haven't done as well as some of us had *hoped.* Some of us are aware of the extenuating circumstances at home, but there are other students here with backgrounds not unlike yours who managed to do a fine job. I can think of several who really tried to pull themselves up. There's a Mexican girl, Andrena Palacios, who will be giving a talk at graduation. We're proud of *her*." He leaned back in the chair. "All right. I'm recommending you for what is called a General Education Certificate. That will indicate that you have completed high school, but it is not a diploma. That would be unfair to those who have worked hard for theirs, and I'm sorry to say you won't participate in the graduation ceremony. Do you understand? " Mr. Potts stapled the papers together and signed his name on top.

"Yeah," Mike said. *You baboon-faced prick.*

"So, Mike. I would say, probably the military?"

"No," Mike said.

"Good luck, Mike." They didn't shake hands. Mike left the office and walked down the hall through the crowd of happy kids. *Wait a minute. I can walk out of here right now; baboon-face signed the paper.* He went to the gym and took the duffel bag and his donut shop clothes and left the school without speaking to anyone. The bag was heavy, but Mike didn't notice.

Who made the decisions? This person will have a hundred friends, and this other will have none. It's okay to put this kid in the trash can, we won't mention it. A tiny part of him had been waiting for a friend to come along, but it never happened. The sudden impulse to walk away sealed it for good, and with each step, he knew he had done the right thing.

The first problem was where to live. He wasn't going back to his mother's. She and the new boyfriend stayed drunk most of the time, and Mike didn't want to be there when the shit hit the fan like it always did. He couldn't go on sleeping in the donut shop. He needed a place, and some wheels. Mike thought about a pickup with a camper, which he could live in comfortably, but that cost real money. Sheree paid him okay, but not enough to buy a rig like that. Mike liked motorcycles. He believed there were three known kinds of people: Jap bike riders, who were beneath contempt; American big bike riders, who were okay but they all wanted the same bike over and over; and the chopper guys. They had the right idea: make your own machine — that was the only way to be yourself. *If you can't unscrew it, you don't own it*, as Dolly used to say. Mike had picked up some welding skills, and Dolly had taught him a basic understanding of gun mechanics: the key was balance and simplicity. Build your design around a single good principle, like the lever action Winchester or the Smith and Wesson revolver. Fancy, complicated things never worked out in the long run, it was true for guns and women.

Mike had a photograph of a bike he had cut out of the classified section of a motorcycle magazine. It was called the "Honest Charlie." This was no mass-produced Harley-Davidson, but a custom-made bike with a vintage Ford sixty-horsepower flathead V8 car motor mounted lengthwise in a long frame. Fat tires and no fenders gave it a rough, badass, take-no-prisoners look Mike loved. "Not for the faint at heart," it read. All you had to do was send two thousand dollars to a shop in Tennessee and wait six months. Two thousand was as good as two million, but Mike felt in his heart that he could make one from scratch. And, if he did, the world would come to understand the secret truth about Mike Brown.

Mike remembered Dolly had a girlfriend, a retired policewoman living around the corner in an old farmhouse with a travel trailer in the backyard. He spoke of her as being hipped on the subject of aliens and alien invasion. *Armed and dangerous, but otherwise nice enough.* The house was set well back from the street, surrounded by oak trees, and three giant ham radio antennas sprouted from the roof. There was a '47 Plymouth coupe in the driveway, with a "Support Your Local Police and Keep Them Independent" bumper sticker. Mike walked up the steps and knocked. He waited and knocked again. A woman's voice called out from loudspeakers mounted in the trees, "I see you.

Who are you?"

"Mike. I work for Dolly."

"Dolly Carney has gone." The door opened against a heavy chain, and the woman stood there looking down at Mike. She was tall, six feet easy, and bone thin but strong looking. She had a heavy-caliber revolver with an extra-long barrel in her right hand, pointed down.

"What do you want here?" she asked, putting the gun away.

"I want to ask about your trailer."

"Not for sale."

"I need a place." *Make it sound good.* "I work at the donut shop. My mom's got a new boyfriend, and I can't sleep. My dad's in prison up north." The woman stepped out onto the porch. "Let's go take a look," she said. Mike followed her up the driveway. She took big strides over the gravel, and her feet made loud crunching sounds. She carried the revolver in a quick-draw holster on her right hip. "The trailer's empty since I moved my equipment in the house."

"What equipment?" Mike asked, trying to be conversational.

"What's it to you?"

"Nothing. I like tools, is all," Mike said.

"Tracking and detecting. I ran out of room in the trailer, plus, there's been some trouble around here lately."

"Trouble?"

"You just bet. I called the sheriffs. They hadn't heard about any B & E locally. I said, this is enemy surveillance, and you couldn't identify B & E on your own assholes." She unlocked the trailer. It was a seventeen-foot Kenskill aluminum single axle, tall enough to stand up in. There was a bedroom/bathroom aft, and a large table and galley stove forward. It was dusty but in good shape.

"I used to pull it behind the Plymouth to meetings — Roswell, Mount Rainier — and it was a pleasure to pull. I don't go to meetings anymore for obvious reasons."

"I could help keep an eye on things. I work late." Mike wasn't sure what the woman was talking about. She was tough like Dolly said, but she wasn't mean.

"Five dollars a week suit you?" she said.

"Thanks."

"Stop in, I'm usually up late myself. It's too bad about Dolly. They take what they want. I've been lucky, so far."

"The paramedics took Dolly, I saw it," Mike said.

"You saw what you were supposed to see. Who called 'em, you?"

"Yeah."

"From Dolly's phone?"

"Yeah."

"He knew he was tapped. How long did it take 'em to get there? How many?"

"Five minutes. Two guys in white coats and a white van."

"The paramedics on Sierra Highway are RFD, and they wear yellow and their truck is yellow. ETA, thirty minutes, minimum. I've got to get back inside and get situated. You got a gun?"

"I got one of Dolly's." Mike held up the duffel bag.

"Bet you got the dirty one. Maybe that's good, maybe it's bad. We'll find out. My name's Gerri." She put out her hand and Mike shook it. It had a soft feeling of strength that surprised him. She went back inside the house. Mike heard the back door locks turn one, two, three times. *Short fuse, high detonation.*

THE PARKING LOT in front of Brakke's CharUrOwn was filling up: There was deputy sheriff Fred Early's Plymouth, bartender Ray McKinney's unpaid for Buick Roadmaster, Smokey McKinney's Mercury station wagon, which he needed to haul his pedal steel guitar and amp, a purple '49 Ford ragtop minus the right front fender, and an unfamiliar Ford Ranchero.

Inside, things were about to get started. Merle Travis had

told Cousin Joe to come by for him; he felt like playing. They loaded Merle's Gibson Super 400 guitar and Standel amp in the Cadillac and headed out, but Merle asked Joe to make a stop at the liquor store, that he needed something for the drive. By the time they got to Brakke's, Merle was starting to slide, so Alice Brakke gave him some coffee and sat with him in the corner while Joe set up the amps. Smokey McKinney was ready with his Sho-Bud pedal steel and the two chairs needed to park his seven-hundred-pound bulk. Once situated, Smokey rarely moved again.

Brakke's wasn't much of a place, more like a roadside bar than a restaurant, but there was always a convivial atmosphere and plenty of music. If you were female and you bought the bartender a drink, he'd get his guitar from under the counter and sing you one. Folks were encouraged to pick out their steak from the kitchen and then take it outside to the barbecue pit, which was fired with oak to a temperature high enough to melt lead. Everyone really enjoyed standing around in the cool, high desert night air cooking their steaks. The results varied, depending on the alcohol content of the individual.

Cousin Joe broke out his trademark Mosrite double-neck guitar, which got a round of applause that prompted Merle to leave the table and walk over. He took his Gibson and strummed a G chord, and that Merle Travis smile appeared. "Well folks, ain't nothin' in this world I like better than a big fat gal," he said. "Well Merle, that goes double," Joe said. Bartender Ray McKinney got seated behind his unpaid for Radio King drum set. He counted off a good swing tempo, and they hit it.

Warm in the winter, shady in the summertime,
That's what I like about that fat gal of mine

Everybody in the place knew it: Joe Maphis and Merle Travis were the perfect combination, like a flathead motor and Lincoln gears. Everybody, that is, except for the four men seated in the back behind the post: Woof Daco, Indian Charlie Small-house, and the Poncey Brothers, looking spooked. If you were paying attention to them instead of Joe and Merle, you'd have figured that a deal was being discussed and the discussion was not amicable.

"It's your choice," Woof said. "I paid you money. You got two days more to get me what I want, or I'm going to start hurting you real bad. Isn't that so, Charlie?" He turned to the Indian.

"They can run, but they can't hide," Indian Charlie said in his hoarse whisper. He smiled at the boys.

Terry Poncey had a little bit of a cool-cat act he'd been working on most of his twenty-two years, but it was all he had. "We lost track of the kid for a while, but we know where he's at now. We'll get it. You ain't got a problem."

"A little problem for me is a big problem for you punks," Woof said.

"Gone be adeeyos, baby," Charlie said. The two boys got up and left. Terry used a piece of copper wire to jump start the Ford, and the car limped off into the night, pulling slightly sideways in the direction of Palmdale.

A woman in a prewar Dodge coupe passed them on the road. She was headed for Brakke's. She turned into the parking lot and drove the car up to the front door. Inside, the boys were just getting started on "Divorce Me C.O.D.," which had been a big hit for Merle. The woman opened the trunk and began to throw items of men's clothing out onto the parking lot. Suits, shirts, underwear, shoes, the works. When she was done, she backed the Dodge out. The future ex-Mrs. Ray McKinney headed north toward Willow Springs in a cloud of oil smoke.

Indian Charlie made his way over to the bar. He held up two thick fingers. A man standing at the bar looked Charlie up and down. "Alice has got a sense of humor, I don't," he said.

"Now, Earl, that's all right," Alice said.

"You're a nice woman, Alice. This is a man's business," Earl said. He was medium drunk.

Charlie turned to the man. "What are you drinkin', friend? I'd be real pleased if you'd allow me to stand you." Charlie smiled his strange Navajo smile and nodded.

"I don't allow no redskin to address me in that style and manner, nor do I appreciate redskins coming inside a place where I drink," Earl said. It was his last remark, followed by a deep gasp of shock and pain brought on by Charlie's surprise balls-in-a-vice grip and the unmistakable sawed-off shotgun barrel that Woof Daco jammed hard into the seat of Earl's Western-style trousers. Nobody noticed as Charlie and Woof eased Earl out the side door into the parking lot.

"It's your choice," Woof said after Charlie got Earl pinned down on the asphalt. "Repeat after me: 'It's a known fact that I am no better than a sack of pig shit,' or we take your pants and shoes." Earl tried hard to talk, but all he could do was grunt. Getting no reply, Woof unsheathed an eighteen-inch bowie knife and cut Earle's pants from the waist down to the cuff. Charlie pulled the pants away and considered. "I say we leave the shoes," he said. The two men drove away in the Ranchero. After a while, Earl felt his groin start to relax, but he had been drinking rye and his head was spinning. He lay there staring up at the stars, trying to focus. The band had switched to a walking bass, honky-tonk ballad he didn't recognize. Someone other than Merle Travis was singing:

Going to Shmengy Town, back to Shmengy Town
Big city life has really got me down
It's a place of sin, there's no room for me
I won't be around, I'm going to Shmengy Town

My dreams of yesterday have all passed and gone
I watched them slip away like a bird that's flown

I saw my chance go by, and the sands of time
Drift through my hands, I'm going to Shmengy Town

The air was cold on his bare legs. Earl made an effort to stand but he stumbled and collapsed facedown on the asphalt again. The disappointment and self-pity in the song got to him, piercing him with a memory of his ex-wife somewhere back in Oklahoma. He started to cry and the crying made his nose bleed.

"Well, folks, I see by the old clock on the wall that it's quittin' time at Brakke's. Happy trails, and may the good Lord take a likin' to yuh."

"Merle, I believe you stole that line from Roy."

"Joe, I believe you're right. Got anything you'd like to add?"

"I don't believe I do. How 'bout you, Kash?"

"Tell 'em to drink up and go home, if they got one."

"That's good advice, Kash, and thanks for stoppin' by and singin' with us."

"My playsure. I think my steak walked out on me. I better go see if I can relocate it before the coyotes do."

Gerri's house was a survivor from a time when people worked outdoors fifteen hours a day and went inside to eat and sleep. Mike came in through the dining room, which was dominated by an oilcloth-covered table and an upright piano. A hallway opened onto a parlor room with a fieldstone fireplace. A TV screen was set into a control panel in the center of the room, surrounded by large hydro transformers scrounged from the local power utility. Gerri sat at the console watching phosphorescent loops and test patterns. Mike sat on a wooden box and watched her.

"I look for a break in the patterns, like a stone in water. Since Dolly left, something's been moving out there. It's small, it can hide, but I seen it here. And here. Take a look." Mike watched the moving lines of light. Some were curved, some pointed up and down. The lines began to speed up. "Here it comes. Watch." Mike watched without recognizing anything. "I'm locked and loaded down," Gerri said. "I scored one hundred in rapid fire when I was on the cops, so don't you worry about that."

"What are you worried about?"

"I'm a watcher. I'm on to them and they know that I know. I used to go to meetings until I discovered the brotherhood had been infiltrated. The new president announced that we had been selected by a group of 'ascended masters.' They were going to lead us into a new golden age. All we had to do was take an oath of secrecy and give the president all our money."

"What's an oath?" Mike asked.

"A pledge."

"Did you pledge the oath?"

"Not on your life. Dolly Carney and I and a friend named Orlando Hopkins split off and tried to form our own group. Orlando was a nice man, but he made a bad mistake, and he paid the price."

"What happened?"

"Orlando went out to Giant Rock on a prayer vigil to amend his sins or whatever he thought he'd done wrong. He was unarmed. All we ever found was his Bible and his flashlight, the rest was burnt."

"You got guns in here?"

"Smith and Wesson police positive, Colt .45 by Pachmayr, .30-.30 by Dolly, .3006 with a nightscope, and a Marlin 12-gauge pump. Five hundred rounds of hollow point and fifty Jap hand grenades. I'm ready."

"Did Dolly believe in these things?"

"Sure he believed, but you know Dolly. He wanted to teach me a dirty trick with cigarettes, but I drew the line there. Now I got to hold the thin white line all by myself, with no help from Fred Early and his deputy pinheads."

"I'll help you," Mike said. "What do I do?"

"Keep watching the skies," Gerri said. "Watch people, especially those known to you. Anyone can be infiltrated."

"How do you know?"

"They look the same but act different. For instance, if someone who was a quiet person starts up talking loud and saying nothing and laughing all the time. I think that whole crowd at Brakke's has been snatched, the way they carry on. Also, people who want to boss you around and make you do things."

"Every son of a bitch at the high school," Mike said.

"A school is the first place they'd go. To corrupt the young."

"Bastards never got me."

"That's RMA for survival. RMA equals Right Mental Attitude."

Mike waited to hear more, but Gerri went back to her TV screen and said nothing further. Mike got up and went out to the backyard and looked at the night. He found himself staring up at the sky, watching and listening.

TERRY PONCEY REALIZED Johnny was starting to slide into panic mode. Stealing the Winchester out of the trailer was going to be a two-man job.

"They'll kill us," Johnny said. "Woof Daco is crazy in his face. You said we could go to Hollywood."

"Listen to me, Johnny. *We* got news for Mr. Woof Daco, which is, *we* got a bonus coming to us, and *then* he gets his gun, and then *we* are going down to Hollywood and find Lorrie Collins, like I told you."

"Tell about it," said Johnny.

"We are going to get her in a room and you are going to fuck her real good."

"That's too fast! Tell it the way I like it."

"We ain't got time for all that. We got business to take care of. You all right now, Johnny?"

"No."

"Sure you are. We're gonna hide that thing out where they can't never find it unless we tell them, and they won't have no other choice but to give us more money."

"I can't walk."

"You stay with the car. Keep the engine running. We can't start it in time if it goes out. You understand that?"

"I keep it running," Johnny said.

"Then, I come back and you slide over and I drive. You got nothing to worry about but to keep the motor on."

Terry figured to go in from the back of Gerri's property where the shallow arroyo ran down to the highway. There were oak trees there, and a man could get some cover. Terry had checked the place out in daylight, and he had a good sense of how far down Gerri's house was. There was no fence along the back, just the trees. It was hard going in the dark. After a while he could see the trailer in the moonlight. He crept up from behind and waited. There was blue light coming from inside the house. Nothing happened, so he went around to the front of the trailer. He had brought along a short crowbar, and he pried the door open in seconds. He got his flashlight out and looked around inside. The table was covered with motorcycle magazines and mechanical drawings. There was a duffel bag under the table. Terry pulled it out and looked inside. He saw gun parts. "The shit," he whispered. Then he heard the sound of heavy footfalls in the dry brush. A voice cried out, "Terry, where are you?" and Johnny came staggering out of the arroyo like the Creature from the Black Lagoon.

The sudden movement triggered the floodlights. A voice came booming out of the trees: "I see you. Who are you?" Johnny froze in his tracks and looked up. "Johnny Poncey," he answered. Terry grabbed the duffel bag and ran. The back door of the house opened and Gerri came out. She raised the Smith and Wesson in both hands and fired at Johnny. The big .38 roared. "Terry!" Johnny wailed, stumbling and clutching at his leg. Terry grabbed Johnny's arm and dragged him down the gravel driveway toward the front of the house. More lights went on. Gerri was following them. She fired again, and Johnny screamed. "Run, Johnny!" Terry shouted. Johnny ran, kicking his right leg out. They made it to the Ford. The motor was still turning over. Terry managed to get Johnny and the bag inside. There was a back road out. The cutout boomed as the car got moving.

Terry had worked it out so that he would get to the meeting place first and hide the gun. He hadn't figured on Johnny getting hurt. He made the turn onto the dirt road and pulled into the dump site. It was pitch dark and dead quiet. He cut the motor and the lights. Instantly, Woof Daco and Indian Charlie Smallhouse appeared, dump zombies on the prowl. Woof yanked the driver's door open. "The early birds. What's the early bird get, Charlie?"

"Give 'em a chance," whispered the Indian.

"What's it going to be?" Woof said. Terry reached in the backseat and pulled out the bag. He threw it on the ground. Woof used his big flashlight to look, then he closed the bag and turned to go.

"Just a damn minute," Terry said. "Johnny got shot."

"Shot where," Charlie said.

"Right leg," Terry said.

"Shine a light on him," Charlie said. He bent over Johnny, looking at one leg and then the other. "I don't see anything. What's the gag?"

"That bitch shot him. What about the rest of our money?"

"Kid, there's nothing wrong with your brother except naked fear. I would sit here for a little while and let him rest. Give us a good start. Woof wouldn't care to see you or this shit car anymore."

The Indian smiled at Terry and walked away into the dark. Terry heard the Ranchero start up, heard it pull out onto the highway.

Mike cut through the oak grove behind the donut shop. He saw police lights; he heard voices as he walked up. Two sheriff's deputies drew down on him. "Stand easy, that's my boarder," Gerri commanded. The officers went into parade rest without thinking. "They hit the trailer, Mike. I think I got one of 'em in the leg, but they got away. I'm out of practice." Her eyes told him to keep quiet.

"Lucky for you, Gerri, 'cause you been wasting a lot of my valuable time with those crank calls of yours," Fred Early said.

"Just do your damn job, Early. I told you I been cased, but you couldn't be bothered. Finally got your lousy B & E. Happy now?" The deputy shook his head and took off in his Plymouth.

"Sorry, Mike," Gerri said. "Your bag is gone. I guess they got the Winchester." She put her hand on Mike's shoulder. "I told Early they took only hand tools."

"Who was it?" Mike said.

"It looked like two guys in an old Ford ragtop. You got to hand it to 'em. They got it down, Mike, they really got it down."

"That's not your goddamn spacemen, it's the Poncey Brothers."

"Oh sure, Mike. Just a couple punks looking for Dolly Carney's famous Winchester and knowing right where to get at it. Tell yourself anything you want to believe. I'm going back inside, I got to reload."

Mike changed out of his work clothes and lay back in the trailer bunk. He thought he had it figured right. The Poncey Brothers were working for the two strangers in the Ranchero. The Brothers knew who Mike was and they assumed correctly that he had the Winchester. Dolly had warned Mike that something like this would happen, but suddenly, it didn't seem to matter so much anymore. Gerri's theory, that the aliens had replicated Terry and Johnny Poncey and their '49 Ford, worked only if you accepted Sierra Highway as a staging area for earth conquest. Mike drew the line there — who'd want it? But just the same, he took a sheet of paper and a black Marks-A-Lot and wrote out WELCOME SPACE BROTHERS in big block letters.

SOMETHING WAS WRONG. One by one, the diners stopped eating and pushed their plates back. The T-bone, the Spencer, the rib eye, the fried calamari and garlic bread just sat there. The laughter died and the talk ground down to a murmur. It was the smell, something sudden and terrible that took over the place, killing the fun.

Deputy Fred Early pulled up and left the engine running. "I need a double bourbon, right now," he said. Alice was tending bar since Ray was out looking for his wife somewhere. She poured the deputy a triple, and he used both hands to hold the glass. The diners watched him drink it down. He turned to face them.

"You all want to know what that smell is, don't you? Well, I wouldn't let you down. It's two men in a Ford Ranchero. They're just sittin' in that car, burnt black, down to the bone. I saw their teeth."

"Electrical?" Smokey McKinney asked.

Early shook his head. "There's an empty gallon gas can on the ground, like a calling card. This is a homicide. It ain't my job." He staggered out to the patrol car and called it in and threw up on the seat. The diners made a beeline for their cars to get a look at the Ranchero before the meat wagon arrived.

Gerri's face was blue in the light of the monitor screen. The lines moved across the screen, up and down, up and down. "It's quiet out there now. They got what they wanted," she said.

"What do they want the Winchester for?" Mike asked.

"I don't know. Dolly's with them now, maybe he wanted it back."

"Dolly got his gun?"

"Makes good sense, don't it?" Gerri had called Mike to come inside the house when he got home from work Sunday night. "Pull up a chair and look at this," she said. "It was on the screen when I came in. Must be an attack weapon or some newfangled torture machine. I don't know how I'd stand up under torture."

Mike studied the image. It appeared to be a three-dimensional diagram, like a blueprint. The image rotated on its axis. "Can you make it stop?" he asked Gerri.

"Well, I just don't know." Gerri said. She turned knobs and switches at random, and the image froze.

"Hold it right there," Mike said. "I seen this before, like a cutaway picture in the hot-rod magazine. It's a motor. Make it go ahead." Gerri turned a big, black knob, and the image righted itself and a framework appeared, then two wheels. "It's a motor-cycle," Mike shouted. "It's the Honest Charlie!"

"They saw you come in," Gerri said.

"Make it get closer. I want to see the transmission linkage," Mike said. Gerri fiddled with the knob, and the drive link got bigger. "That's it! How the hell they know what it is I need to know about?" Mike said.

"Told you before, they know about everything we think and do."

"That's all right with me, now I can get the job done right, I can feel it," Mike said. He got paper and pencil and made a sketch of the transmission section. When he was done, the screen went blank.

"Did you get it?" Gerri asked.

"I believe I did," Mike said. The wavy lines returned.

Mike walked into the front office of the Hammond Lumber Company. He was looking for someone who could tell him about the old flathead-powered band saw contraption they had in the back. Out of service and rusty, but it had the original clutch and transmission, and he could get started on his motorcycle if they'd let him take it. The office was empty except for a Mexican girl sitting behind the cashier's desk, crying. The girl looked up and saw Mike. "Please excuse me," she said, wiping her eyes. "Can I help you?"

"Sorry to bother you." Mike felt embarrassed for her.

"I'm okay. Just a stupid family problem," she said.

"What's the matter?" Mike asked.

"I talked to my sister. Her boyfriend is bad. She is young, what can you do when there is no father?"

"My father's in prison somewhere," said Mike.

"Our father went back to Mexico, or who knows?" The girl smiled at Mike. He noticed there was something wrong with her teeth. They looked damaged, and he got embarrassed again. A pretty girl with messed-up teeth, that was tough.

"Are you from around here?" Mike asked.

"Yes. I went to Canyon Country High School."

"I went there," Mike said.

"I never saw you at school," the girl frowned, trying to remember. "Did you graduate?"

"They passed me out, I didn't get a diploma."

"I didn't get one either. I did something that made them angry."

"What?" Mike leaned forward on the counter. This, he wanted to hear.

"They wanted me to speak to the class at the ceremony. I asked, 'Why me?' They said, 'Learn these lines.' It was all about the way Meskins should think and act. I said, 'But I don't feel this way.' The vice principal said, 'Don't you want to help your people?' I said, 'How does this help them?' She said, 'Do as we say, or you won't graduate with everyone. You can do better for yourself, or be just another Meskin.' I said, 'But the white girls will hate me standing there.' She said, 'How dare you say such a thing.' I didn't make the speech, and I didn't get my diploma." The girl looked like she was going to start crying again.

Mike got excited listening to the girl's story. "Look, they are nothing but bald-faced liars. I heard about you. Mr. Potts told me all about the Mexican girl who was smarter than me. The same thing happened to me, I didn't do what they wanted, whatever it was. So what? You don't have a thing to worry about." Mike laughed, and the girl laughed.

"What's your name?" she asked.

"Mike Brown."

"Andrena Palacios," the girl said. She reached across the counter and took Mike's hand and squeezed it, sending an electrical current through his body like a dual ignition Vertex Magneto.

Mike looked up from his drawing as two men came in. They were dusty and hot looking, like they'd been outdoors for a while.

"I'm so doggone hungry I could eat my right hand if it had bread," said one man.

"Dry bread, shore ain't greasy. Hard work, shore ain't easy," said the other man.

"Dry bread and hard work is always comin' my way," the first man sang in a voice Mike recognized instantly.

"Merle Travis," Mike said.

"And Missus Bigsby's boy, Paul," Merle said. "What's your name, son?"

"Mike Brown. I used to work for Dolly Carney. You remember Dolly."

"I certainly do," Merle said.

"Last of the best," said Paul Bigsby. "What do you recommend for a couple of old timers just in from three days of racing at El Mirage?"

"We got cheeseburgers, new on the menu," Mike said. "Get 'em for you in a jiffy."

Mike put two deluxe cheeseburger plates down on the counter and went back to his drawing.

"What you doing there?" the man named Paul asked.

"I'm trying to design a motorcycle, but this drive link's got me stumped," Mike said.

Merle Travis said, "Well, Mike, today is your lucky day, because Paul here is the greatest genius of mechanical design in Downey, perhaps the world. Take a look, Paul, help the boy."

Mike passed the drawing over to Paul. He studied it while he ate his burger. He looked at Mike and said, "Now, this here is very interesting. This is your idea?"

"No, sir, I picked it up. I'm trying to put it together with flathead power. I just don't understand it so well."

"I suggest you bring us two more cheeseburgers. I don't know where you got this, son, but it is very intriguing and very unusual. See, Merle, it's a kind of a planetary drive, like the old Model T used to have. Constant gearing, so's you don't shift it. Controlled from the handlebars. That, and the open driveshaft instead of a chain. Very nice, very neat. Where'd you say you got this?"

"Well, I got it off television."

"Son, there is nobody on the TV with a mind anywhere near this good, but nobody."

"It wasn't local TV." Mike felt he couldn't begin to explain.

"I tell you what, I will fabricate this in my shop back in Downey. If you bring me the frame and motor, we'll hook it up there. Give me six weeks, I got to build a new triple-neck for Buddy Emmons." The two men finished their lunch and got up to leave.

"Mike, that was the flat out best cheeseburger I ever ate in a lifetime of cheeseburgers," Merle said. "It was round, firm, and fully packed."

"Come and look at what we got in the trailer," Paul said. Outside was a pickup with two motorcycles tied down on a flatbed. Every feature was molded into sculptural shapes that curved and flowed and joined. The big bikes were buffed and polished, and the metal had a rich luster, unlike steel or chrome.

"That's all cast aircraft aluminum, built from scratch," Paul said. "Got 'em up to a hundred and fifty yesterday, didn't we, Merle?"

"I never noticed," Merle said. He pointed to the sign in the front window. "It says, 'Welcome Space Brothers.' You expectin' 'em anytime soon?"

"Maybe," Mike replied.

"Sure hope they like Recorded Country Music, because my sales are startin' to slide pretty bad. The hip-swivellers are gonna put me out of business."

Paul started to drive away and then paused. "Only thing might be the weight for a feller your size. That Ford 60 will be heavy and hard to handle. Think about a four-banger. There's ways a four can be just as rockin' and fun as an eight, with half the size and twice the cruising range. Just a thought." The truck pulled out in a cloud of dust.

Sheree watched Mike bring the donut trays out. "Andrena Palacios is a nice girl, Mike. I saw you and her talking the other day. You could ask her out, and we could double date. We could go to Brakke's. I always get the Spencer steak, it's just my size."

Mike kept working with the trays. "So who's your date?" he asked.

"I was thinking of asking my golf teacher from the Antelope Valley Country Club. Vic is a little bit older than I am, but he's taking a personal interest in me. He says I have a natural ability and I could be competitive if I lose weight. He's helping me with my diet and my nutrition."

"How'd you get interested in playing golf?"

"From croquet, when I was little."

"What's that?"

"It's like golf for kids, that's how you get them started." Sheree stared at the rows and rows of fresh donuts in the trays, each one as perfect and beautiful as the next: the plain, the chocolate, the crumble, the fried, the glazed, the jelly filled, and the new lemon curd Mike had invented. She tried one. "This is fantastic, Mike, this is a winner," she exclaimed with her mouth full. "You are the man."

"I don't know if Andrena is ready for Brakke's, I don't think they like Mexicans in there. That might be rushing things. I'm in no hurry, she ain't going anywhere. Guess I'm not going anywhere either."

Mike was closing up at the donut shop when he heard the car — a flathead with the cutout open. He stood in the parking lot and watched the Ford ragtop come around the corner by the shopping center. In the moonlight, the car was a dirty purple with the right front fender in gray primer. *Where's Johnny?* Mike wondered. Then he remembered Gerri said she winged one of the killers from space. Mike waved. Terry Poncey didn't wave back. The car kept going up Sierra Highway. Hollywood Spinners, the hubcaps of the doomed.

Smile

1950

—∾—

G ET THIS AND get it straight: Crime is a sucker's road, and those who travel it usually wind up in the gutter or the morgue . . . or the dentist's chair.

I'm Sonny Kloer. I'm a dental technician and a steel guitar player. You don't know me, but I got a story to tell you. What's that you say? Nothing ever happens in Los Angeles? Sit down, take a load off, try some pork fried rice. It happened like this.

When the phone rang, I knew the voice: "Hey Shonny, ish Ray." Old Ray Randucci, the King of C6th. Ray Randy, as he is, or was, known in the profession. I hadn't heard from him in quite a while, but I don't get a lot of calls anymore.

"Ray, old buddy," I said, my standard greeting. "Where you at?"

"In town," he said, the standard musician's answer. "Nobody

won't hire me no more. Ish my teethsh. Can you do shomething to help me?"

I still had my old job at the Walgreen Dental Lab, so I'd be the guy to call. Plus, we were musically acquainted since all these years, even though I was never in Ray's league.

"Well, Ray, I don't know," I said. "I'm the only technician at the lab, and I'm all backed up." Not exactly true. "Got any money?"

"No. But I'll trade shoo for the work, Shonny."

"What you got to trade?" I already knew the answer, but this I had to hear to believe.

"I shtill got the Bigshby. You ushed to like it, now you can have it."

The Bigsby triple-neck — the holy grail of steel guitars. The one thing every player wants but a prize only a few could ever have. For an ordinary guy like me, it's unheard of.

"Okay, Ray. I'll take care of you on the QT. The Belfont Building, Seventh and Main. Take the elevator, third floor, in the back. Nine o'clock."

I worked nights, so I never saw the boss, Puss Walgreen. "Any moonlighting, I touch half," Puss told me when I started at the lab ten years ago. But a Bigsby — it's like King Solomon and the baby — you can't cut it. Paul Bigsby would have made a great dental technician if he had gone in that direction. You should see how the little parts fit together just perfectly, all hand cast from aircraft alloy. And the sound! I used to play a Fender Stringmaster, which was nice, but I traded it for an automobile that I needed to get to work. I can't go chasing streetcars. The Stringmaster is an Oldsmobile to the Bigsby Cadillac. Naturally, we can't all be Cadillacs. I do the best I can with what I got, bum legs and all.

They pulled me out of Leyte in '45 and did what they could. The army doctors said something about progressive nerve damage. I walk with a cane, but it's getting harder now. The G.I. Bill offered a course in dental technology, and it seemed like a good choice for me since you sit down. Dentistry really took off in Los Angeles after the war, what with the new materials they'd perfected in the airplane factories. No sense kidding myself, there was little future for me as a steel player, and the instruments and the amplifiers are so damn heavy that a guy with bum legs had better keep it as a pastime and get a steady job. But I like to stay in touch with the music and the players out there, and that's how I knew Ray Randy.

Ray came through the office door at nine sharp. "I'm shcared," he said. I had a blank prepared out of casting alba stone. It's a mold of fine-grained cement, shaped in a curve, like teeth in the mouth. The patient bites down and waits for it to set up. But not too long, because it gets hard suddenly and there ain't no way out! Ain't a doggone thing in the world you can do. Ray was nervous, but he did fine. It took about ten minutes.

"Here's what we do, Ray," I explained. "I build each tooth as an implant, and an implant man installs them one by one. Then there's another way. I go ahead and remove the teeth you got left and build you up a whole set and install them as a unit. A bridge, we call it. The implant man is a good extractor. He gets paid in cash, but I'll handle it on my end."

"What shoo need him for?"

"I'm just a technician, but Houseley is a real doctor. He'll do the extractions, then I make the set, then he comes back for the fitting. We'll get the job done right, 'cause I want that Bigsby!"

"Will it hurt?" Ray asked.

"You won't feel a thing. If we try and save the teeth you got, then we have to go in all over again when they fall out, and I believe they will."

"Jush do the whole dang shebang," Ray said.

"I'll get a message to Houseley," I said.

There was a heavy fog in Chavez Ravine. I parked off the road, just below the old Barlow Sanitarium, according to

Houseley's instructions. It's a pretty remote spot: hills and trees and dirt roads — and a few rough shacks where Mexicans live, if you call it living. I didn't see one other car going in or out. I smoked a cigarette and listened to the radio and waited. The fog settled all around my Oldsmobile, a prewar job with one of the first automatic transmissions. It was a crap transmission, but I didn't have to clutch it.

I first met Houseley around the time I started at the Walgreen Dental Lab. Puss Walgreen brought him in for specialty jobs that he offered customers at half what a regular dentist would charge. Puss even undercut Dr. Beauchamp, the friendly credit dentist, whom he hated. Houseley seemed to make the patients uncomfortable, but he was good, his work was real artistic so they kept quiet. We had a routine. He'd give me an address over the phone and I'd go pick him up. He was never in the same place twice, and he only worked at night.

The door opened and Houseley slid over like a shadow. He smelled of damp earth and wet eucalyptus trees.

"Cigarettes! Can't stand the stink of 'em!" he said. "Whiskey?"

I passed him the bottle. I drove down through the Ravine and turned right on Broadway. Houseley was getting old. His face was creased, his hair was white, and his eyes were stuck way down deep in the folds of his drooping eyelids. His clothes were dirty, and he needed a shave.

"Been doing a little consulting at the Barlow," he said, "they're interested in my work on schizophrenia."

"This is just an extraction for a friend of mine, nothing fancy," I said.

"Won't work for Puss Walgreen! Can't trust the man, he threatened me."

"Threatened you with what?"

"He had me do a scrape, some years back. Seems the girl died. Beauchamp found out about it."

"Beauchamp, the credit dentist?"

"Walgreen and Beauchamp were partners. Beauchamp forced him out and took over the operation. He's a rich man now, and Walgreen's got a piddling little lab on Main Street. When the girl died, Walgreen blamed me, said Beauchamp put me up to it."

"Did he?"

"I don't make mistakes. Last I knew, the girl was fine. Nice girl, a vocalist. Sang that hillybilly stuff you like. Can't stand it, sounds like cats fucking."

"How come I don't know about all this?" I said. Houseley held the bottle in both hands and drank, spilling whiskey down his shirt.

"My advice? Mind your business." Old Houseley was right that time.

I gave Ray enough sodium pentothal to put him out for two hours, and Houseley yanked his few remaining choppers. I had him leave the incisors: two on the bottom and two over top. You need 'em to anchor the bridge. "I'll call you when it's ready," I told him.

"Don't be too long," Houseley said. "This man's got gum disease, needs a gingivectomy. Can't guarantee the long term otherwise, won't be held responsible." I gave Houseley some money and he drifted out.

I played the radio and waited for Ray to come out of the gas. It looked like the best solution was to utilize individual teeth I had on hand. You might be surprised how often that happens. Somebody needs dental work but then they don't show up, or they can't pay for it. I had drawers full of teeth, in all shapes and sizes; men, women, and kids. It would save time, and I didn't want Puss Walgreen poking around asking questions.

Ray panicked when he woke up and saw himself in the mirror. He looked like a wino from San Julian Street. I gave him an old, store-bought set, the kind they made twenty years ago. "Walking-around teeth, just temporary." I told him, "Bring the Bigsby when you come back."

"Gahnammeh, Shonny! Ish worsh! Ah luh lah *hell!*" I told him not to worry.

The real work is in the structure of the bridge. If your structure isn't strong then your bridge is going to flex and shift around and come loose when you talk or eat or what have you. I used the impression I'd taken of Ray's gums for my mold. I set up the plastic material around the wire frame in the usual way, and put it in the icebox to harden. I closed the lab and used my elevator key to get down to the street, since the elevator operator quit at ten at night.

On the way home, I stopped off at Sammy's Hot Spot, a storefront joint in an old Chinese business block on Ord Street. It's the only place around there that stayed open that late. I sat at the bar, and Sammy came right over.

"Haryew, SonnyBoy! Pokeflylice?" Sammy said. My usual.

"Skip the flies and the lice, SammyBoy." My usual line. Sammy featured this clear rice wine with a kick like moonshine, which is what it was.

"Houseley come by, he payed cash!" Sammy said, like it was an event.

"We're working together," I said. Sammy brought my rice bowl over and set me up with chopsticks and hot sauce. Four Chinese girls were sitting at the corner table laughing and drinking. They were all excited about the dance hall where they'd been and the swing band they saw and the musicians they liked. I knew the place, the Zenda Ballroom, on Seventh and Figueroa. Tetsu Bessho and his Nisei Serenaders played there every Monday night. Jimmy Araki, the sax player, he was sharp. Joe Sakai was cute. The girls spoke English with a lot of hip slang like musicians use, and as far as I could tell they were no different from any other American girls, except they were Chinese. One of the girls kept playing the same mournful Mexican tune on the jukebox and dancing around by herself. I watched her in the mirror behind the bar. She had on a jade green sweater over a tight black skirt, white socks, and Chinese-red shoes. She was a good dancer. She held her head sideways with her shoulders up around her chin and her hands out in front like a French nightclub singer. Where did she pick that up, I wondered. "Hit me again, Sammy." I said. He poured me a tall one. It burned like mad. "Crazy hooch, Sammy," I said.

"Yah, crazy. Top come off! Chinese girl like sad song. She break up wit boyfriend, say adios muchacho."

"The boyfriend was Mexican?"

"Yah, pachuco boy. No good fo' Chinese girl. Bad boy got funny hand." Sammy held up his left hand and spread the fingers out. "Got too many, make six! Bad sign, bad boy."

"A pachuco with six fingers? I better keep it in mind. Hasta mañana, SammyBoy." I paid and left. Chinatown was dead quiet. The girls left Sammy's and walked north on Broadway. They made a lot of noise in the foggy, empty street, laughing and singing the jukebox tune in high, screechy voices. If I get my hands on that Bigsby steel, maybe I could get a job at the Zenda, I thought. Tetsu Bessho never thought of hiring a steel player. That would be something new. I could make connections. I hadn't worked in a long time, so it would be like starting all over again, but it was worth a try. Got to be more to life than cut-rate teeth and pork fried rice. I almost didn't notice the old Ford panel truck pulling out of the alley behind Sammy's. It drove off in the direction the girls had gone. Just a night man like me, on his way home.

Old Woody Dickpants, the elevator man, was dozing on his bench when I got to work the next evening. "Hiya, Woody," I said. "Third floor."

"Gosh, I guess I know your floor, Mr. Kloer. Been knowing it good for ten years, haven't I?"

"I might surprise you one of these days and quit," I said.

"Ain't nothing ever going to surprise me again," Woody said.

"How long you been on the job here, Woody?" I asked.

"I been right here since back when they had a lobby man with castanets. This was a nice building, they used to sweep up."

A woman came in from the street and tap-tapped across the bare marble lobby like she was late. "Wait there, boy!" she called. We waited. She was a nice-looking woman, about thirty, in a fur coat and high heels. Blond hair, done up. No hat. "Four," she said. She faced the front looking up, like most people do. Woody closed the cage door and pulled the lever, and we started. He watched the woman's back. He got the sad look, and then his pants bulged out in front about a foot. Poor old Woody, it happened every time a woman rode in the elevator. He didn't do it on purpose; it was a kind of medical condition.

Woody called three, and I got out. What's a juicy uptown blond doing in the Belfont at this time of night? I wondered.

I took Ray's bridge from the icebox and set it down on my bench. It looked very good. Ray was going to be a new man. Whatever happened next was not my problem. He could get another steel guitar. I had a feeling the Bigsby was going to change things for me. I might be moving up. I picked up the phone and dialed. Sammy answered.

"Ha' Spa'."

"Sammy, it's Sonny. If Houseley comes in, tell him to get a cab over here. I'm ready for him."

I left a similar message with Ray's landlady. I smoked a cigarette; I had a drink from the bottle and played the radio. It was Thursday night and that meant swing music live from the Hollywood Roosevelt Hotel. I counted five saxophones, minimum. I bet a blond like that blond in the elevator knows all those sax players by their first names, I thought. Bet she could get real chummy at the Roosevelt. I heard knocking. I was expecting Ray Randy, but it was Woody Dickpants.

"Help me, Mr. Kloer." Woody was vibrating like a tuning fork.

"Come on in, have a seat," I said. "Drink?"

"Oh, thanks, you're a pal. I need a drink bad. Something terrible happened."

"Elevator stuck again?"

"It ain't funny Mr. Kloer, don't laugh. She laughed at me, that's what started it."

"Just tell it, Woody," I said.

"The blond, you remember, you saw her, in the fur coat? All I said was, 'That's a mighty nice coat.'"

"You let her out on the fourth."

"Yeah, but this was later. She rang the buzzer, and I went up. I was going off duty, but I figured it won't hurt me to go back. It's dark on the stairs. I didn't mean nothing, Mr. Kloer, I'm a sick man."

"You went back up. Take it from there." I looked at the office clock. It was 10:30.

"I went back up to the fourth. She says, 'Down, boy.' I says, 'Going down.' Like I always say. Then, she came up close and leaned on me. She says, 'I said, *down*, boy.' I says, 'Lady, I'm trying to operate this elevator.' She says, 'Do you pull that trick with all the girls, or do you like me special?'" Woody started to cry.

"What happened?"

"She laughed at me with her big mouth. I pushed her off. Maybe I pushed a little too hard, I don't know. The Good Lord knows how sick I am. She fell. I think she hit her head. Please help me, Mr. Kloer."

"Where is she?"

"Right here, on the third. In the elevator."

I walked down the hall to the elevator cage. The hallway was dark. The light in the elevator was an outdoor bulb and it was too bright. She was lying on her back with her head jammed in the corner. She looked all wrong, like the strings had been cut — the way they look in police photographs — one arm pinned underneath and the other flung out to the side. One shoe was off. Her dress was hiked all the way up, and her panties were torn. Good old Dickpants. There was blood. It made me feel sick. I checked her purse, like they do in the movies, but then I heard somebody walking toward me. I panicked. I put the purse down and tried to stand up and I stumbled. A hand steadied me. It was Houseley. "He's gone," Houseley said, after I got my balance.

"Who?" I asked.

"Office door is open. Whiskey bottle's empty. Woody, I presume, has ankled the scene and left you holding the proverbial bag."

I felt faint, sick. The army doctors had warned me about what they called "overstimulation."

"I think she's dead, but I'm afraid to touch her," I said to Houseley. "You're the doctor, you want to make sure, don't you? I got to call the cops."

Houseley shook his head. "She's dead as she'll ever be. I'm wanted in five states, please allow me to step gracefully off. *Au revoir, mon vieux.*" He disappeared down the back stairs, and then there was nothing on the third floor except the dead girl in the light and the ringing in my head and the radio in the lab. The announcer was signing off: "Be sure to tune in again next week for the uptown sounds of Harry Spivak and the boys, featuring the glamorous vocal stylings of Miss Josephine Hutchinson! This program was transcribed for broadcast on the Armed Services Radio Network. Roy Rowan speaking."

"Kloer, get your stuff and clear out," was all Puss Walgreen had to say. The thanks I get. He claimed Woody absconded with five thousand dollars' worth of his dental gold supply while I was out of the room. He implied I might be in on it. I figured Puss was going to stick it to the insurance company. He never kept that much gold around; you order it as you need it. The cops took my statement and told me not to leave town. I told them my car couldn't get past the city limits.

They put out an APB for Woody. *May be carrying a concealed weapon, approach with caution.* Detective Spangler didn't buy the Dickpants story: "This was penetration with instrument. We'll find it."

The cops wanted to know what the girl was doing in the Belfont. She didn't have much money in her purse, so it wasn't a payoff. Unless I took it? She was going up to the fourth, but she didn't say why, not in my presence. I never even been up there. How would I know if this was a grudge screw? I make teeth, that's all I know about. Woody had never been in trouble in the building before. He's an old man, he doesn't have any known associates.

"He's a deviated sex-killer," Spangler said, "It's another Black Dahlia. This baby is mine."

The police turned me loose from headquarters at seven in the morning. I hadn't been outdoors at that hour in years. I drove over to Philippe's on Alameda and got breakfast. Ordinarily, I didn't eat breakfast, but I ordered bacon and eggs. I hadn't had bacon since I was in the army. Army bacon was mostly fat.

I am what you call a methodical person, that's the steel player in me. Steel guitar is a very methodical instrument and very logical, and that's why I like it. You sit there and you put your steel bar down on the strings and you play your patterns. That's how we do it. It's fine for a genius like Joaquin Murphy to play free and easy and just wing it, but the average Joe has to plan ahead.

The citizens cleared out, and Philippe's got quiet. I tried to do a little thinking. I couldn't do any work that meant standing up for long periods, and I didn't have skills you need for office work. The one thing I knew how to do besides making teeth was playing the steel guitar, and I didn't even own one. But that could change.

Ray Randy: Why didn't he come back for his teeth? It must have been something drastic. I wrote down all the places he might be: The Sunshine Hotel on Bunker Hill; the Musicians Union in Hollywood; The Riverside Rancho, a Country-Western joint in Glendale. Any bar between here and the Pacific Ocean. Turned out to be none of those.

Woody Atkins, AKA Dickpants: He slept on a cot in the basement, and the building superintendent paid him in cash. The police found an old copy of *Mankind United* under his pillow. *Happy Birthday Woodrow from Gertrude* was inscribed on the flyleaf. I figured Woody was just a lonely, old man who ran the elevator and had a weird nervous disorder, and now he was gone. Not my problem. Turned out it was.

Houseley Stephenson: If I could locate him, maybe he could help me. I found him all right, but when I did, he was no help at all.

The Barlow Sanitarium had been a tuberculosis hospital back in the 1800s. It was very rundown and very quiet. The reception area was dim and smelled like floor wax.

The usual nurse was sitting at the usual desk, and I had a flashback to the army hospital in San Diego. I should have worn my medals, and I've got plenty.

The nurse stared at me. I leaned heavy on my cane. Up close, she was not so usual: about thirty, with very smooth, clear skin and black hair. Her eyes brought you up short, though, they stopped your show. Violet, for real.

"Howdy, ma'am," I said, with a little salute thrown in. "My name is Loren Kloer. They call me Sonny. I'm looking for Dr. Stephenson."

"There's nobody here by that name," she said. I liked her voice, she wasn't army.

"I'm talking about Dr. Houseley Stephenson. He told me he was consulting. So maybe he's not on the regular staff, see?"

"Just a moment, please," said the nurse. She went through a side door and came back with a man in a white coat. He was very tall and thin with a very tall, wavy hairdo, like a gospel singer. He had big red lips that he poked out in an aggravated way, and dark beady eyes. He sighted down his long nose at me and said, "I'm Dr. Cross. This is a private hospital, what do you want here?"

"Very little. I want to see Dr. Houseley Stephenson, if he's available. If not, I'll come back later," I said.

"You've made a mistake. There's no such person as Houseley Stephenson."

"I make mistakes, but I don't think this is one of them. I bet he's here somewhere. How 'bout I look around, how would that be?" Dr. Cross didn't like that at all. He pursed his lips and twitched his eyebrows, and pointed his clipboard at me.

"Nurse Bari, show this man out immediately. I object to these intrusions." He turned and went back through the side door. The nurse came around from behind her desk and stood next to me. She was just my height, but plenty strong looking.

"If you please," she said.

"Okay, but why the big display? Houseley's a good friend of mine. I picked him up down the road two nights ago. He told me he was working here; it had to do with schizophrenia. See, I'm not making this up, why would I?"

"Dr. Cross is a very busy man," she said. She held the door open for me.

"I'm in the way of being a medical man myself," I said. "You better take the doctor's pills away from him. He's all strung out, he might collapse at any time." I was kidding around, but Nurse Bari paused. Her eyes changed, and then changed back. With the clear violet, you could see it happen. I hobbled out and down the steps. She waited until I got in the car and then went back inside and closed the door. Absolute quiet returned.

Houseley Stephenson was an unusual name, a mouthful, and Dr. Cross had shot it back at me a little too fast. I decided to do recon, like we did back in Leyte. The army taught us the best way was to get some altitude so you can look down on your objective and get the picture. The Barlow was situated low against the hill, called Palo Verde, or "green hill." I followed the road up to the top and parked. I walked through the tall grass to where the hill sloped down, where I could see the whole layout of the hospital. The top of L.A. City Hall was visible just over the next ridge. The city had grown up around the Ravine, but the Ravine itself hadn't changed much since the old days when the Barlow was first built. I spread my jacket on the ground under a eucalyptus tree and sat down to rest my legs. I figured it wasn't a military operation, so I had a smoke. After a while, I fell asleep.

My commanding officer in Leyte used to say, "You do recon, you do not engage, I don't care what you find out there." This was toward the end, when we were mopping up, or so we thought. We came across a company of Jap infantry in a little clearing by a pool of stagnant water.

We watched them, and it was terrible to see. They were starved and emaciated and their uniforms were in shreds. One soldier was eating gravel and whimpering like a frightened child. Another soldier went over and struck him. The first man held up his hands and begged and pleaded, and the other guy stopped hitting him. Then, the whole routine started over.

We fell back and had a powwow. One said he was for wasting the whole bunch, but another said, "Let's take 'em back to command, we might learn something."

Another fella said, "I say shoot 'em and keep moving."

We couldn't decide, so we voted. The vote was four to two in favor of taking them back, even though it went against direct orders. We advanced in a circle formation. When the soldiers saw us, they fell on their knees and went into a prayer routine, it seemed. They showed us they had discarded their weapons, so we got them to stand up and fall in line.

Then all hell broke loose. Suddenly, we were under fire. There must have been fifty more Japs up in the trees waiting for us, and they let us have it. The fact is, these guys were just decoys. They figured Americans are soft and they figured right. You know, democratic. It was a massacre for us as well as the poor starved soldiers. I grabbed one and started running back into the trees, using him as a shield. He was crying the whole time, really crying, and it made me sick, but he took the hits and it saved my life. It was just me and my buddy named Clark that survived and got back to the unit. I got hit in both legs and Clark had to carry me most of the way.

The CO didn't want trouble, so he reported to the high command that we were heroes. I was decorated. My CO said if I ever breathed a word about what really happened, he'd track me down and kill me. I heard he died recently, so I'm not worried about him anymore, but he was right, in principle. Do not engage, because you don't know the enemy's strength. Remember the Japs in the trees.

A motor was running, and it woke me up. A little Mexican girl with pink hair ribbons was sitting beside me in the grass. It was getting dark.

There was an old panel truck parked down below in front of the hospital. The girl pointed to the truck. "Cousin Beto," she said. She was holding a homemade rag doll that looked like it could have once belonged to Pancho Villa. "I like your doll," I said, "what's her name?"

"Lydia."

"You know Cousin Beto?"

"Yes."

"Does he live around here?"

"Yes. There is my house." She pointed to a lopsided wooden shack down the road from my car. A goat was tethered to a tree in the front yard.

"Regreso a la casa para comer. Adios." Something about going to the house to eat. I hadn't eaten since Philippe's. She waved good-bye and took off with her doll.

There was only one other car in front of the Barlow. It was a prewar Plymouth convertible, a cute car, a lady's car. I'd seen it earlier. That might mean Nurse Bari was still on duty, or maybe it belonged to a black-jack-wielding orderly. I'm not one of those guys you read about in the dime-store murder books with the crazy covers, the kind of sharp cat who can break in a second-story window and get the girl out while he cuts the bad guys down with a .45 and cracks wise the whole time. Not old Sonny, not with his shot-up army hospital legs. But I had to find out if Houseley was there, so I got back in the Olds and drove down the hill. I parked right in front, next to the Plymouth. The registration on the sun visor read, "Lynn Bari, Barlow Sanitarium, Chavez Ravine Rd., Los Angeles."

The main building was dark. There was a lighted window in one of the cottages, and I tried to walk there as quiet as a man with a cane can walk. The window gave on a small sitting room where Nurse Bari was reading a book by the light of a floor lamp. She was wearing a housecoat with a flower design, not very fancy or stylish, like she was in for the night and wasn't expecting anyone. I watched her. She had an allure women in artistic paintings have when they're just sitting alone doing nothing. Organ music drifted out the window from a table radio next to her chair. A man was speaking in the sorry tones of an undertaker: "Korla Pandit will now conclude this hour of blessed meditation. Send your prayer requests together with your dollars to *The Brighter Day*, care of this station." The organ died away. You wouldn't have figured the violet-eyed, alabaster-faced Nurse Bari for the likes of Korla Pandit.

She put the book down and walked through a connecting door, and I moved to the next window. Somebody was stretched out on a bed. Bari stood there for a few minutes checking a pulse and then left. There was a pair of French doors with curtains, which were unlocked. I opened the door a little and waited. No bells rang; no orderlies came running swinging rubber truncheons. Whatever the Barlow was, high-security it was not. I went in. It was Houseley. His eyes were closed, and he was breathing deep and regular.

"Houseley, wake up," I whispered. I bent down closer and whispered again. "Houseley, it's me, Sonny." I took his arm and shook him. He stirred. "Won't enlist," he mumbled. I shook him some more. His hands reached in the air. "Whiskey!" he croaked.

"You can have a drink, but you got to answer one question," I whispered. His hands went back down. He frowned. "What are you doing here?" I asked him.

"Make me a sergeant, charge the booze!"

"Listen, I been in the army, it's hard to get liquor. Where you going to get it?"

"*Captain* Cross." Houseley gave a mock salute. "Big shot, army hospital, gets what he wants."

"The war is over, Houseley, you're back stateside now. What's Cross want you for?"

"He threatened me! Won't work for him! Won't be bothered!"

"Nurse Bari went to get you a drink, she'll be right back." He smiled, he liked Nurse Bari. I heard the radio. I went to the door and looked in. Now she was doing needlepoint. The radio was making noisy, echoing sounds. "Live from Temple City, it's time once again for *Championship Bowling*, brought to you by Miller, the champagne of bottled beer!" Bari turned the dial.

"The Slavick Jewelry Company brings you *Music Into The Night*, with your host, Thomas Cassidy." An orchestra fiddled around. Bari went back to her needlepoint.

In the army, they told us be decisive. Consider your options, but don't take too long, because someone might get the drop on you and get you hurt. I put my money on violet and walked into the room. Bari looked up and saw me and put her needlepoint down — it was one of those framed panels with the old-time lettering: "For Cozy Comfort to Serve My Guests" — that was as far as she had got. I pointed to it. "What's the rest of it, Nurse Bari?" The violet eyes gave away nothing. "I always like my kitchen best,'" she said in her low voice. I sat in a chair across from her. "My legs are killing me," I said.

"I guess we underestimated you," she said.

"Most people do, if they even bother. I want to know what is going on with Houseley. He told me he was a doctor here. Cross said, 'no such person.' Now you're watching him. Go on from there."

"The man you call Houseley Stephenson is a patient here, has been for years. He and Dr. Cross knew each other in the Army. He has an unusual medical condition which Dr. Cross has been treating him for ever since."

"He's an alcoholic, what's so unusual?"

"He needs special medication." Her book was facedown on the table by her knitting basket. It was more of a pamphlet than a book, entitled, "A Sample Talk for Those Who Invite Small Groups to Meetings." She noticed me looking at it and covered it with a ball of yarn.

"You could talk me into most anything, Lynn, since that's your name, but I make false teeth for living, so I'm sort of an expert. The other night, Houseley told me he was doing research here, and just now he babbled about something he has that Cross wanted. I think it has to do with the war, like my legs. What makes it a secret?"

"I don't know what to say, I only came to work here four years ago. No one ever comes to see Mr. Stephenson." Bari saw something over my shoulder, and her eyes got big. I looked around, already feeling the crazed orderly's viselike grip on my windpipe, but it was only Houseley standing in the door. "Where's my drink?" he said. "Told you I don't make mistakes, the girl was fine all along. Why'd you tell everyone she died? Cross promised me bonded, can't trust anybody." Bari got up and took Houseley back in the other room. She was gentle with him, he went quietly. In five minutes, she was back.

"This dead girl keeps coming up, she bothers him," I said. "I can't follow it. Have you got anything to eat here?"

"No. And I think you had better leave, it's getting late."

"Why? I'm a night man, I'm used to it. I thought we were just getting acquainted."

"If the doctor comes back, there's going to be trouble. I can make you a cup of coffee, that's all there is," she said.

I was getting light headed. The army doctors had warned me about low blood sugar. There were too many doctors in Los Angeles. If you laid them end to end, they'd reach all the way from Chavez Ravine to the Belfont Building.

"I think Houseley's in some kind of danger, and I'm going to take him with me. I have nothing to offer you, but why stick around here? Los Angeles is the land of the brighter day."

"Well, thank you," she said, but she didn't budge. It was time to go. I went back to the bedroom. Houseley was sleeping. I got his arm over my shoulder and stood him up. Leaning hard on my cane, I dragged him over to the French doors and got them open. By that time, I was sweating. Then there was the yard. It wasn't a big yard, but it was big enough. "If you're going to make a move, make it," the CO used to say. I moved.

It was cold and damp outside. The ground was soft and my cane didn't help much. It was a snail's pace, but we managed. Around the front there was gravel, and it was easier. I got

Houseley up to the Olds and rested him on the front fender, trying not to throw up on him. Then suddenly the headlights snapped on, nailing us like coyotes on the road. Someone got out of the car and walked toward us on the gravel, stopping behind the lights.

"Órale. Buenas noches, amigos." The words trailed off like wind in the trees.

"What are you doing in my car?" I said. It was a stupid thing to say, but my pulse rate was up too high and I couldn't think.

"I like these ones, the tranny es *coool*."

"What do you want?" I said

"I am known as Cousin Beto."

"You work for Dr. Cross?"

"Si. Claro. It's so tranquilo in Palo Verde en la noche. Why you have to rush away?"

"I'm taking this man out of here. Step aside."

" 'Step aside'? Is this hospitable? Is this *polite*? You, mi amigo, are in no position to give orders." Behind the lights, he was just a shape. In the darkness, other shapes joined him.

"We're leaving." It was a stupid thing to say. I wasn't going anywhere. Weak as I was, I couldn't even drive the car fifty feet.

"Watch the left hand. Knife," Houseley whispered. The shapes darted forward.

"Pa'tras, cabrones!" Cousin Beto hissed, and the shapes moved back. He stepped into the light where I could see him. He was short, but his pachuco hairdo gave him an extra four inches. He was wearing a white undershirt and a long coat that didn't match his pleated trousers. "You are expected," he said, bowing like a maître d' in an Olvera Street taco joint.

Beto and the boys locked us in what seemed to be Cross's office. "El doctor is busy just now, pero he will attend you very soon," Beto said. He tended to keep his left hand out of sight in his coat pocket.

Houseley came to life and started going through Cross's desk drawers. "Cross is a doper, but he might have something around for medicinal purposes."

"I never knew you were in the army, Houseley."

"'Disarm the world,' they said. Ah, but first, they wanted something to demonstrate their power, something big and showy. I told them, fine, no problem, I'll get the amplitude up so high, their eyes will vibrate right out of their sockets for hundreds of miles! They loved it! Told them, charge the booze and I'll do it! Idiots! No such thing, of course."

"Disarm the world? Who, the army?"

"Used to be called 'Mankind United.' Got into trouble during the war. Got a new moniker now, can't think what it is. Cross is slipping. I don't make mistakes."

"What's Cross up to around here?"

"'Divisional Superintendent,' he calls himself! Wasn't supposed to have a lady friend, the faithful didn't like it. F.B.I. claimed the organization was seditious, tried to subpoena her. Cross put it out that she died as a result of the operation."

"But she didn't die," I said. "Where'd she go?"

"Made a deal with Cross. Silence in trade for a new name, new face. I did the job. Damn good work, I don't mind saying."

"Where is she now?"

"You need to sharpen up the old gray matter there, Sonny. Pay attention, start taking vitamins, if you're going to come to work for the organization. They have a use for everybody, even Mexicans." Houseley started going through the medicine cabinets. "My opinion? Diabetic," he said, looking over at me.

"I've got to eat something, I can't stay here," I said. There was another door in Cross's office, and it led out into a dark hallway lined with a few doors with glass windows. One showed light. I looked in, and it was a tiny room with padded walls and a narrow bed. A man was lying on the bed trussed up in a straitjacket. He must have felt me looking at him, because he turned his head toward the door. I figured the window was one-way only. I could see Woody, but he couldn't see me.

The door was unlocked. Woody panicked when he saw the door open, but then he recognized me. "Mr. Kloer! Help me, for God Almighty's sake!"

"Who tied you up?"

"They kidnapped me, the Sponsors think I'm a spy for the Hidden Rulers. They hurt me! I'm not a spy, Mr. Kloer. I been a faithful servant all these years, make them stop!"

"The police are looking for you. Who was the girl, Woody? I'll help you, but tell me the truth. Don't bullshit me that you didn't know her."

"I swear I didn't!"

"I'm leaving, Woody. I'm going to find Nurse Bari and tell her you been lying."

"No! Not her, not that! She'll tell Dr. Cross, and he'll take me to Ward Seven! Don't let them take me to Seven," Woody sobbed. He was terrified. My CO used to say, every prisoner you take alive is a mad dog from hell unless proven otherwise. The point being, there was no positive proof available on short notice. I told Woody I was going to do a little recon. With the door closed, you couldn't hear him crying and begging.

There was one time we made a mistake that cost plenty. A Jap soldier was badly wounded and the medic said he was dying. The medic spoke a little Japanese, and he said, the man was begging to commit hara-kiri with a sword for the sake of family honor. He had lost so much blood, we didn't see any harm, so Clark gave him his bayonet. He managed to spring off the stretcher and stab Clark in the stomach. Me and two other guys tried to grab him, but he was too quick for us, and he ran past us with the bayonet, screaming "Banzai!" and slashed the medic, whose back was turned. I brought him down with my army .45, but he had done plenty of damage. The CO really chewed us out that time.

Down the hall, Nurse Bari and Dr. Cross were in a room with the door open. I was curious about Bari's voice and the way it could change, like her eyes changed. One minute, she was just a nurse, and the next, she was the boss, the one with the chops, like we say in music. You need chops to play good, or to think fast, or control the situation. Joaquin Murphy has chops, Sonny Kloer doesn't have chops, never did. I listened, and it was quite interesting, especially on an empty stomach.

"You're a fool, Richard, you've always been such a fool. You're tall, and that look in your eyes makes people want to believe what you believe, but you've become entangled in the physical world. The Sponsors are displeased. I've done all I can."

"I'm tired, I've been under a very great strain." Cross was a ham actor at heart, but his voice was a real instrument too, like a radio bishop.

"The Sponsors have ordered me to find a new location immediately. I can't keep making excuses and lying to people. I didn't fool the man with the cane, he came back, you see. He even propositioned me, in a way."

"The man's nothing but a simpleton. You never tire of throwing other men in my face, it seems."

"Oh, I don't know; he's some kind of a man. Brave, even. You, on the other hand, remind me of a bowerbird who collects shiny things so he can admire himself. I'm sure the Sponsors won't object to your staying here, and you can play doctor to your heart's content. The Sponsors have ordered me to move, not you."

"And you expect me to step gracefully off? 'Thanks ever so much, don't mind me?' I rescued you, I brought you into the organization, I'm still Divisional Superintendent!"

"The Sponsors have decided to close down the division. We need to move the organization forward. People are frightened of Communism; it's a perfect time for us to reappear," Bari said. "And as far as throwing men in your face is concerned, at this point in my life, I just might prefer the simpleton with the cane to a spiritual cripple like yourself. In any case, I'm leaving."

"What about Atkins? The police are looking for him. What would the Sponsors like me to tell them?"

"Woody is like a bad dog that wants to sleep on the couch. Tell him if he doesn't get down off the couch, you'll take him to Seven. The police aren't coming here, why would they?"

"My dear, you are perfect, promise me you'll never change. Stephenson did a magnificent job. The Sponsors have nothing to fear."

Nurse Bari and Dr. Cross finished their talk, and there was silence for a while. They seemed to understand each other. I walked back down the hall to the office. The window was open and Houseley was gone. It was just getting light in Chavez Ravine.

The day I left the army hospital for the last time was a great day. It had been raining, and the clouds were big and fat over San Diego. I picked up my duffel bag from the redistribution station and caught the first thing smoking, which was a Greyhound bus bound for Los Angeles. A buddy of mine had given up his place on Monte Vista Street, in Highland Park. It was just a two-room shack behind a grocery store, but I wouldn't have to climb stairs, and the rent was so low, I didn't have to worry. Riding north on that Greyhound, I felt like a million, who knows why. I didn't have a job, or a girl, or friends, or anything except my old Fender Stringmaster, but I felt good just to be alive. All us G.I.'s thought we'd licked the bastards for good, and the world could stop worrying about Hitler and Hirohito and even Joe Stalin.

I drove down the hill and headed for Chinatown. A double order of pork fried rice will just about fix it, I thought. I had heard about Communism, but I didn't understand it, so I wasn't going to worry about that, or anything. I had made up my mind to quit worrying. Los Angeles was the Land of the Brighter Day, something good was bound to turn up.